SUE GEE is the author of ten novels, including *The Hours of the Night*, winner of the Romantic Novel of the Year award, and *The Mysteries of Glass*, long listed for the Orange Prize. Her most recent novels are *Reading in Bed*, a *Daily Mail* Book Club selection, and *Coming Home*. She has also published a collection of short stories, *Last Fling*.

Sue Gee ran the MA in Creative Writing at Middlesex University from 2000–2008 and now teaches at the Faber Academy. She is a mentor with the Write to Life group at Freedom from Torture. She lives in London and Herefordshire.

SUE GEE

Trio

SALT

CROMER

PUBLISHED BY SALT PUBLISHING 2016

2 4 6 8 10 9 7 5 3 1

Copyright © Sue Gee 2016

First published in Great Britain in 2016 by
Salt Publishing Ltd
12 Norwich Road, Cromer, Norfolk NR27 0AX United Kingdom

www.saltpublishing.com

Salt Publishing Limited Reg. No. 5293401

A CIP catalogue record for this book is available from the British Library

ISBN 978 1 78463 061 4 (Paperback edition)
ISBN 978 1 78463 062 1 (Electronic edition)

Typeset in Neacademia by Salt Publishing

Printed and bound in Great Britain by Clays Ltd, St Ives plc

Homage to Catalonia by George Orwell (Copyright © George Orwell, 1937)
Reprinted by permission of Bill Hamilton as the Literary
Executor of the Estate of the Late Sonia Brownell Orwell.

For Timothy

BOOK I

PART ONE

I

1936

WINTER WAS CLOSING in: propped up against the pillows, she could see through the one small window that the moor was speckled with snow. There was nothing else to see: no other house, no livestock; only the frozen ground, the pitiless pale sky from which more snow would fall today. That was a certainty.

He had lit the fire, before he left for work. Two weeks before the end of term, and he had to leave her, with coal in the scuttle, a box of wood - off-cuts and logs from the freezing shed - and a bowl of porridge on the chair at the bedside.

'Just a little,' he said, standing there in his old jersey, un-ravelling at the wrist. Something else she had not done, nor mended. 'For me, Margaret - do it for me.' His tie was askew, the collar of his shirt was frayed. Another thing. 'Please,' he said, and lightly - oh, so lightly - kissed her cheek. Then he clattered down the narrow stairs, took his jacket, hat and coat from the peg, called out goodbye again. The door slammed: keep in the warmth, keep it in! And he walked away down the track.

Small flames still leapt. She turned slowly from the window, saw firelight reflected in the dark varnished wood of washstand and skirting board and door. I'll scrape that all off one day, he'd said, when they moved in two years ago, but he hadn't. Too many other things to do: mend the roof, replace the rotting window frames, and the ill-fitting door that led straight from kitchen to moor. He had to fence in the little garden where they were growing vegetables, and make a gate. He had to replace the missing quarry tiles on the kitchen floor. He did everything well, like his father.

Geoffrey Coulter, Cabinet Maker, Birley Bank, Near Hexham

Steven had learned carpentry from him as a boy, could have followed in his footsteps; instead, went to university, the first person in his family ever to do such a thing. But the skill was still there: he sawed and planed and hammered, out in the old farmer's woodshed which became a workshop. She took out a chair and sat sewing curtains in the shade of the thorn tree, looking up now and then to watch him through the open door. Birds flew by. It was summer then. To teach, as she used to do, with a long journey to and fro each day: over the windswept moor, with its single, sheep-worn track, down to the road where the bus to Kirkhoughton came only every hour. Who, except a lonely old farmer, dead a twelvemonth, as they'd said in town, would want to live here?

She tried to move a pillow behind her, up against the bars of the iron bedstead. Like washstand and dresser, it had been bought at auction. They'd walked, hand in gloved hand, amongst chests and tallboys and dismantled beds stacked up against a wall. This will be our marriage bed, they told one another. This one. The brass needed polishing. I'll polish it, she said, her hand in his.

Farmers were looking at scythes and pitchforks, straw still on their boots; stout women in coats and felt hats went through china in boxes. The auctioneer mounted his steps as she found a mildewed mirror. They looked at their reflection; he reached out, touched her face within the glass, ran his fingers over her lips. She stood very still, and watched him do this.

The cold iron bars pressed through the pillow: nothing was comfortable to her now. Not leaning back, nor lying down on the mattress, on which, in the first year of their marriage, they had taken one another over and over again, the window open in spring and summer to their cries, to the calls of peewit and lamb, the scents of grass and heather.

The window was tight shut now. They had told her that fresh air was crucial, that if she insisted on staying at home it should be open day and night, but no, it was too cold, it was intolerable.

She shifted, just a little, reached for the bowl of porridge. Every movement had to be made so slowly. Every breath felt dangerous. He soaked her stained nightgown and sheets in a bucket; hung them over the range. She sat on the chair and watched him remake the bed, again and again. He helped her to wash, to brush her teeth; he took down the washstand jug and basin, and the chamber pot.

Don't draw the curtains, she murmured sometimes at night, when he had done all these things, climbed the stairs and undressed, and gone to the window. He got carefully in beside her, turned out the paraffin lamp, lay still. He took her hand; they turned to look out at the stars. It felt as if it were the last thing left they could do together.

Not every day was difficult. She had rested and rested: this, as she had been told, over and over, was what she must do. If she were in the sanatorium, they told her, if she were sensibly down in the sanatorium near Barrasford, that was what she would do. If she – and if he – insisted that she stay at home, then rest was essential: no exertion, nothing, not even washing a teacup. Eating was what was needed, to keep her strength up. So he cooked, and she did nothing all spring and summer: he could manage, he told her in term time, and in the holidays what else would he want to do but bring her back to health?

On good days he took one of the chairs his father had made as a wedding present, when no one was thinking of illness – why should they be thinking of that? – and put it by the kitchen door he had made himself, that first year, and she sat there and watched him, digging in fitful spring sun. Clouds blew over the moor and curlew called. Sturdy sheep trotted up the track with their lambs from the farm below: white-faced Cheviots, bred for this particular stretch of the moor, as all Northumbrian sheep were bred for their own patch. The farmer lifted his cap, stopped, called his dog to, while they talked about sheep, and the weather, and she looking stronger now. And broad beans and potatoes were in flower, those onions doing well, look at that, that was a good sign.

It grew warmer. She brought out her sewing bag again, and stitched in the summer sun, making a quilt from scraps left over from bedspread and curtains, a small one because there weren't that many scraps, and one day – oh, one day! – they might have a baby at last.

He dug up potatoes, brought them into the kitchen in a box, and she heard him pour rain water over them in the sink. She heard him scrape another chair over the tiles and turned to smile at him as he set it down beside her on the turf, and cleared her throat, and then a scarlet spray as fine as pinpricks speckled the quilt, and then there was suddenly more.

And then everyone said it was madness, to go on living up here. She should be in the sanatorium, flooded with light and air from the wide open windows and doctors on call and nurses to nurse you, you silly lass, so he wouldn't have to, it was too much for him, surely it was.

They all said it, in letters which Steven picked up after school from the box on a tree at the bottom of the track: her mother, writing from Cawbeck; his mother, from Birley Bank. Then came one from Miss Brierley: they wanted her back to health, the girls had never forgotten her, they sent their best wishes, they all did. *Would it not be better to take advantage of the sanatorium, my dear . . .*

The district nurse, Miss Douglas, wheeling her bicycle up the track, taking her temperature, shaking her head: she said it, too. 'Look at you, Margaret Coulter.' She brought the spotted mirror to the bed, showed her the thin white face, eyes huge in dark sockets, the colour on her cheekbones bright as blood. 'Hectic, we call that colour,' she said, taking the mirror away as she closed her eyes. 'Not a natural colour, my lass, and when will you two see sense? You know you could infect him, don't you, you do realise that.'

She lay still as a mouse, and listened.

Autumn was coming, wind and rain blew hard. And perhaps she should do what they said, she told him that evening, as he sat beside her and held her hand. But he wouldn't be able to see her, he said, they won't allow visitors at Barrasford; and they looked at one another, unable to imagine nor bear it.

Especially, she thought, she could not bear it, because she had never known a time when she had not loved him, not since the day she had looked across the Museum gallery as her girls made notes from glass cases, and saw him shepherding in his boys. 'Quiet, now, lads, that's it.' And something about the way he spoke, the way he reached out his arm to bring in one of them, small and hesitant—'Come along, Moffat,' - such a simple, ordinary thing, but all at once it wasn't ordinary, it was his way of doing it. And everything fell into place.

'You belong with me,' he said on that wild autumn evening, as she lay back against the pillows. 'Let's see how you go on. If you're not better by Christmas . . .'

He went downstairs again, and came up with two bowls of very hot soup on a tray and made her drink hers to the last drop and she did feel better then, and slept well, for once, knowing she wasn't going to leave.

The fire was beginning to die, but the light at the window grew brighter. She turned her head once more, slowly, slowly, and saw the snow beginning to fall again, flakes blowing here and there entrancingly, the room filled with whiteness, until it was falling thickly, on and on, so she could no longer see the empty miles of moorland, only the whirling white. For a long time she lay there, watching, imagining its fall on the thorn tree and shed and water butt, coating them thickly; on the river far below, dark and racing. The bowl of cold porridge rested on the quilt. She had eaten three mouthfuls, for him.

Then she slowly put the bowl back on the chair. She must use the chamber pot, she must see to the fire. Slowly, slowly, she pushed back the blankets and quilt; unsteadily set her feet, in the socks her mother had knitted, down on the rug. If he were here, she'd be reaching for his arm.

She sat down on the edge of the bed, sat there for ages, hearing the last log fall to pieces in the grate; breathing lightly, from her upper chest, as she did all the time now, though what good fresh air could get into you like that, Nurse Douglas had asked her. 'And if it's dangerous to breathe more deeply you should be in the sanatorium, my girl, I'm not going to say it again.'

She got to her feet, bent down, reached for the pot and squatted over it. Oh, that was better. Slowly she pulled herself up again, and perhaps the porridge had done her good, she did feel a bit stronger now, enough to carry the pot to the door and put it down on the tiny space at the top of the stairs. She could hear the clock ticking in the kitchen, and the shift of wood in the range. Such a long time since she had been down there.

Now then. The fire. She shut the bedroom door again, saw the room filled with miraculous snowy light, so beautiful, and walked over the bare boards to the fire box and bent down to feed the flames with fresh wood, just a little at first, that was it, and she blew, as much as she dared, just a little, to fan it all, and a fresh flame leapt up towards her. She blew again, and sparks glowed and little bits of ash flew up, and she coughed.

Up the blood came.

She pulled herself to her feet and coughed again, impossible not to. She reached for the washstand as something to clutch at and steady her, something to hold on to, but the blood came up, chokingly, more and now more. She leaned over the bowl and saw its whiteness and blue-painted flowers disappear in a clotted crimson flood.

Help me – the words swam through her. She was gasping, her hands to her terrible mouth, then clutching at bed, bedclothes, anything, as the marvellous light went black and she crumpled to the dusty floor.

Which was where, hours later, after stumbling up the track, clearing the bank of snow at the door with the spade he had left there, pushing it open, calling her name, pulling his coat off and racing up the narrow stairs, he found her.

PART TWO

I

SNOW WAS FALLING again as he crossed the playground.

'Sir!' Footsteps came running after him. 'Mr Coulter, sir!'

He turned, saw Johnny Mather racing up.

'You forgot this, sir.'

He shook his head, took the textbook. 'Silly of me. Thanks, Mather.'

He remembered cleaning the blackboard, as the boys went noisily out, and stacking up the exercise books at the desk; remembered putting them in his bag and leaving the classroom. He didn't remember who he'd said goodbye to in the smoke-filled staffroom, nor putting his coat on, nor walking across the playground, though here he was, almost at the gates.

'Wouldn't have been able to do your marking, would you, sir?'

Mather was class monitor: it was one of his jobs to collect things left behind and hand them in to Miss Aickman's office. Or to go running after a teacher with his mind elsewhere.

'Thank you,' he said again. 'Off you go.'

And Mather touched his cap, and ran back to fetch his own stuff, half-skidding on an icy patch, shouting out.

Frozen slush was still heaped up by the railings; the sky was a yellowish-grey. He put the book in his bag, and went out into the street.

Snow was falling on snow: piled up in the gutters, all round the square, coating the war memorial and the great tall Christmas tree in the middle. Paths had been scraped along the pavement.

There were boys everywhere, ragging about until they saw him, then walking away down the hill to Bridge Street or along the side streets, Middle Lane, Milk Lane, as the Kirkhoughton town clock struck the three-quarter hour. Tea time. Lights from the shops shone out. The afternoon ebbed away.

'Never known a winter like it,' said an old lady, half to herself and half to him, walking slowly along with her basket. It was what people said every year. He nodded, walked on to the bus stop.

'Come on, come on.' Snow fell down his collar, he stamped his feet. Then the bus came into view, lit up, the wipers going steadily. He climbed on, a few boys behind him, threw his bag on the seat. As they pulled away, a snowball suddenly hit his window, and he jumped, hearing Thompson splutter behind him. He looked out, saw Donald Hindmarsh, his hand clapped to his mouth. Not such a dreadful thing, but everyone was tiptoeing round him these days, pretending that they weren't.

Deepest condolences, the card had read on the wreath. Miss Aickman would have ordered it; Mr Straughan had written the words: black ink, his strong distinctive hand.

They drove out of the town, as light on the ring of hills faded.

The house smelled of ash and cold air. He dropped his bag and stood in the unlit kitchen, putting his hands to his face. Each day it was such a relief to do this: after the greetings, the smiling, the 'Come along, lads,' the 'Get out your books,' the 'Silence!' Though he didn't have to say that often. They were quiet and respectful, on the whole.

He shut his eyes, drew the deepest breath. That, too, felt an immeasurable relief.

'Margaret.' Each day he said it. He said it when he woke, and when he shaved at the washstand—

How long had she lain there, before he came home?

He said it as soon as he came in from school.

'Margaret. My Margaret.'

You can't stay in that house, said his parents, her parents. You mustn't be up there all on your own. And, He's stubborn, they said, when he'd shaken his head and left them. Like her. Neither of them would be told, and if only they'd listened—

He took his hands from his face, lit the paraffin lamp on the table. He refilled the range and sank into the chair beside it, where she used to sit and sew, or read. They used to read together, when he'd done his marking; reading together was one of their deepest connections.

'Margaret?'

She'd look up at her name, put her hand out. They never tired of looking at one another. And they talked, they talked all the time. Until they learned the great beauty of silence.

'My love.' A murmur. And then—

They lay in the deepest quietude, the window open on to the cropping of the sheep, the calling of curlew and chough, and then the starlight.

Now – there were so many places where she was not. She was not in that chair by the fire, her head bent over her book, her sewing. She was not in her place at the table, passing his plate, listening as he told her about his boys. She should have been telling him about her girls, as she'd done when they were getting to know one another. Teaching was in her blood.

'Good morning, girls!'

'Good morning, Miss Ridley!'

The Ridleys had been teachers for as long as anyone could remember. Her grandfather had taught maths at the Board School in Hexham. Her father was Head of the Cawbeck village school. But then she became Mrs Coulter, and a married woman was not allowed to teach.

'What shall I do all day?'

'We'll have children, won't we?'

'Margaret,' he said to the empty kitchen, where the clock ticked on the wall. Where had she gone?

She was not sewing a quilt for the baby who never came, not humming as she took down her coat from the peg, pulling her gloves from the pocket as they set out at weekends to walk.

Sometimes they went down to the river, tumbling out of the forested hills, a great plantation dating back a hundred years or more, and picnicked on the bank. In summer, kingfishers flashed. 'Look! Look at that!' Sometimes they struck out across the moor, hand in gloved hand swinging as she sang: folk songs, border ballads.

'You shall have a fishie, on a little dishie,

You shall have a fishie, when the boat comes in . . .'

She sang songs from her girlhood, too, heard on the wireless in her parents' house in Cawbeck: 'Tea for Two'; 'Happy Days are Here Again'. Sometimes he joined in, though he didn't think he had much of a voice, beside hers. She was the musical one.

'We shall have a family, a girl for you, a boy for me . . . '

Her sweet clear voice rang out. Sheep bolted into the bracken. Five miles across were the remains of a Roman fort: they ate their sandwiches leaning against the broken stone wall, the wind in their faces, hearing the high sad pipe of lapwing.

The schoolchildren knew all about the Romans, as if they were part of their own families, their ancestors.

Margaret had been in her first term at Kirkhoughton Girls when she walked Class One in pairs along Milk Lane and up into the Square. A fine day in early October, 1933, sun shining on the weathered sandstone of the Museum. Many of the great buildings in the Square - the Assembly Rooms, the Museum, the Judge's Lodging – were sandstone, designed in the early eighteenth century, she had told her class, by a pupil of William Newton. In they went, through the big oak doors.

'Ssh, now, girls. Take a sheet, each of you, that's it.'

They gazed at coins, pots, fragments of pots, little figures, beaten bronze necklaces. The morning sun came in at tall windows. They pressed their faces to the glass-fronted diorama: women cooking, men marching over the hills. Then the rooms were suddenly noisy and crowded, as a class from Kirkhoughton Boys arrived.

'Quiet, lads!'

She looked across, saw their teacher, tall and nice-looking, shepherding in a straggler. He caught her eye.

They knew, almost at once, though neither had ever thought it could happen like that.

Back at the school, the girls began a frieze. She painted an enormous backdrop in sections: long straight roads cutting across moorland and valley. She wrote in the names of real places and features – places the children would already know about, or could go to, on a trip: the Cheviot Hills to the north-west, Hadrian's Wall, to the south; a long wavy blue line for Fallowleys Burn, which ran down from the hills and through Kirkhoughton, with its fine stone bridge. Their brothers fished there in the summer holidays. She marked pikes and crags. Hencote Moor had been just a name to her then.

One afternoon, coming out of the school gates, she found the young teacher from the Boys' school waiting for her.

Her first years spent history classes drawing, painting with powder paint, cutting out: great grey stones to build the Wall, the barracks and milecastles set along it, the sally ports, the turrets and forts and settlements. They painted the helmeted figures of centurions, added foot soldiers, patrolling garrisons, to march along the wall, and along those great roads, rising and falling over the land.

The afternoons darkened, the gas lights went on. They cut out women in togas, huge amphorae, heaps of coins. There was a village, a bathhouse. Stables. Everything was glued on with flour paste, and by the end a whole Roman world ran round three walls of the classroom. Miss Brierley came in to admire.

All this, she had to give up.

'But you still want to marry me?'

'Kiss me again.'

Walking up the track to Hencote Moor one Saturday, the fifth they spent together, they'd come upon the empty little house. They peered in through dirty windows, tried the door. Someone must own it, surely, they said, sitting down on the grass. They looked out towards the distant town. They could ask at the agent in the Square.

You don't want to live all the way up there, said her parents, out in Cawbeck, a thirty-minute bus ride from Kirkhoughton. That's not very sensible. She and her brother had always been sensible, competent and clever. They were proud of them. She said it was what she and her fiancé both wanted, and since until then she had done almost everything she was asked, they said, Well, if that's how it is.

When she fell ill, all sense deserted her.

Her coat still hung on the kitchen peg, and would always hang there, next to his. It smelt of wood smoke and paraffin, like everything else. Reddish-brown hairs still clung to the collar. One day, she might come back, and need it.

'Margaret.'

Sometimes, saying her name aloud like this, like an incantation, he half expected to see her, singing as she ironed their clothes with the flat iron, or put the heavy kettle on the range. 'Tea for two and two for tea . . .' He saw her lighting the lamp, climbing the stairs to their bedroom, washing at the stand, there in her nightgown, splashing her face, brushing her teeth, turning to smile at him, saying his name as she climbed into bed beside him.

'Steven.'

They say you know you love someone when you hear them speak your name. As if it had been waiting to be spoken, by just that voice. That was what it had been like, for both of them, when they went out together for the first time: Mr Coulter and Miss Ridley. Finding out each other's first names, hidden behind those titles, was almost like undressing.

She was kneeling up before him while he slipped the gown over her head; looking into his eyes, smiling, murmuring, 'Here I am,' as he enfolded her.

There was no one to say his name now, no one to call it. He made tea, put the pie his mother had made in the oven. He got out his books and sat at the table, trying to do his marking. End of term essays.

'The Battle of Alnwick took place in 1174, when William I of Scotland invaded Northumbria. He was met by Ranulf de Glanvill, leading four hundred knights . . .'

Snow blew against the window. The clock ticked into the silence. When she was here, he had hardly noticed it.

2

1937

THE NEW YEAR began with the setting of her stone. On a freezing January afternoon they all stood round her grave in the Cawbeck churchyard.

Of course this was where she must lie, with all the old Ridleys around her, but although this was where they had married, her father walking with her through the village and along the grassy lane, so that today made it all of a piece, in a terrible way; it felt as lonely and pitiful as on the day of her funeral, to have her so far from him. Left to himself, he would have buried her up on Hencote, marked with a stone from the moor.

In life she had been his. In death she belonged to everyone: her white-faced mother; her father, biting his lip; her brother Andrew, silent all through lunch, who'd been the top student at Kirkhoughton Boys and now was studying law in Edinburgh.

Rooks cawed from the elms. Steven stood between his parents and they all looked at the fresh new stone, and its carving.

Margaret Coulter, née Ridley, beloved wife of Steven
19th June 1912–3rd December 1936

A June baby, born in the loveliest month of the year, sun and shadow dancing over the churchyard grass on the day of her christening, birds flitting into the yew. He thought that was how it would have been.

'He's made a good job of it,' said his father, clearing his throat.

Her father nodded. Her mother began to cry. Andrew stood stiff and apart.

The pale winter sun was sinking. They walked back along the path to the lych gate, the grass stiff with frost, great big icicles hanging from the guttering on the church.

'What will you do now, Steven?' her father asked him, back at the house, by the fire. The cat was stretched out like a dead thing. Teacups chinked. He couldn't answer. He stood looking out at the darkening garden; birds beat their way to the trees.

He went home, climbed the track up the moor, climbed the stairs, flung himself down on the bed.

A young man sobbing in an empty house.

This is it, this is it, this is it.

3

SPRING CREPT OVER the moor. It came in the faintest green on the thorn tree by the shed, where one half-term morning, fetching in fresh wood for the range, he disturbed a hedgehog.

'Hello.' It lay in a corner beyond the log pile, uncurling with the sudden flood of light from the open door. At once, with his shadow, the sound of his voice, it curled up again, and he stepped quietly away. Next morning, it had gone. He felt painfully disappointed.

He stood looking round: at the saw on its hook, the work bench and planer, and remembered the carpentry he'd done in the first year of their marriage: the new kitchen door, the window frames. He thought of Margaret on summer days, sewing and watching him work, as his father had worked all his life, the finest cabinet maker for miles. He wanted to tell her about the hedgehog, felt a new wave of loneliness as he carried the logs out. It had rained in the night, and the branches of the thorn tree were dusted with fresh green, the tightest buds. Pools of peaty water lay in the grass.

Spring came with the sheep trotting up the track again, the farmer touching his cap and saying how sorry he'd been to hear the news, lambs racing and butting and crying as the flock spread out in the sun. The thorn tree was thick with white blossom, the tough moorland grass and the bracken greened up, the heather was a purple haze. Then came the call of the curlew.

He took down his coat and went walking. He was looking

a bit less peaky, his mother told him, when he went home to Birley Bank at Easter. Ducks were nesting on the riverside, daffodils blew in the garden. 'Got a bit of fresh air on your face again.' She put lunch on the table. 'Still too thin, though.' 'Leave him alone,' said his father, carving spring lamb. 'He's too much alone as it is,' she said. 'How can you stay up there, Steven, love?'

Back at school the talk in the staffroom was suddenly of the bombing of Guernica, a little Spanish market town no one had ever heard of. 'Have you seen this?' Frank Embleton flung *The Times* on the table. 'The boys must be made aware of this,' he said. Then the bell rang, and the day's routine began.

Routine was saving Steven. He had started the first years on border raids, fortifications, castles and peel towers. Things they had learned in infant school, but it did them good to come to it all again. They traced the outline of the county, marking in castles: Haydon Bridge; Alnwick and Bamburgh on the coast, Lindisfarne on Holy Island; Featherstone at Haltwhistle; Kirknewton, Newcastle. There were more castles to the mile in their county than anywhere else in the British Isles, he reminded them. More battle sites.

As the boys went up through the school they had local history under their belt, a solid foundation to anchor them for the rest of their lives: that was what Straughan said he wanted – another historian, and a Northumbrian to the last cell of his body. Then they could look at the world. He spun the great globe in the hall.

Everyone sensed that the world was changing: here, with men out of work and women scraping by; with the great march from Jarrow to London last autumn. Here, and in Europe: civil war in Spain, Hitler and Franco in alliance, women and children blown to pieces in a market square.

'Listen to this,' Frank Embleton told his sixth-formers, reading out from *The Times*.

But the bell rang, homework was given, exams loomed in the summer.

The second year was Steven's own class. Each morning he took the register. Archbold, Aickman – that was Miss Aickman's nephew. Here, sir. Bell, Carr and Cowens. Dagg. Here, sir. Herdman and Hindmarsh. All the old names. In medieval times they'd have been feuding in *graynes*, clans. There were one or two feuds here now.

'Mather.' 'Here, sir.' 'McNulty. Moffat. Moffat?' Moffat's father had died two years ago, after months in the sanatorium. 'He's poorly again, sir.' He put a cross. Later in the morning a note would come. Potts. Rigby. Stoker. 'Here, sir.' Neat ticks in the column all the way down. Wanless. Wigham.

Margaret had wondered if your place on the register affected your sense of yourself. Sometimes, she'd said, she started at the bottom with her girls: she thought it did them good, suddenly to be first and last when you weren't used to it. And it made them laugh.

'Wilson.'

'Here, sir.'

'Good.' He closed the register. 'Get out your books.'

The room smelled of chalk dust and boys. By break-time they could smell pot-pie, wafting from the kitchen along the corridor, where everyone walked to the left.

In the staffroom he took his tea from the trolley. 'Have a bun,' said Frank Embleton, fresh from the Lower Sixth, and the Boer War. He passed the plate.

'Do you good, sir,' said the girl behind the trolley.

'That's right,' said Embleton, giving her a smile. Molly-on-the-Trolley was what Armstrong called her, a pretty girl. She brushed crumbs off her flowered pinny and smiled with a blush.

Embleton and Steven sat by the open window, away from all the smoke. Gowens had his pipe in his mouth almost before he was through the door; Armstrong and McLaughlin sat in clouds of Navy Cut. David Dunn stood in a corner, leafing through a heap of papers. One or two dropped to the floor.

Shouts of the boys came distantly from the playground at the front: on this side of the school they looked out over the hills. Frank Embleton's mind had left Spain and the Boers for now: he talked about Tom Herron, deputy head boy, whom he was preparing for a scholarship. Steven listened. Frank had been to Oxford, he was very bright: Straughan had made him Head of Department as soon as old Ogilvie retired. Dunn hadn't liked that, but no one had thought he would get it.

The morning sun shone on Embleton's fine young face and fair hair. He polished off his fruit bun, changed the subject.

'How were the holidays?'

'Quiet.' Steven looked away. 'I saw my parents. You?'

Frank said there'd been a little concert at home. He had a sister, Diana, a cellist, who played in a trio of friends.

A boy and a girl: that was the family Margaret had said she wanted. At once, it was what Steven had wanted too, though until they met he had scarcely given it a thought. Perhaps only children didn't. He'd had a dog as a boy.

Frank was still talking. He'd hardly heard a word.

'Shall we go for a drink one evening?'

'All right – thanks.' It was a long time since he'd been out and about.

The bell rang from the playground and they got to their feet. Year Three: the Industrial Revolution. Railways taking coal down from Tyneside to the river, Puffing Billy, colliers taking coal down the Tyne to open sea, and to London. Stephen-

33

son's Rocket. Stephenson's High Level Bridge at Newcastle, an amazing achievement.

'Me great-granddad worked on that, sir.'

'Me uncle's out of work, sir.'

Shipyards were closing. Steelworks were closing. The Jarrow march down to Westminster had changed nothing.

'He's on National Assistance now.'

Summer unfurled. In May they had a day off for the Coronation: bunting all around the Square, trestle tables set out beneath the trees. When Edward VIII abdicated so shockingly in December, it was days after Margaret's funeral, and Steven had barely noticed. Now Miss Aickman played the National Anthem in Assembly as if she were at the Proms. She was all excited about the little princesses.

Then it was cricket, exams, meetings.

The yearly school exams were held in the classrooms; the big public ones, School Certificate, and Higher, in the hall: Miss Aickman welcoming the invigilators, Mr Straughan in his gown at Assembly, tall as a Scots Pine, telling his boys he knew they would be a credit to him. Kirkhoughton Boys, one of the best in the county, and don't forget it. His general kindness made his rare anger all the more terrifying: unruly boys who were sent to him were sometimes sick whilst waiting outside his room. He used the cane rarely, but he used it.

Papers turned over, pen caps off, eyes down. You may begin.

Before that, as every term, came the departmental meetings, and in the summer Straughan sat in on them – summoned the staff to his office, in fact. It was like having an inspection, one or two new, younger staff muttered now and then, but it certainly focussed the mind.

'Come in, gentlemen.'

His windows were open on to the fresh May morning; they

34

could hear Miss Aickman clattering away next door, the ping of her typewriter as she came to the end of a line.

'Have a seat.'

Embleton, Steven and Dunn took the chairs before the mahogany desk.

Straughan, an historian, was also something of a philosopher. He thought there were questions to be asked about the past, and the progress of mankind, liked to engage his staff in discussion. Frank had responded to all this at once, when he arrived in '34, and Straughan had at once been alert to that, to his gifts and intellect.

And he'd passed over David Dunn, as everyone knew he would have to: a man who'd come back from the Somme with a smashed leg and shellshock, who was now in his fifties and still not quite right. Fit to teach? Just. Better in class than out of it, apparently. A man like Straughan wouldn't get rid of a man like Dunn.

Steven had been passed over, too, or rather not encouraged to apply for the departmental headship when old Ogilvie retired, but he hadn't expected anything else: a local boy who'd made it to university, he knew he needed a good few years under his belt before promotion. And now he was glad that he had no more responsibility: teaching steadily was as much as he could manage. Even in meetings, her face sometimes swam before him. It swam before him now, and he briefly closed his eyes.

Straughan lit his pipe. 'Shall we begin with the reports?'

They went through them all, year by year, noting the rising stars, the strugglers. From Jack Bown and Tom Herron, destined for Oxford, to Donald Hindmarsh, who'd only just scraped through the first year. But a good lad, they all agreed.

'History is about how men have learned to live, is it not?' said Straughan, tamping down his pipe. 'If a lad like Hindmarsh can be brought to understand that – how Alcibiades lived and suffered, as Aristotle had it – he might be a bit more interested.' He dropped a match in a vast wastepaper basket. 'How did men learn to make tools, build somewhere to live, use the wheel, reckon time? How did they learn to write? Even within the constraints of the syllabus we can go back to first principles, can we not, Mr Coulter?'

Steven said that they could. Straughan's rhetorical questions could make you feel as if you'd been told to get up from your desk and stand by the blackboard.

'And of course the individual man is subject to great events, is he not?' Straughan went on, puffing away. 'Why do men live where they do? Because of invasion, colonisation, war.'

Dunn was tugging at a long loose thread on his shirt cuff. Was he listening?

Frank was: he leaned forward intently, as Straughan went relentlessly on.

'When did men begin to think about themselves, and the world?' he demanded of the smoky room. 'These are the kind of things I hope you're discussing with your sixth-formers, Mr Embleton. If you try to answer them, you cover the history of religion, politics, science. History itself, do you not?'

'Of course!' You could see that Frank loved all this. He raised his hand, flung it open, as if he were making a debating point, or taking part in an animated tutorial, college windows offering a view of the quad's immaculate lawn. 'And to get the boys thinking about how history is described – that's so important, isn't it? To understand that nothing is neutral, that historians have their own drum to beat.'

The thread round Dunn's finger grew tighter, and snapped. He sat up, as if he'd been discovered doing something foolish at the back of the class.

'There are times when the same drum has to beat for everyone.'

'You're absolutely right.' Frank looked at him warmly, and with that look Steven saw, not for the first time, how compelling he was: clever, but always generous, wanting a man who had been through hell, and perhaps would never quite recover, to feel equal and included. How some girls might fall for that, he thought suddenly. Fall deeply, even.

'Now for instance,' Frank went on. 'Europe – Spain – that little town bombed to bits – the boys should know about it, we should all be discussing it in class. Are we?'

'I believe Mr Coulter is on the Industrial Revolution at the moment,' Straughan said drily.

'But history is now!' said Frank, as the bell rang out in the playground.

'And now we need to get the boys through their examinations,' said Straughan, reining him in, turning from philosopher to pragmatist in a moment.

'But Mr Dunn is right.' Frank flung out his hands, and knocked the ink well on the desk. 'We need to be standing together against what looks like the rise of something terrible, don't you agree?'

Straughan reached for the inkwell and rose. They rose with him. 'Thank you, gentlemen.'

They gathered up their papers. Dunn dropped a heap, and bent stiffly to scoop them up. Out in the corridor, as the boys swarmed by, he said: 'If there's another war—' He gave his strange, exploding laugh, and Steven looked away, seeing a few boys snigger.

Cricket was out on the playing fields at the bottom of the hill, next to the recreation ground. In winter, football, and hockey for Kirkhoughton Girls; now it was cricket again, and the girls played tennis on the court behind their school. The boys poured out on to the Square in the afternoons, walked in pairs beneath the trees and down along Main Street: Armstrong up at the head, Embleton or Coulter, as Steven thought of himself at school, bringing up the rear.

The talk was of County cricket, of how Wisden had once named Frank Townsend cricketer of the year even though Northumberland had never won the Cup. When they passed the turning to Milk Lane he looked away, though he noticed one or two boys from the Lower Sixth turning towards it now and then at the sound of girls' voices.

'Sir, Mr Coulter, sir? When are we playing Hexham?'

He thought it was July, once the exams were over.

They were crossing Bridge Street. A bus rumbled by. Elaborate summer clouds sailed over the hills ahead of them, dotted with grey stone farmhouses and dry stone walls, sprinkled with the sheep which were always there, always grazing, moving this way and that in sun and enormous shadow.

Windswept and rain-washed in winter, splashed now with sunlight as the clouds moved slowly by, the hills and enormous feudal fields were part of the great continuities which, amidst talk of unemployment, of dark events in Europe, still anchored all their lives: sheep on the hills, farming, football, cricket; the piano at assembly, the bell ringing out between lessons, the lessons themselves. And sometimes all this was enough to make him forget, for half a morning, or part of an afternoon, what had happened.

Then she returned to him, her sweet clever face and red-brown hair before him, and he blinked, or shook his head: what could he have been thinking of? And it all began again.

'All right, boys, go and change.'

They raced to the pavilion.

Towards the end of the summer term came two more annual events: the Governors' meeting and the Sixth-form dance, held with Kirkhoughton Girls in the Assembly Rooms.

'Will you come?' asked Frank Embleton, as he and Steven sat outside the Queen's Head. The evening sun slanted along the Shambles. Inside, in the snug, they were playing darts as usual.

'I don't think so.'

When he and Margaret had gone together, the summer of their wedding, she'd spun beneath his arm, and skipped in and out of the stamping, clapping line, the bows of the ceilidh band on the platform going so fast you'd think they'd fly out of their hands. Everyone was there, as always, Mr Straughan twirling Miss Brierley like a spinning top, the sixth-formers with their exams all behind them whooping and shouting. At the end, when they stepped out into the dusky street, they'd passed a boy and a girl pressed tight up against one another in the shadows, and he'd pulled Margaret to him and kissed her hard.

'It might do you good,' said Frank now, draining his glass.

Darts thudded into the target in the snug; the pub cat came out and wound herself round his legs. Steven bent down to stroke her.

'I'll see. Let me get you another.'

When he came back, the cat was on Frank's lap. He talked, as he caressed her, about taking his sixth-formers to walk in the Bavarian Alps for a week at the end of term. The trip had been planned with Duggan, Head of Geography, for months, though with things as they were now in Germany it felt—

'Well, I half-wonder if we should be going. On principle, I mean. But it gives us an opportunity to get to know the boys properly – I'm sure we'll be safe.' Frank had such confidence, such charm, you felt he'd be safe anywhere. 'Then it's home with the family,' he said. 'Usual sort of summer, I expect.'

The usual sort of summer at Great Whitton, it seemed, was tennis, boating on the lake. Steven sat listening to this talk of another world, unable to imagine it, really. Lunch parties, drives. Frank was one of the few members of staff to run a car, which he parked on the Square, attracting glances. A Riley Imp, he told the boys who clustered round it at the end of the day. It was red. *Red!* They gazed at its open top, and long sleek bonnet.

'Want a spin?' he'd ask sometimes.

'Yes, *please*, sir!'

'Hop in.'

Now he said to Steven: 'Come over one day, we'd love you to.' And he mentioned his sister again, Diana, who played the cello, and her best friend, Margot Heslop, whom he might invite to the school dance, and who lived out at Hepplewick. The garden of Hepplewick Hall, like the one at Great Whitton, had been done by Capability Brown.

'Diana and I spent our early childhood there. Shared a governess.'

And as he had done once or twice before, Steven wondered that someone with this kind of background was not teaching at some great public school, instead of an old Board School turned Grammar. But Frank, on the face of it cast in an upper-class, Oxbridge mould, was individual, alert to a world beyond his: he made that clear in every meeting. '*History is now!*' He read widely, belonged to some kind of left book-club in London, said in the staffroom that George Orwell was changing his life. Gowens had growled.

But now he was talking again about the summer. Margot played with his sister in the trio he'd mentioned in the staffroom, with another old friend, George Liddell. 'We all grew up together, it was a lot of fun.' He hesitated. 'I know it's hard for you, Coulter – what's happened – but do come over if you can. We'd love it.'

'Thank you,' said Steven, and wondered: why would someone like Embleton stretch out a hand to someone like me? The beer on an empty stomach was making his head swim. 'Let's get something to eat.'

They ate bread and ham in the snug: mellow evening light at the windows, old men at their dominoes in a corner, the darts game concluding with a sudden shout.

He didn't go to the dance, but the Governors' meeting, held the week after, was something you just had to do. A hot July evening, almost the end of term, walkers out on the hills, windows flung wide. Straughan, in his gown, stood at the door to greet the little group: Arthur Shaw, the vicar of St Peter's; two retired teachers; Ernest Bradbury, the head of a tannery in Gosbridge, whose son was shining in the Lower Sixth.

Straughan looked taller and craggier than ever.

'Good evening, gentlemen. Splendid to see you all.' He was good at welcomes, always finding something to make people laugh and unwind a bit.

'Do sit down.' And as Miss Aickman gave out the agenda he made the same little joke he made every year. 'Six items to get through before the main business of supper.'

A good spread was laid out in the dining hall; Miss A. had done the flowers. The only woman in the school, apart from the cooks and the cleaners.

'Now, then. Item One: raising funds to renew the Science lab.'

And so it began, with talk of a grant from the Local Education Authority, and the announcement of a donation from the tannery. 'Very generous, Mr Bradbury.' Then it was on to the appointment of a new classics teacher, with Thompson's retirement; the possibility of a music teacher, which Mr Embleton had raised.

The hymns at Assembly were generally accompanied in workmanlike fashion by Miss A. The piano was scuffed and unremarkable, had stood in the hall for ever. But some of the boys sang pretty well, she said, looking up from the Minutes –

you could hear Benwell and Naylor, for instance, and what about young Stote in the first year, whose voice was lovely, really. Wispy Mr Shaw said he'd heard Stote sing at St Peter's, coming now and then with his parents, and though music had never been on the curriculum – wasn't an academic subject, after all – perhaps they should develop it a bit.

'I think we should,' said Embleton. 'I think we should have a school orchestra. Piano lessons at least. I have a friend—'

Dunn gave an embarrassing yawn. Embleton always had a friend. It was very hot; the agendas became fans. But Straughan was never one to make a meeting longer than it had to be, and within the hour music had been put on hold, the interview date for the classics applicants arranged, and they were on to the annual prizes.

Steven proposed Wanless for the history prize in the second year and Johnny Mather as the best all-rounder. Duggan put forward Tom Herron for the Sixth Form Cup. And then it was over, and everyone milling into the dining room, complementing Miss A. on the flowers, talking about the holidays.

'You'll be getting away, I hope,' people said to Steven, one after the other. Wispy Mr Shaw pressed his hand. And he felt their unspoken thoughts: that he was too young to grieve for too long; that what had happened was a tragedy, of course it was. But life lay ahead, did it not?

4

THAT SUMMER, HE began to write to her.
Dearest Margaret . . . My dearest love . . . .

He wrote sitting at the kitchen table, the door open on to the grassy track and the paper lifting a little in the breeze. When it rained he kept the door open still, listening to its patter into the water butt beside it, and on to the slate roof, watching it soak into the ground.

He wrote after breakfast. *Last night I let myself think you were in my arms again. I held you to me, as if you were well again . . .*

He wrote before he climbed the stairs to bed, the evening light filling the kitchen with shadows. *I'm praying I'll dream of you tonight. Perhaps I should murmur a spell . . .*

Sometimes he did dream of her, once had a nightmare from which he woke shouting her name. *I dreamt you were dying out on the moor, and I couldn't find you . . .*

No, he couldn't tell her that, it would upset her too much.

That was how close he felt to her now, in this solitude.

He did the same things every day: it was like settling a coat round his shoulders. In the mornings he tended the vegetable garden, weeding, digging up potatoes, picking the beans and carrots his father had got him to sew in the spring, telling her how they were getting on. The hawthorn tree was in dark leaf now, chaffinch and stonechat flitting in and out.

I remember you sitting beneath it, my love. I remember you watching me while I made the new door. You would have watched our children in that way – they would have thrived, doing things under your eye.

In the afternoons he went walking, and the letters ran within him, over and over.

The gorse is so bright, and the air is full of lark song – the larks are everywhere now. I stand and listen, and watch them drop like stones to the nest . . .

Today, by the river, I saw an otter. He slipped into the water when he heard my footsteps, and I saw him as clear as anything – a big dog, his head above the water as he swam with the current. The river is very full and fast, after all the rain we had last week. You would have loved him . . .

A card came from Frank Embleton, walking with Duggan and the boys in Bavaria.

We've tramped round ice-age lakes and bogs. Everyone pretty fit. Do come and have lunch when I get back. I'll be in touch.

Steven propped it up on the mantelpiece above the range. He didn't want to go to Great Whitton for lunch, or meet new people. These weeks were for Margaret, for the two of them, close to one another again, and if nobody understood that, so be it.

School fell away. From high on the moor, on the clear summer days, he could see the distant buildings of the town, which he visited only for provisions, rumbling in on the bus. Sometimes, passing the shut-up gates, he saw some of the boys, out of uniform.

'Afternoon, sir.'

'Afternoon, McNulty. Hindmarsh.'

He put bread and cold meat and groceries into a bag and rode home. The bus was full of holiday-makers. After supper, he lit the lamp and settled to writing once more.

There's a great big moth just come in at the door, I think it might be a Puss Moth . . .

44

The letters gave shape to the days, comforted and uplifted him as nothing else had done. He saw her bright intent face as she read of the otter, the larks, the fat lambs taken down to market, the bubbling call of the curlew, which was everywhere now. It all went in, with news of their families, the only people he could tolerate. *Dad's had a commission from a house outside Haydon Bridge, quite a grand place, he says. They want a new sideboard, something modern. He says everyone's after Art Deco now.*

Sometimes, visiting his parents, he almost gave them her love.

He packed boxes of vegetables to take them for Sunday lunch in Birley Bank, or to take to her parents for Saturday supper in Cawbeck. Not that they were really in need, with their own well-tended gardens, but still – he knew that they liked it. On Saturdays he took the bus out across country: the windows open, the summery wind blowing in from across the fields. In Cawbeck village, he walked slowly in the afternoon heat, along to grassy Church Lane, and through the churchyard. Tall cow parsley was fading now in high summer, but the scent of it hung in the air. Up on the moor there was only the heather and gorse.

Margaret Coulter, née Ridley, beloved wife of Steven
19th June 1912–3rd December 1936

I set gorse on your grave, my love, just a few sprigs in a jar, as you used to have it in the kitchen, and I felt you so close beside me. They've put sheep in the churchyard again, and the grass is cropped neat round your stone . . .

Andrew Ridley was home for the long vacation, talking more easily now: of his finals coming up, of his lodgings, his tutors; of criminal law, of something called tort. They had supper out in the garden, the four of them, where there should have been five. The cat came prowling out of the flowerbeds, sometimes with a mouse or a vole. Bats flitted about as the sun went down, and the scent of roses was everywhere.

'Take some home with you, Steven.'

Her mother wrapped them in newspaper, wet at the stems. Back at the cottage, he put them in one of the stone jars they'd found in a cupboard when they moved in, and set it on the washstand, once filled with that terrible blood. The scent filled the room like a prayer, or benediction.

Your mother has sent me home with roses again. They're up in our bedroom, darling.

He washed, went to bed, took her into his arms.

The town was almost empty now, everyone gone to the coast. Long summer days by the sea.

I'm thinking of that time we walked out to Lindisfarne from Alnwick, and almost got cut off by the tide.

He was cut off by the tide now, and on many days had no desire at all to return.

It's just us, as it used to be, darling.

The town was very hot, away from the moor's cooling breeze.

Just us, just us . . .

But there was Miss Aickman, walking with her basket along Market Street, stopping in the Square and greeting him. He almost jumped. Yes, he was keeping well, thanks, and hoped she was, too.

'And there's Mr Embleton,' she said suddenly, and he turned and saw him, in jacket and open shirt, walking down through the Square and waving. A young woman was beside him: tall, in a straight green dress and straw hat.

'Steven!' Frank was striding up. 'Miss Aickman, good to see you.'

Introductions, smiles, Frank so easy and kind. 'Our school secretary. My friend Steven Coulter. My friend Margot Heslop.'

She held out her hand with a smile. 'How do you do?'

Dark hair was visible beneath the rim of pale straw; she carried herself as if a book lay flat upon her head. She was Margot, not Margaret, and Frank had mentioned her before, but the name was close enough for his stomach to do a nosedive.

'How do you do?' He took her hand awkwardly, and at once released it.

Then Miss Aickman said she must be off, and the three of them stood there in the shade of the trees, Frank saying how he'd hoped he might see him, and how was he, and do please come up one day this week, come up tomorrow for lunch, everyone was there. Margot would be joining them. He touched her arm lightly; she gave him a smile.

'That's very kind.' Steven floundered for an excuse. 'May we leave it for a day or two? I'm a bit - well - I'm keeping to myself at present.'

'Of course.' Frank gave his own easy smile. 'Just come when you can.'

And they said their goodbyes, and he turned away from them.

Was he tipping a bit towards madness? Unable to make conversation with a woman just because of her name? Unable to accept an invitation? He was too much alone, they all said it: his parents, her parents. But he'd been an only child, he reminded them all, he was used to solitude. In the long summer holidays of his boyhood, he'd often been out alone day after day, with his dog and his sandwich, walking lanes high with cow parsley and rose bay willow herb, meeting no one but a farm worker, or pony and trap, clip-clopping along in the heat.

This is different, Steven, love.

It was. But those days had made it possible for him to be

47

alone now. To long to be alone with her, just the two of them.

You need to be with people sometimes, it's not good for anyone—

Andrew Ridley came up, bringing a cake from his mother: they went walking together, taking bread and cheese. That felt good, because he was a part of her. They talked again about Edinburgh, Andrew hoping to get articles in the autumn with a firm in Prince Street.

'You don't want to come back here, then?'

'We'll see. Edinburgh's a good place to start.'

They ate their lunch near the Roman fort, saw a line of young men in uniform marching down the hillside. Back at the cottage, he made tea and they polished off most of the fruit cake. The moment he'd seen Andrew off at the bus stop, walking back up the stony track in the dusk, he was writing again.

Andrew was here this afternoon - we walked out to the fort. Caught sight of a group of the Fusiliers, out on exercise . . .

The evenings grew shorter; wind whipped over the moor. He got out his books, from the case beneath the clock. For a morning it felt as if he'd never seen them before. Then Romans and raids and monasteries began to tick away in him as he looked at the syllabus; he planned lessons, pulled out a book about Bede, pulled out more about Henry VIII, for the Upper Fifth. Wolsey in power; the breach with Rome. He knew that he had to go back to school. Not once since her death had he ever thought he would leave, except in the week leading up to the funeral. Then, he had thought he would never do anything, ever again.

I'm getting ready for term as usual, darling . . .

And he knew that once it all began he probably wouldn't write to her again. Not like this, with this sweet, comforting intensity. On the last day, before the first staff meeting, he put all the letters in a pile, and re-read them. Then he put them into a brown foolscap envelope and kissed it, and tucked it into the bookcase, next to her childhood copy of *Jane Eyre*.

He climbed the stairs to bed, took her into his arms once more; lay with the window open, looking out at the last summer stars.

PART THREE

I

A NOTHER FOUL WET autumn afternoon. But here, in
the drawing room – music! Diana's fair head was bowed
over the cello, skinny little George held his violin aloft, and
Margot, now and then, caught sight of her hands and dark hair
reflected in the upraised lid of the grand. Half-past three, but
the fire and the lamps were lit and the room shone against the
rain sweeping across the garden and beating against the tall
squared window panes.

The last bars faded. They were still for a moment. Then
Diana sighed, George lowered his bow, and Margot turned on
the piano stool to look at them.

'Yes?'

'I think so.'

'Can we just take that from letter K?'

'If we do it any more we'll have nothing left for tonight.'
George almost shook himself, like a shivering little animal, and
walked across to where the violin case lay open on a chair. His
feet in scuffed brogues sounded loud, then soft, moving from
board to rug. He laid down his violin, and closed the lid.

Whimpering and scratching came from outside the door. He
tiptoed over, flung it wide.

'My friend!'

'Oh, George! You've made him jump.'

He bent to the sleek black head.

'In you come.'

Wag wag, patter patter, over to the fire.

'Good dog, that's it.' He flung himself into the wing chair

and patted the seat. A black nose poked in, a head squeezed adoringly against his thigh. George leaned back, patting the sleek coat, closing his eyes. 'Any chance of tea?'

'I expect you'd like us to make it.' Margot closed her score. Diana was resting her cello on its stand, wiping the bow.

'How kind.'

It was freezing out in the hall. 'Must light the fire after tea.' They hurried down the passage, with its row of bells which nobody rang any more, and into the kitchen. A huge room to heat, but warmer in here with the range. The big black kettle hummed.

'Are you nervous?' Diana pulled out a tray from the rack.

'I'm always nervous.' Margot opened the pantry door. An ice-house. 'You know I am,' she said, and then: 'I can almost see my *breath*.' She drew a covered half fruit cake from a shelf and came out shivering, closing the door behind her with her foot.

'It never shows. And George always pretends he's not.' Diana put a cotton-lace cloth on the tray, set out cups and saucers, pulled open a rattling drawer for knives and teaspoons. She'd been coming here since childhood, knew every shelf and cupboard. There had been Nanny, then, of course. Nanny and Miss Renner.

The day nursery had beeen made into a schoolroom; the four of them sat round the table, Miss Renner at the top in a high-backed chair. Maths books, poetry anthologies, a globe. French conversation.

'*Bonjour, mes enfants.*'

'*Bonjour, mademoiselle!*'

Miss Renner had a fiancé, she told them, fighting in France. Captain Gibson. She pinned little flags in the map on the wall, to show them important places. As the years went by, so the pins moved. Liege. Ypres. Neuve-Chapelle. Loos. Verdun. The Somme. None of them ever forgot the Somme.

'Shall we have toast?'

They carried it all back to the drawing room, the grandfather clock in the hall just striking four, the rain going on and on.

'What good girls you are.'

'Make yourself useful and put another log on.'

The Hepplewick Trio, taking tea. George had come up with the name.

'This is where we met, where it all began.'

Margot Heslop, Diana Embleton, George Liddell.

'Frank would have made it a quartet.'

'But Frank isn't musical, is he?'

'*Political.*'

A general sigh.

Hepplewick Hall lay well back from a quiet lane, the entrance shielded by trees. A broad, left-curving drive swept up to a flag-stoned terrace. The house was elegant, built of stone, with tall chimneys, and the plans which William Newton had drawn up in 1761 were still kept in the bank in Morpeth. Newton had grafted the house on to the fifteenth-century pele tower, empty and looming. Margot's father said he wasn't sure if you could graft something grand on to something much simpler, but that was the word they all used.

Once, the Hall had had staff: generations of Heslops had rung those bells, summoning cook, parlour maid, footman. Grooms had run out at the arrival of carriages, horses had clip-clopped over the stable-yard. One of them, a tall black hunter, had a portrait up in the dining room, whose walls were hung with Heslops: Margot's father said it was good enough to be a Stubbs.

These days a Ford Model T stood in a loose box. There were no horses, and almost no staff at all, for in the 1930s the idea of service had given way to the idea of work – when you could get work. It was only the gardener, old Barrow, whose name they'd long since stopped laughing about, who'd been here for ever and still came up twice a week, with Mrs Barrow. She cleaned, and sometimes cooked, while he worked in the kitchen garden, tended the rose beds and the beehive, heaped up bonfires, mowed the endless lawn.

A towering cedar stood on the grass, on the right of the curving drive, and darkened the fine casement windows at the front, but no one had ever wished that cedar gone: generations of Heslops had taken tea in its shade on summer days; a swing still hung there.

'Push harder! I want to go *high!*'

They took it in turns, out in the garden after lunch, whenever it was fine. Frank was the tallest, the most in demand as a pusher, strong as a horse at seven, able to bat the ball which Miss Renner threw right into the shrubbery.

'I'll get it!'

'No, me!'

Margot – 'tall for a girl' as Miss Renner said, and she herself lean and rangy – went racing over the grass, little George hurtling after. Dreamy Diana stood dreaming.

Cricket and croquet and the swing. And races.

'Go!'

Down from the sundial and over the lawn, down to the ha-ha, quite a long way. Capability Brown had put it in, riding over from Capheaton in his carriage on a hot afternoon in the summer of 1762, walking with Sir Thomas Heslop over the unmade ground: that was how Miss Renner thought it might have been. Sir Thomas had made his money in coal. He wanted something to show for it: grand house, grand garden. Brown's elegant plans, too, were kept in the vault in Morpeth.

The children stood on the edge of the ha-ha, panting. Slow-moving cattle grazed the field on the other side. Frank almost always won.

And at the end of the afternoon, the pony and trap came for him and Diana to take them back to Great Whitton, and another for George, to clip-clop him home to Coquet Bridge. Miss Renner went to clear everything away in the schoolroom, and Margot ran looking for her mother.

'Here I am, darling.'

Up in the broad airy bedroom, up at her dressing table, fastening an earring, smiling at the reflection of her daughter as she came running in, over the blue and green rug. They leaned together, watching the endless images of themselves in the triple glass.

'So many of us!'

Often, before bed, her mother would play the piano. Sometimes she sang.

'Now the day is over,
Night is drawing nigh;
Shadows of the evening
Steal across the sky . . .'

The grandfather clock in the hall struck the hour. Margot leaned against the piano and watched the shadows lengthen over the garden.

When it rained – and it rained a good deal – they played inside, allowed in the drawing room to read on the window seat, dress dolls in the corner, spread soldiers on the floor. Miss Renner talked again of her fiancé. She played them marching songs on the piano, singing away. 'Pack up Your Troubles in Your Old Kit Bag', 'It's a long way to Tipperary', 'Here we are, Here we are again!'

They stamped up and down, they sang as the rain poured on. Sometimes the songs were gentle and sad, not war songs at all: 'The Eriskay Love Lilt', 'Loch Lomond'.

'And I'll be in Scotland *afore* ye . . .'

The Scots had always raided, and the Northumbrians raided back. The pele tower had been built so strong that no Scot could get in there: that was what Margot's father told her, and she told the others, thinking pele was spelled peal, and thinking of bells.

Alone in the great big drawing room, she ran her fingers over the piano keys. She gazed at Miss Renner's music, and at her mother's, turning the pages. She banged about, she loved it. When she was six, she began to have lessons. By the time she was seven, they knew she was going to be good.

By then, her mother had stopped doing pretty things at her dressing table, or playing the piano in the evenings. She was lying in bed all the time.

'But I want to *see* her!'

'Later, my duck. Mummy's resting now.'

When Margot was eight, it was 1916. That was the year her mother died, and when Miss Renner pulled her on to her lap and rocked her, she was sobbing not only for Evelyn Heslop but for Edward Gibson, who had taken a lock of her hair to France, and written letters beginning *My darling Emily* (she pressed the page to her lips), and died in the Battle of the Somme.

'For me and my true love will never meet again . . .'

They never sang 'Loch Lomond' after that. They looked away from the bright little flag on the map. And after that everything changed. Frank and George went off to prep school, Miss Renner stayed bravely on. But a motherless only-child could not be at home with a nanny and a governess for ever, even if there was another little girl sharing lessons.

In 1918, Margot and Diana were sent to boarding school. Thomas Heslop hugged them both to him as Barrow heaved their trunks up into the trap.

'Please don't cry.'

'Don't *you* cry, Daddy.'

They clip-clopped away down the autumn lanes.

'Here we be, Miss Heslop.'

They held hands as they looked at the long flight of steps.

Margot's memories of her mother faded. The great deep house remained. When she came home for the holidays she jumped down from the trap and ran over the flags. She kissed the brass knob above the letter box, stood looking about her as Barrow led the pony back to the stable yard. The branches of the cedar rose and fell in the wind; the swing swung to and fro. To the right of the door, at the corner of the house, stood a huge old forsythia, which tossed in the long wet spring, shaking yellow flowers all over the flagstones, floating in pools in the hollows. Her mother had painted a watercolour of it: windy sky, grey stone, lemon-bright flowers and shining water. It hung on the landing now.

Indoors, Margot put down her schoolbag and kissed the case of the grandfather clock. She stood in the shadowy hall, feeling suddenly very alone, and watched the rose-pink smiling sun above the face move infinitesimally to the right. She waited for the chime to welcome her. Her own grandfather had listened to it, when he was a boy: her father had told her that.

'You're back!'

He came out of the library to greet her, his dog behind him, as the clock began to strike. She flew into his arms.

A ND NOW THE pale profile of the moon rose slowly behind the faded numerals, trailing his dusky-mauve clouds. Half-past six on this October evening, the whirr of cogs and wheels, before the chimes began. 'Dah-dah-dah-dah,' as Margot and her mother used to sing it, climbing the stairs to the candlelit nursery, and Nanny. 'Dah-dah-dah-dah!' Next morning it was Miss Renner, putting out the school books at a quarter to nine: 'Dah-dah-dah-dah, Dah-dah-dah-dah! Dah-dah-dah-dah . . .'

'Bong! Bong!' Frank and Diana and George, arriving on the stroke of nine for lessons.

That was a long time ago, before Miss Renner became too sad to sing; and now the half-closed eyes of the moon appeared, smiling his secret smile as the clock began to strike. Already people were arriving. 'Dah-dah-dah-dah!' sang Margot, churning with nervous energy, running downstairs in her long dark dress and jacket.

'All right, darling? All set?'

'Yes, thank you, Father.'

He stood with his back to the hall fire, the dog beside him. Firelight played over the hearth. A car swished up in the wet. Old Barrow's daughters were on duty as usual: Grace at the door, and Nellie in the kitchen, setting glasses on trays, smoothing back her hair. Footsteps came hurrying over the flags, and umbrellas were shaken out in the porch, a Victorian addition to Newton's plain facade. The doorbell rang commandingly.

'Good evening, sir, madam. May I take your coats?' Little

Grace Barrow, soon to be married and saving hard, carried wet wool and tweed to the stand. The dog left Thomas Heslop's side and nosed his way to the cold hands of every guest. Wag wag, pat pat.

'Hello, boy, hello, hello. Good evening, Tom.'

'Good evening! Good to see you.'

A Hillman, a Rover, then a purring Bentley, slowed and turned in from the streaming road. The cedar tossed above them and the swing swung wildly.

'A terrible evening!' Umbrellas dropped in the big brass stand.

'But lovely to have a concert to look forward to.' A little cloche hat starred with raindrops was lifted carefully off a glossy bob. 'Thank you, Grace.'

The Lindsays, the Gills and the Rutherfords, driving through the dark from Coquet Bridge, Wallington, Morpeth, Fenrather.

'Look at that fire!'

The doorbell again. The Liddells, bringing old friends.

Then: 'Nanny!'

Diana pressed forward, took her old hands.

'Hello, pet.'

Then: 'Miss Renner – how lovely of you to come.'

'You're looking very well, my dear.'

Miss Renner herself was looking as straight and composed as ever – but perhaps the lines round her mouth had deepened, thought Diana, as Grace took the long brown coat. All on your own, for twenty years! How could anyone bear it?

'Emily.' Thomas Heslop straightened up from the log basket. 'Come and get warm. And you, Nanny, that's it. We'll go through in a minute.'

'I hope the fire's stoked up in that drawing room.' Nanny held out her hands to the blaze. 'Where's my Margot?'

'Here I am!'

Into her arms, still so warm and strong.

'Remember me?' asked George, swanning up in his bow tie.

'I wouldn't forget a scamp like you, Master George.'

'Mr Liddell, thank you, Nanny. *Mr Liddell!*' He shimmied away.

Ring ring.

The Embletons! Diana greeted her parents with a kiss.

'You look lovely, darling.' And she did, thought her mother, stroking the soft fair hair, so pretty against concert midnight blue. 'Nervous?'

'Just a bit. Hello, Frank. Having a good half-term?'

'Very good, thanks. Let me introduce you—'

Yes: who was this, standing tall and so pale beside her brother?

'My friend, Steven Coulter,' Frank announced, and to Steven: 'My little sister.'

And then there was talk of how Diana and Steven knew one another's names, and of course, he taught with Frank, didn't he, and how nice of him to come. Was he musical?

Stephen shook his head. 'Not at all, I'm afraid.'

'But I twisted his arm,' said Frank, as the clock began slowly to strike the hour. 'I dug him out of his lair.'

'I say!' George was beside them. 'Anyone remember we're giving a concert? Hello, Frank. Hello, whoever you are. This way!'

A snow-white programme on every chair, the shutters closed against the rain, the room lit by lamps and candles. A buzz, as people took their seats. Sitting down next to Frank, Steven looked about him: at plaster moulding, pictures, a table heaped with books and copies of *The Field*, a silver cigarette case shining beneath a lamp. The room smelled of logs and candle wax and expensive scent: he knew it was expensive, though no woman he had ever known had ever worn anything like it.

Soap. Lavender water. That was what he knew. There was also the smell of dog: leaning forward, he saw the black Labrador, flopped before the fire with its marble mantelpiece. It felt like the one thing here he could connect with. A boy with a dog, out walking through the past.

The musicians had taken their places at the far end of the room, were opening their scores.

'I'm so glad you're here.' Frank, beside him, was bending back the programme, and Steven opened his own. Piano trios. Of course he knew the composers, but these pieces meant nothing to him. Brahms: Piano Trio No. 1 in B major, Op. 8 – he had no idea. Would he even be able to absorb it? Beyond hymns sung at church in childhood, and now at school assembly; beyond an occasional concert at Durham, he knew so little of music. And though Frank had said he didn't know much either, that couldn't be true. His usual kind modesty was surely at work: he'd grown up with it, through his friends and his sister, even if he didn't play.

It was Margaret who had been musical, who sang about the cottage, and on their walks together.

'We shall have a family, a girl for you, a boy for me . . .'

Her hand swung in his. The words blew away across the windy moor.

Illness had reduced that high clear voice to a whisper.

Someone was tinkling a fork against a glass: the room fell silent. Then Margot Heslop stepped forward from the piano, and gave her welcome – such a dreadful night, so good of you all; Brahms and Schubert, do hope you enjoy. She sat down again with the others: the tuning-up began.

Steven watched them: on the right, Diana Embleton, so pretty and fair in a full dark dress, bent over the cello between her knees; on the left, George Liddell, the eager little violinist, whose name Frank had told him as they came through, now tightening a string. Between them, in profile, Margot Heslop was composed, graceful, straight-backed. She struck a note or two; George and Diana drew their bows across the strings. A girl he hadn't noticed stood up from her chair beyond the piano, and stepped forward.

'The little page turner,' Frank murmured. 'One of Margot's pupils.'

'She teaches?'

'They all do – family support only goes so far. And it's good for them.'

The tuning-up was over. Somebody coughed, and was silent. The Hepplewick Trio glanced at one another, and Steven saw a connection, a swift understanding run between them. That same sense of a team seen out on the cricket pitch. And then the Brahms began.

Nothing could have prepared him for its effect. The gentlest tune, something instantly inviting, so lyrical and tender that he felt tears prick his eyes, and at once—

Oh, Margaret. Oh, my love . . .

He hadn't written to her for weeks. With the start of the autumn term he'd made himself concentrate: up at first light, striding down the track, his mind on the Lower Fifth: Henry VII, Wolsey, the Star Chamber. At night, when yearning and solitude filled him, he murmured her name, drew her to him, but soon fell exhausted to sleep. No letters, no river of love on the page.

But now—

The cello was taking the lead, repeating that lovely phrase, and now the violin began to soar.

I want you here, I want you beside me. I want you listening to this . . .

❦

At the interval, they all poured across the hall to the dining room. A fire burned here too, beneath another marble mantelpiece, with a portrait of a horse hung above it.

'Thank you, thank you.' Everyone had warmed up now; they took drinks from the trays which Nellie and Grace grasped tightly, moving through the throng. 'Well, wasn't that good?'

They all knew each other, it seemed, all talking away. Steven was used to boys, and the staffroom; he couldn't remember when he'd last been at a gathering like this, knowing no one. Frank said, 'I'll get you a drink. And you must meet my sister.' And he stood there waiting, like a new boy on the first day of term.

'You're a big lad now,' he heard his mother say suddenly, at the gates of his infant school. 'Be off with you.' But then came his father, a man of few words, liking best the long quiet hours in his workshop, with its sweet smell of sawdust and planking. 'If you've nowt to say, say nowt.'

Steven had nowt to say now: he was still full of the music, which he had no idea how to talk about; still so full of longing that for a moment he almost saw her, moving easily through the crowded room, her loose red-brown hair glinting in the lamplight, talking and laughing with a teacher's confidence; then coming to stand by his side, slip her hand in his.

Oh, darling . . .

'Hello.'

Diana Embleton was suddenly before him: he took in a cloud of pale hair and light scent, pink-and-white skin above rustling taffeta. 'My brother's not looking after you, he's so naughty. I hope you enjoyed that.'

'Very much.' He cleared his throat, gave a smile. 'I'm afraid I don't really know about music, but—'

'There are a million things I don't know about,' she said.

'I can vouch for that.' Frank was back, glasses in hand.

'Oh, you. What have you been doing?'

'What does it look like?' He gave Steven a glass, and his sister another. 'Well done, Di: that was lovely.'

'How kind.'

Frank put a hand on Steven's arm. 'You must meet some more people.'

'He's only just met me.'

Listening to this banter, not really knowing how to match it, Steven glanced away. That was a very fine horse, above the fireplace, a fine black hunter whom someone must once have ridden at a gallop. A little knot of people was gathered by the fire beneath it: a stout, middle-aged couple and a tall greying man in a grey silk tie. Beside him stood Margot Heslop, and he saw that she had the same brow as this man, who must be her father, and the same dark eyes.

He sipped his drink. And he noticed the sombre eyes of her father in particular, because although Heslop appeared to be listening attentively to the talk, his gaze was often not on Margot, nor on their companions, but directed across the room – to his own little group, in fact, where Diana and Frank Embleton stood laughing together, two young people so attractive, so at ease with one another, you might almost have thought them a couple.

The rain beat on against the windows. Back in the drawing room, the Trio was tuning up once more as everyone took their places. Steven opened the programme again.

Schubert: Piano Trio No. 2 in E flat major. He thought Schubert might have been played at Durham, in one of the concerts he'd gone to, as he'd gone to exhibitions now and then, to broaden his mind. It had needed some broadening. On the whole, looking at paintings had moved him more.

The windows shook in their casements. Margot turned from the piano, and the delicate precision of that glance between the three of them caught at him again. Their heads went down. They began to play.

The opening was so strong and energetic that at first he felt overpowered. He sat gazing at Margot's hands, the extraordinary speed and control with which they ran over the keyboard, her arms outstretched. And then, as the piece developed, he became fascinated by all of them: by George's complete authority, and immersion – the way he lifted his bow at the end of a phrase, almost flung it; how he bent to the violin once more, as if they were in the deepest relationship – which, beginning to listen more attentively, Steven realised they were. As for Diana: she was transformed from the laughing, bantering young woman he'd just met to someone serious and intent. She frowned, she bent low. Once, when she took the lead, she raised her eyes from the music as if listening to something else, something beyond her own playing. Then she turned once again to the score.

He'd been too full of emotion in the Brahms to take in what he began to understand a little now: that the whole piece was a conversation between their instruments, a move from question to answer, from gentle enquiry to passionate response. He realised that he was never unaware of the piano, and that the physicality of such playing was extraordinary – for all of them, hugely demanding; but when he watched Margot's slender body half lift from the stool in a fast, dramatic passage, as if she couldn't stop herself, he began to wonder at what it must do to you, to play like this. And at who you must be, to want to make it your life.

The mood of the music was changing. What had been forceful and emphatic was all at once offering a theme which tore at him: soft, enquiring, oh, so sad.

And now he couldn't look at any of them. He put his head in his hands.

'You're not well?' Frank asked him, as the applause broke out at a triumphantly dramatic finale. He was full of concern.

'I'm fine.' Steven straightened up, feeling dazed. 'Sorry. That was wonderful.'

Before them, the Trio were making their bows, and someone called out 'Bravo!' They bowed again, then stood before their audience, faces alight. 'Bravo!'

You would love this, darling—

He made himself stop – *Pull yourself together!* He joined in the clapping as Diana Embleton bowed low, like a flower bent by the wind. Margot was smiling at her father, who was on his feet, with others rising behind him. And though he had been so moved, so swept up by feeling, for the second time this evening Steven now noticed something: George Liddell, energy and emotion crackling off him, was raking the audience intently, clearly looking for someone, until he smiled quickly, flushing, and looked away.

Supper, and they returned to the dining room, where the long mahogany table, china and glass on snowy linen, had been pushed up towards the far wall. Another portrait hung there, above the heads of the Barrow girls, serving in white aprons: a couple in eighteenth-century dress beneath a feathery tree, a long-nosed hunting dog at the man's side, two children leaning against their mother. A landscape stretched mistily away behind them.

Steven nodded towards it as he and Frank took their places in the queue.

'Who are they?'

'That's the first Thomas Heslop and his family. He looks like a landowner, doesn't he, but he made all his money in coal.'

'Like a lot of old families,' said Steven, wondering how the Embletons had made theirs. Coal, shipbuilding, tanning, engineering: mighty Northumbrian industries, something to be proud of, as Straughan told the boys in Assembly every year; and every one of them now in decline.

'*Me uncle's on National Assistance.*'

Around them the talk was of the concert, but not only of that, and Steven sensed that perhaps he wasn't the only person here who didn't know a great deal about what they had heard; that friends and neighbours were glad of an evening out, but had other things on their minds once it was over. Hunting. Politics. He heard 'Mussolini,' and turned to see a large fair-haired man holding forth, and then his pretty wife protest: 'Oh, Charles, please not now.'

Someone was lightly touching his arm. He turned to see Margot, dark and straight as an arrow, almost as tall as he was. After all she had given to the music, her composure, it seemed, was recovered.

'May I introduce you to my father? Father, this is Steven Coulter. He teaches with Frank at Kirkhoughton.'

Beside her, Thomas Heslop held out his hand. 'How do you do.'

'How do you do, sir.'

Small talk followed. Yes, Heslop knew the school, or rather its reputation. Harry Straughan was a good man, it seemed. And Steven taught history?

'Frank's my Head of Department.'

Frank gave a bow beside him. 'I try to keep the place in order.'

'You've done well,' said Heslop. 'We always knew you would.'

'Unlike the rest of us,' Margot said drily, and he patted her arm.

'You know I didn't mean that.' He turned back to Steven. 'You enjoyed the concert, I hope. Good, aren't they?'

'Very good,' Steven said, and didn't know what else to say. How could he tell them it had made him want to weep?

People were moving away from the table with their plates.

'And what do you want?' Heslop asked his dog, nosing over to him. He patted the hopeful head. 'You've had your supper.'

Steven looked down, felt a lift of the heart, and bent to stroke him.

'What a beautiful creature you are.'

Despite the formal phrase, it felt like the first natural thing he had said all evening, and as everyone laughed, small talk and courteous questions evaporated, in talk of dogs, of walking them, breeding them, feeding them. By the time they reached the table, where George and Diana were handing plates and glasses, he felt he might be among friends.

'Glad you came?' asked Frank, as they drove away. Rain gleamed in the headlights and pattered down hard on the roof. The wiper was swishing like mad.

'I am.' Steven was trying to get his legs organised: it was tight as a drum in there. 'It was good of you to ask me.'

And he was glad – unexpectedly so. How isolated he had become. An evening he had viewed with apprehension, with music which had both interested him and plunged him back into grief and longing, had ended in talk and laughter. For a little while he had been diverted.

'My sister enjoyed meeting you – everyone did. You must come to another.' Frank slowed as they came to the village, the headlamps shining on unlit cottages, then drove on past the church, picking up speed again. On this wet night only the cars of the concert guests were out, and most had left long before them.

'Thank you.' Steven yawned, and leaned back in the little bucket seat, closing his eyes. His mind was full of smoky candlelit rooms; of Margot's dark head bent over the keyboard, of her passionate engagement with the music; of fair hair falling in a mesmerising mass as Diana Embleton bowed low. Amidst all his impressions, he found himself recalling particular glances.

One was the swift *Yes: now!* which ran with a nod between the trio. But also: those two gazes across those crowded rooms. In the interval, Margot's father had let his eyes rest sombrely on a laughing girl in a sheen of taffeta. And at the end of the concert, George Liddell, lit up with applause, had searched in the audience for one especial face. Then he had found it, had flushed with a smile, and looked rapidly away.

'Frank?'

'Yes?'

'I—' He stopped himself, though he didn't know quite why. 'Nothing.'

They drove slowly on past the darkened fields.

It was very late. Nellie and Grace had piled up plates and glasses. 'Leave it, leave it,' said Margot, seeing them yawn. 'It can all wait until tomorrow.'

'If you're sure, Miss Heslop.' They pulled on their coats and galoshes, took their umbrellas and gazed at the rain from the open door. A mile down the road to the village. 'Our dad'll walk up to meet us,' said Nellie.

'Nonsense. I'll take you home.' Margot's father was beside them in the hall. 'Keep the dog in,' he said, and to the young women: 'Wait there.' And he put up his own umbrella and strode out to the stable yard.

Grace and Nellie stood shifting from foot to foot in the porch, until the engine started up, and the Ford came bumping out over the cobbles. 'In you get!'

They hurried out over the flags. 'Bye, Miss Heslop!'

'Goodnight! Thank you again!'

Margot closed the door behind them, drew the great curtain

across. And stood there quite still for a moment, logs breaking up in the hearth, the grandfather clock ticking steadily, the dog beside her.

'*What a beautiful creature you are.*'

She said it aloud, bending to stroke his dark head.

'Sweet of you to say so.' George appeared like a sprite, his bow tie loosened. 'Cocoa is served.'

They sat round the kitchen table, where a candelabra burned. This was one of the best moments, always: the concert done, everyone unwinding. And especially when, as tonight, they had played not in a church, or village hall, not in the drawing room of someone else's house, with separate journeys home; but here, where it had all begun: here, where Diana could stay the night in the nursery, and George in the guest room, breakfast in dressing gowns, everything easy and known.

'Pretty good?' said George, tipping his chair back. 'Are we agreed?'

'If Miss Renner saw you do that she'd have something to say.' Diana tapped on the table. '"That chair could slip and you could crack your head open, George Liddell, and then where would you be?"'

'Sorry, Miss Renner.' He leaned sharply forward, and the mugs of cocoa shook.

'"You're over-excited,"' said Margot, in Nanny's reproving tones.

'I am, I am!' He scraped the chair back again over the tiles; he danced round the kitchen, declaiming. 'It was good, it was good, it was very very good.'

'There'll be tears before bedtime.'

He pulled out his handkerchief and made to sob.

Diana was stirring her cocoa. 'An audience of over thirty on a dreadful night.'

'And who,' asked George, pulling his chair back and sitting down again, 'who was the shy new chap with Frank?'

'He teaches at Kirkhoughton,' said Diana. 'Steven something.'

'Steven Coulter,' said Margot.

Both of them looked at her. She reached for the sugar bowl. George moved it away.

'Give me that bowl.'

The front door banged, and a tail thumped beneath the table. Footsteps came along the passage.

'Father! We didn't hear the car.'

'You can't hear anything in this rain.' Heslop bent to the dog as George got up. 'Hello, boy, hello. Do sit down, George.' He pulled out a chair. 'Well, that was splendid. Well done, all of you.'

'Thank you, sir. Cocoa?'

'If there's any left.'

'I'll make it,' said Diana, picking up the jug.

He smiled at her. 'That's very kind.'

'I wonder what you thought of the Schubert,' said George, passing Margot the sugar bowl at last. 'The second movement – I'm afraid we missed a few notes.'

'You mean I did.' Diana was at the range, pushing back her mass of light hair, pouring milk into a battered old pan she had known since she was six. In the candlelight, her bare arms were creamy against the taffeta.

'Sir?' George asked Heslop. 'Did you notice anything?' And then again: 'Sir?'

3

THE RAIN POURED on and on. The boys came pelting across the playground as the bell rang out each morning, clamping their caps to their heads. The doormats were wet and muddy, there were puddles in the corridors, the cloakrooms smelled of wet wool and gabardine. The football pitch down across the burn was a sea of mud, and football was cancelled. The burn itself rose to the top of the bank. At this point in the long winter term everyone was tired and the wet gloom made them irritable.

'Quiet! Quiet, boys!'

It was only Straughan whose very presence had them silent at once, striding into the assembly hall, announcing the morning hymn.

'For all the *Saints* who from their labours rest,

Who Thee by faith before the world confessed,

Thy name, O Jesu, be forever blest . . .'

A rousing one like this got everyone going, Miss Aickman pounding away and the boys shouting out at the tops of their voices.

'A-a-le-LU-ya, A-a-a-le-LU-ya!'

Lessons afterwards could feel interminable; they were cooped up at break-time, gazing moodily out through the streaming windows, playing endless games of Hangman on the board.

'Music doth soothe the savage breast,' said Frank in the staffroom, thick with tobacco smoke. 'I'm sure we could do with more of it.'

Molly-on-the-Trolley rattled in. No one was really listening.

'I'm having a word with Straughan,' he said to Steven. 'Margot might come in and give lessons. The Trio might give a concert – do you think that would go down well? At Christmas?'

Steven said he was sure that it would. He got out his stuff for the third years: essays to return on the Wars of the Roses. Since the concert, he had been preoccupied with practicalities, waking in the cottage next morning to the sound of pouring water, stumbling downstairs and opening the kitchen door to see broken tiles strewn across the grass. He set buckets beneath the leak in the bedroom and hauled the mattress downstairs to sleep in the kitchen. It might be days before he could get up to the roof.

Returning on dark afternoons, he got out his torch as the bus swished away, and checked the wooden letter box on the tree at the foot of the track. He dug out damp envelopes once or twice a week: letters from his parents, Margaret's parents.

Terrible weather, love. How are you managing up there?

He read them as he stood, dripping, close to the range. The mattress with its tangle of bedclothes lay on the floor and made everything feel wrong and out of sorts.

There were days when he wondered if it was madness to go on living up there. Then he thought of leaving and knew that everything that had brought him happiness was in the cottage. 'Margaret,' he said aloud. He still did that.

'Father?' She knocked at the library door. 'May I come in?' No answer. She went in anyway. 'Father?'

He swung round in his chair. 'I didn't hear you.' Music was on the gramophone, the room full of rainy light.

'Schubert,' said Margot. 'This is the trio we played.' She stood listening to the record hiss and scratch, as her father took off his spectacles. He was at his desk in the window, overlooking the stable yard. Rain blew across it, the door of a loose box banged.

'Must get Barrow to see to that.'

The desk was piled high with letters and ledgers. Framed photographs stood at the back. Beneath it, the dog lay snoring. Schubert wound slowly down.

'I'm interrupting you,' she said, crossing to lift the heavy head. 'Just wondering what you might like for lunch. Will leftovers do?'

'They will. Thank you, darling.'

For years they had lived together, she and he; for years had had such conversations.

She keeps house for him, they said in the village. The Barrows go in, of course, but she keeps it all going.

There were other households like this, though more where an unmarried daughter cared for an elderly mother. Look at Emily Renner, living in Lynn Cottage with old Mrs Renner all these years, since poor Captain Gibson was killed, his name on the memorial in Kirkhoughton with all the others. The Hepplewick children had been sent away to school, Miss Renner went home to her mother.

Sometimes, fed by the Barrow girls, the talk turned to wondering how it was that Miss Margot had not found a husband yet. Of course, she was musical: that might put them off.

'What do you mean?' A shopping basket was shifted from one arm to another. 'Some men like it. Songs round the piano.'

'I mean she's *professional*.'

'Oh. Oh, I see what you mean.'

The dog came out from beneath the desk and stretched. Margot sat down by the fire and put her hand out.

'Poor old boy. Cooped up all the time.'

'I took him out first thing.'

'Yes, I heard you.'

She heard it every morning: the bang of the front door as she lay in bed, footsteps and pattering over the flags, a whistle. Her bedroom overlooked the drive, the lawn, the cedar, whose sigh in the wind she had listened to every night since she was sent away to school and returned to find herself moved out of the nursery, into this vast strange room at the front.

'You're a big girl now,' said Nanny, who had packed her trunk and now had come home for the holidays. She pulled open drawers and showed her the neat piles of underwear, night-clothes and woollens; pulled wide the huge doors of the tallboy to reveal skirts and dresses on hangers. 'Your uniform can go in here, my duck. You're growing out of that school coat already, I must tell your father. Going to be tall, like him.'

Margot stood in the middle of the carpet. The room felt forbidding and enormous, like everything else: the great high bed, the towering furniture, the curtains which fell to the floor, that huge dark tree beyond the window, where the swing swung to and fro like a ghost. It was different when you were on it, looking up into the branches, somebody giving you a push.

'*Higher! Higher!*'

Along the landing lay the emptiness of where her mother used to be. Her father was in there all alone; there was no one to sit at the dressing table, put on an earring, reach out an arm as she came running in.

'*Look at us!*' Their faces, pressed together, had been reflected endlessly, on and on. Now the porcelain boxes and bottles of cream and scent which had stood so prettily on the top had gone.

She swallowed. 'Can Diana come and stay?'

'Of course she can.'

'Will you call me "My duck" again?'

Nanny closed the wardrobe doors and turned round.

'Oh, don't cry, my duck, don't cry.'

She sobbed, and was enfolded.

That was a long time ago. And now – now she loved her room, as she had always loved the house. When she was fifteen, her father gave her a desk, a slender rosewood thing with a soft leather top and a set of three drawers on either side. It stood at the window and she prepared for the School Certificate there, looking out on summer days past the cedar, down the long lawn with its rose beds and summer house and shrubbery, to the ha-ha and the fields beyond, where cows swished their tails in the heat.

In the evenings Diana and George came over to practise, down in the drawing room, the windows pushed up high till dusk fell. Sometimes Frank joined them, sprawled in an armchair, listening, or outside hurling a ball for the dog – a different dog then – over the grass.

'Fetch! Fetch!'

When she was sixteen, her father asked if she would like to have her mother's dressing table, still in his room.

'I could easily move it. Barrow could give me a hand.'

She thought of the dusty space it would leave in her father's bedroom, of the dents in the carpet its legs would have made, of how it must comfort him, having it there. She shook her head. And night and morning, when she brushed her hair, she went on looking into the mirror above her chest of drawers, into the dark eyes so like her father's, though her mouth, she knew from photographs, was her mother's mouth, shapely and soft.

When she was seventeen, Frank kissed her. They were walking back from the tennis court, long summer shadows darkening the grass. His arm went round her, his lips met hers, gently and then insistently. She pushed him away, very hard.

'You're like my brother,' she said, though part of her trembled.

'You're not like my sister. Come here.'

'No.'

'Please, Margot. Please.'

'No.' She ran through the open door of the house as the grandfather clock struck six.

It struck the half-hour now, on this rainy morning: they could hear it out in the hall, the chimes like the heartbeat of the house. Each week her father stood on a chair and took down the key kept on the top of the casement. He turned it thirty-one times in the beautiful, round, calm face, with its glimpses of sun or moon. When she was little, and watched him get down and ease open the door, it had felt as if she were seeing the clock's secret life: the huge heavy cogs on their chains, the soft brass gleam of the pendulum. He touched it, and the slow steady tick began. Life came back.

Life came back!

Dah-dah-dah-dah! The chiming ended. Rain streamed down the library windows. After lunch, her father would take the dog out again, as always, rain or shine, and she would practise until it was time for tea. Tomorrow her students would come. This, like the weekly winding of the clock, was the pattern of things, had been for a long time now.

She said, stroking dark silky ears, 'Frank has suggested I might do some teaching at Kirkhoughton. He's made an appointment with the Head.'

'Harry Straughan,' said her father, putting his specs on again, turning back to his desk, where a photograph of the Trio stood by a pile of papers. He gave it a glance. 'Good idea.'

The rain blew away at last. With a great gust of wind over the hills it was gone overnight, and then the world was all shining puddles, gleaming wet grass on moor and garden and football field. With a whoop, the boys were out. More mud on shirts and shorts, but a good strong wind to blow the washing lines out in the gardens and cobbled back yards of the town.

For a day or two it was almost spring-like, the November sun pouring through the school windows, lighting the scratched veneer of the piano at Assembly, and the plates set out on the dining hall tables for lunch, which most of the boys called dinner. It poured into Steven's third-year classroom in the afternoons, and with the huge old radiators roaring away it was almost too hot in there, one or two boys taking off their jackets, please, sir, and Moffat coughing at the back.

'The Battle of Tewkesbury,' said Steven, up at the blackboard. 'The end of the Lancastrian cause. Who remembers the date?' He turned to the class. 'Moffat?'

Another cough: he coughed too much, that boy. Then another, and one or two heads were raised, and Johnny Mather said all at once, 'Sir? Sir!'

Everyone's head went up. Stephen strode down the aisle between the desks. A blood-stained handkerchief was clamped to Moffat's white face. And then it was suddenly soaking, flooding the open exercise book and the Wars of the Roses.

Chairs were scraped back, boys got to their feet.

'Mather, fetch Miss Aickman. Run!'

The classroom door banged, they could hear him shouting in the corridor. Michael McNulty, who always sat next to Moffat, had thrown off his jacket, was tugging off his tie. In a moment he was stripped to a singlet, his shirt pressed up against the sodden handkerchief, blood everywhere.

'Mr Coulter?'

Miss Aickman was at the door. He looked across at her, saw her take it in.

'I'll ring Dr Maguire.' And she was gone, another classroom door and then another opening along the corridor as she ran.

The bloody shirt was lowered to the desk. Moffat dropped the handkerchief on top of it. His face was a battlefield. He whispered, 'It's stopped now, sir.'

There was a silence. Steven was shaking so hard he could not speak. Then Donald Hindmarsh, who was always made to sit at the front to stop him larking about, said, 'Moffat, I've told you before not to be greedy with the jam,' and the class erupted.

Nobody ever forgot that afternoon.

The bus drove away and he walked to the foot of the track. It was almost dark. Moffat's ashen young face – he could not get it out of his mind, nor that soaking scarlet handkerchief. He flashed his torch over the letter box, felt inside. Empty. He began the climb.

For weeks, getting up and down had been almost as difficult as in the great snow of last year. He had taken a stick, but still slipped and slid and waded through the mud. But the sun and wind had dried it now, and walking was easier. The torchlight flashed on caked ruts and winter grass, cropped low by the sheep all summer. Now they'd been taken for lambing down to the farm, whose buildings he could just make out in the distance, far to the left. And now there was only the sound of the wind, and the first pale stars appearing, growing brighter as he climbed.

There was the cottage.

And there was Moffat, gasping and choking at the back of the class.

Miss Aickman had taken him, slowly, slowly, her arm around him, out to the washrooms, and then to sit waiting in her office until – he and the boys could see from the sunny window – Dr Maguire pulled up at the gates and walked briskly across the playground. Straughan was waiting at the door. Mrs Moffat came running in her old winter coat and headscarf. Then came the ambulance.

'All right, boys, settle down.'

'Where will he go, sir?'

'I expect—' Steven cleared his throat. 'I expect he'll go to the hospital in Hexham.'

'Or Barrasford,' said McNulty. 'That's where his dad was, in the sanatorium. That's where he passed away.' He stopped abruptly.

There was a silence. Pages turned. After a few minutes the bell rang out, and it was time for maths.

Stars lit the leafless hawthorn tree, the woodshed. Steven let the torch beam light the blue door of the cottage, put down his bag and turned the handle. And not since that terrible evening in January, after the setting of the stone, had a return here been so difficult, nor the place felt so entirely desolate.

'*It's stopped now, sir.*'

Brave boy. Would he live, if they took him into the sanatorium? Might Margaret have lived, had she gone there? Might he have had her beside him still?

He kicked the door to, lit the lamps.

4

THE CHRISTMAS TREE went up in the Square. It was huge and full, cut from Harwood Forest, and brought down by bull-nosed lorry in the first week of December.

'Look at that!'

'That's grand!'

Paper chains went up in the shops, everyone's mood was lifted. At school, though people thought about Moffat - how could they not? - they rarely spoke of him. He had been taken to Barrasford: Straughan telephoned once, the following Monday. He told them in Assembly next morning that he was doing as well as he could. Nobody knew what that meant, or if they did, did not say so. The great waters of school life washed over everything, and the term hurtled on. Amidst the writing of reports, there was talk of a concert.

Of course, they could never be professional: George knew that, though he never spelled it out. He knew, too, that in any trio or quartet there might be a weaker player, and that with them it was Diana. She was good, she was passionate and intent, but it was for her, in rehearsals, that they most often had to stop, and repeat a passage, often at her own request. But still: no matter. They made a very fine amateur group.

George knew these things because he was the one who'd come closest to success: the only one who'd gone to the Royal College.

'But we must *all* go! Of course we must.'

A June afternoon in 1926, the windows open wide to birdsong, Barrow mowing away in his shirt sleeves, petrol fumes rising into the balmy air. George had bicycled over from Coquet Bridge; he waved the letter at them.

'There's still time to apply.'

Margot was on one window seat, Diana on the other. They looked like something out of Leighton, he thought, striding up and down before them. It wasn't their clothes: Margot's straight linen skirt and Diana's low-waisted dress were indisputably Today. But Diana was somehow not of this age, never had been, and it was their air, the composition, which made him think of Leighton reproductions seen in art classes at school: two languid young women – who would guess at their musical energy? – dreaming at an open window, waiting for something to happen.

Something should! He waved the letter again.

'London awaits!'

Footsteps came over the flagstones: a man and his dog. Margot waved, then sat clasping her knees.

'I can't.'

'What do you mean?'

'I couldn't leave him.'

'But surely – he'd want you to go. Let me ask him!'

She shook her head. 'Even if he did – I just couldn't bear to think of it—'

'But you were away at school – he sent you!'

She thought of their partings, Diana beside them in the hall; of the way her father had kissed them both, and turned quickly away. She thought of her return, of his coming across from the stable yard, or out of the library, his face lit up.

'You're back!'

She ran into his arms.

'The house is alive again.' He kissed and released her. 'And where's Diana?'

84

'She's coming to stay next week, if that's all right.'

'Of course it is. Now – come and tell me everything.'

She turned away from the window as the front door banged.

'I just couldn't,' she said again. 'I'll go on having lessons here. We can all play together in the holidays.'

George gave an exaggerated sigh, but he meant it. 'You're hopeless. But Diana – you must have a try.'

She shook her head, lifted her mass of hair.

'I couldn't go without Margot.'

'Oh, for heaven's sake.'

Footsteps came along the hall to the door of the drawing room. He sprang to open it.

'Good afternoon, sir! I've had some good news.'

Heslop raised an elegant eyebrow. From the window seat Margot made complicated gestures: Don't ask him about me, I'm not going.

They took tea in the shade of the cedar, the dog flopped down on the grass, pigeons cooing above them, and the idea that the girls might audition wasn't even mentioned.

And so it was that George took the train down to London alone, seen off by his parents, by Margot, Diana and Frank, soon to go to Oxford, all waving and waving amidst the clouds of steam. And in London he was tutored and encouraged, and invited to join a quartet. He could have been a soloist, even: George Liddell, on London concert platforms. In Vienna! But as the end of the final year approached he found himself refusing all the offers made to him, as Margot and Diana had refused to leave Northumberland. He had his own reasons for wanting to return.

A free double period. Steven sat in a corner of the staffroom, writing his third years' reports.

A *good term's work*. That was Mather.

Satisfactory. That was Carr. And Dagg. And quite a lot of them: too many, Frank would probably say. We want more than Satisfactory.

His eye went from mark-book to report form, all down the register.

We expect more of him next term. That was Hindmarsh. Would he pass the School Certificate in two years' time? *He needs to work considerably harder.* Hindmarsh looked set to leave at the end of the Upper Fifth: and then what? An apprenticeship? The Army?

He blew on the ink, set the form on top of the others as the bell rang out and the door opened.

In came Armstrong, with a heap of maths books. He nodded, thumped them down on the table, lit up.

An excellent term's work. McNulty. McNulty looked set for university, he and Frank had agreed at the last departmental meeting. There'd be another in half an hour, the last in the Christmas term, and always a bit awkward, Dunn twitching away, saying little.

Here came Moffat. *We very much hope to welcome him back next term.* He stopped, let the ink dry, thought of that sheet-white boy lying by an open sanatorium window as the fresh cold air blew in, listening to the waters of the North Tyne racing past the village. He'd send him a Christmas card.

Smoke drifted across the room as Armstrong opened a text-book, inhaling deeply. Steven coughed.

'Sorry.'

'Doesn't matter.' He coughed again, he sat suddenly rigid.

You realise she could infect you, Mr Coulter? Dumpy Nurse Douglas, standing at the door with her bicycle. *The pair of you want your heads examined, I'm not going to say it again.* She bumped away down the track.

Now the anniversary of that terrible death approached, and

how was he going to get through? For a moment he shut his eyes.

'Everyone's coming down with something,' said Armstrong, flattening a page. He stubbed out his cigarette in a filthy ashtray. Sometimes it felt like a pub in here.

Steven cleared his throat, and got out his handkerchief. His mother washed and ironed them every other week, with his vests and shirts, giving them back after Sunday lunch. He spat very carefully into it, had a careful look. Nothing. Not a hint, though he found he was trembling. Slowly he reached for the next report form. Benjamin Potts. *A creditable term's work.* Armstrong lit up again.

Every year, there was a carol service, as traditionally a part of school life as the Nativity Play had been in Kirkhoughton Infants, down in Shaw Street.

'I remember you, McNulty, with a tea towel round your head.'

'Shurrup.'

Every now and then in a break they could hear little Alfie Stote from the second years, rehearsing in the hall for his big moment, Miss Aickman tinkling away.

'Once in Roy-al D-a-a-v-i-d's City,' warbled Hindmarsh, passing him in the corridor on the way home on Friday, and Stote kicked him.

'Boys!'

Then, in Assembly, Straughan announced something new. Not only the carol service to mark the Christmas term, but a concert, to be given by friends of Mr Embleton. The Hepplewick Trio – perhaps one or two of the boys had heard of them. Most of the faces before him were blank, but Steven saw Tom Herron give a nod. Herron was not unlike Frank, perhaps, he thought suddenly: had a background where certain

87

things were taken for granted, though his parents had not sent him off to public school. Perhaps they were principled. Perhaps they just couldn't afford it.

'I understand they're fine musicians, and that we are in for a treat. Afternoon lessons on the 15th of December will be cancelled. Homework—' he gave his dry smile, as a murmur ran round the hall, '—homework will not be given. And now we will stand and sing our closing hymn: "Hark! A thrilling voice is sounding".' Miss Aickman struck up, everyone got to their feet with the usual clatter, off they all went, and within moments the music was sweeping staff and boys along.

'You didn't tell me,' Steven said to Frank in the staffroom, as they gathered their books. 'About the concert.' Boys went thundering past the closed door. 'Quiet!' roared Jack Halpin, out there on corridor duty. 'Keep to the left!'

'We've only just arranged it with Straughan. You know what he's like about new things.' Frank made a Straughan face, a mixture of caution and implacability, and Steven laughed. 'Glad to see you looking better.' He made for the door. 'And it should be good.'

Now, on the afternoon of the carol service, they all went trooping out of the school gates after dinner – 'Lunch, Dagg, lunch,' – and, as every year, the pupils from Kirkhoughton Girls came to join them, walking in neat pairs along Milk Lane and out into Main Street, before they reached the Square.

'Eyes front,' said Gowens, bringing up the rear.

It was freezing. The two long crocodiles made their way at a brisk pace, past the towering Christmas tree, past the lit-up shops, the butcher hung with game, past the Museum and the war memorial and down Battle Street to St Peter's, where an ancient coke furnace did its best. As Gowens said every year, it was still as cold as charity.

A crib stood inside the west door, and the girls went ooh

and ah as they walked past and the boys pretended to take no notice. Wispy old Shaw was waiting before the rood screen in his purple Advent stole and the organ softly played. Candles burned, up on the altar, and here and there on the deep window ledges. The place smelled of wax, coke fumes, boys.

Everyone was there: every member of staff, with Straughan and Miss Brierley greeting one another at the door, each to read a lesson. Steven saw Frank usher his sixth form into the pews at the back, giving them all a smile. It was the kind of smile which would make the most recalcitrant boy want to do his best, and Steven, moving slowly forward with the lower forms, thought that only Frank could have persuaded Straughan to do something different for once, and that if he put his mind to it he could probably persuade anyone to do anything. And he knew that he himself, as the bleakest day of his year approached, was somehow looking forward to the concert.

He settled down with his third years, next to the aisle, Dunn at the other end of the pew. Everything was just as it always was, with its atmosphere of sentiment, boredom and expectation. He looked across at the girls. Before they were married, Margaret had been with them, down at the front with her first years, and the Christmas after they met, when they'd become engaged, he had craned his neck to see the back of her head, a little felt hat on her piled-up hair. Nut-brown, he had said, the first time she unpinned it for him, sitting on the grassy moor outside the empty cottage they had come upon, on an autumn afternoon. The wind blew strands back from her face; he smoothed it and stroked it, leaned forward and kissed her—

Oh, darling, darling.

This time last year he had been at her funeral.

'Margaret?'

Banging the front door shut against the snow, running up the narrow staircase, numb with cold.

'*Margaret?*'

Knowing, in the silence, that something was wrong; pushing into the unlit bedroom, the snow at the window falling on and on—

The organ played a last few bars. People were checking the number on the boards, opening their hymn books: no need for old Shaw to announce a thing, after his welcome: everyone knew how this service began. And unmusical though Steven felt himself to be, here was music he had known all his life and still loved. He drew a great breath, pushing that dark afternoon away. He made himself push it away. He opened his own book and found the page, as Alfie Stote made his way from the front pew up to the chancel steps and stood before them.

Stote was a scrap of a boy, really, like Moffat. Sometimes the only decent meal some of these lads had was at school. Some of the parents, Steven knew, could barely afford the second-hand blazers the boys arrived in – that had certainly been true of Moffat, one of five, his father gone and his mother cleaning six houses a week. That was what Miss Aickman had said, as the ambulance drove away.

Behind the rood screen, Mr Shaw got to his feet. They all rose with him. There was a hush. Then little Stote, his mousy hair watered down within an inch of its life, looked straight ahead down the aisle and began, unaccompanied, to sing.

'Once in Royal David's city,
Stood a lowly cattle shed . . .'

His voice was as clear as a moorland stream, as pure as winter air.

'Where a mother laid her baby
In a manger for his bed . . .'

Steven felt the hairs rise all along the back of his neck as the top notes in the next two lines rang out, and knew that this was probably happening to everyone around him.

'Mary was that mother mild,
Jesus Christ her little child.'
Stote finished, and stood very still. Then the organ sounded
and he made his way back to his seat as they all began to sing.
'He came down to earth from heaven,
Who is God and Lord of all . . .'
Two hundred voices, maybe more, rose in unison. Beside
Steven, Mather and McNulty were singing at the tops of their
voices; along the row he could hear them all, his lads, his class,
doing their best: Dagg and Cowen, Potts and Herdman and
Wanless, and he felt that to be singing with his boys now was
one of the best things to have happened for a long while: he
loved them, he was proud of them.
He hadn't quite known that he felt like this.
'With the poor and meek and lowly,
Lived on earth our Saviour holy.'
On they sang, and you didn't have to believe a word of any
of it to be moved by upraised voices as united as a swirl of
sheep on a moor. Only Moffat was absent from all this, and
Steven winged a thought towards him, fifty miles away from
his family, his mates.
The organ was thundering out; all at once the church was
lighter, brighter. He turned to look at the windows, and saw
it must be snowing, whiteness softening the old stained glass.
And then he saw something else, and felt a shiver run right
through him.
'Not in that poor lowly stable,
With the oxen standing by . . .'
At the far end of the pew, David Dunn was standing with
his hymn book held out before him. As always, he looked set
apart, poker-stiff, the weight put on his good leg to ease the
pain of the other. But it wasn't just that. He was weeping, tears
streaming unstoppably down his thin hard face.

Had any of the boys realised? Steven glanced at Wigham, standing straight as a cornstalk next to him, and at beefy Hindmarsh, gazing steadfastly ahead, and knew that they had. For a moment he thought: if they snigger, or make something of it afterwards, I'll send them straight to Straughan. But he sensed that they wouldn't, that something had touched them, tough lads as they were, and as the last lines rose to the rafters and the organ pealed, Jack Halpin made his way to the front to read the first lesson, a Head Boy rising to the occasion, and Dunn got out a handkerchief and blew his nose. He wasn't the only one to do so, and for all you knew half the congregation was pretending to go down with a winter cold.

They sat, they waited. Halpin cleared his throat.

'And they heard the voice of the Lord God . . .'

At the end of the service, when they all filed out, it was snowing really hard.

The snow settled on the town, lacing the Christmas tree and the bare trees round the Square, piling up on the roof tops. It settled on Hencote Moor, where each evening he tramped slowly up the track, flashing the torch before him. Starlight and glittering snow and silence. Indoors, he heaped up the range, let his socks dry on it; stirred soup; heaved down the mattress again, sleeping in the warmth, waking each morning in the winter dawn to the ashy smell of the last of the wood burning down. He heaped it up again, made porridge, pulled on his boots.

'Margaret,' he said aloud, and bid the empty cottage farewell, for it was here that her spirit resided. He closed the door.

As he set off down the track again, the sky was flushed with rose and gold, and he beheld the limitless great stretch of white moorland beneath it, empty and sparkling, and knew that he was in a place as beautiful as anywhere on earth, which was why he and Margaret had chosen to live here. And that perhaps it had killed her, choosing not to leave. And he knew that without her, though he might say her name aloud, day after day, trying to hold on to her, its meaning was beginning to slip away.

He stood by the snowy bank on the road, waiting for the bus which would take him into the roar of school life, and thought that his life had become a sequence of soliloquies and crowd scenes. Perhaps, until his marriage, it always had been. Until his marriage he had always kept something back. The only thing he actually felt settled into now was teaching. Which was just as well, because he didn't know what else he was going to do with his life.

'All right, boys, we're having an end-of-term test today.'

'Sir! Si-ir! You never said.'

'I'm saying it now. Get your wits about you, I'm going round one by one. McNulty: the date of the Battle of Bosworth.'

'1485, sir.' Quick as a flash.

'Herdman. The Battle of Tewkesbury.'

A slight hesitation. '1471, sir.'

'Very good. Hindmarsh: which battle took place in 1455?'

A deep frown. 'You're going backwards, sir.'

'I am. Where are you going, I wonder.'

A ripple of laughter round the class. In forty minutes like this he could forget almost everything. He knew he wasn't really a philosopher, like Straughan. He wasn't fully alert to current events, as Frank was, all the time, though he knew that what was happening in Europe was disturbing. He thought of himself as a jobbing historian, a teacher who believed in middle-year pupils getting a lot of facts under their belts, anchored in a good solid sense of the past. Then, with someone like Frank, they could begin to think critically about the world they lived in.

'The Battle of St Albans, Hindmarsh, wasn't it?'

A look of relief. 'Yes, sir.'

'I knew you knew. And what was its significance?'

A long pause. 'Its significance, sir?'

'Which war began after that battle?'

A long pause, a sudden cheerful light. 'The Wars of the Roses?'

'Exactly. Well done.'

He gave them this test two days after the carol service. Then they all went hurtling out to break. He was on playground duty, pacing up and down as the boys kicked a ball or ragged about, the snow scraped into heaps against the walls. Though it might still lie deep on moorland – you could see it on the tops of the hills everywhere you looked – here in the town it had thawed a little, and the roads were clear. The sky was empty, a radiant blue in the sun. A car pulled up at the gates.

He noticed it because you always noticed a car. He noticed it because it put him in mind of Frank's Imp – not that it was a sports car, but it had a sleek, distinctive look. He noticed it because a woman was driving, something you rarely saw, and he saw Margot Heslop get out, and come walking through the gates. Her height, and her hat, and her long dark coat, brought kicking a ball about not to a halt, exactly, but to a head-turning pause. Apart from the cleaners and cooks and Miss Aickman, Kirkhoughton boys did not often see women.

Steven did not often see women. And though he had begun to feel at ease with everyone at Hepplewick on that rain-filled autumn night, now, as Margot stopped, with a funny little frown, and said, 'Oh, hello, Mr Coulter,' he felt as awkward as a lad in the Lower Fifth: away from his mates, voice newly broken, shaving cuts all down his neck, nothing to say for himself.

'Good morning, Miss Heslop. Have you come about the concert?'

It sounded so gauche, so clumsy, as if he were asking if she'd come about the drains, and she laughed, and he blushed.

'I have,' she said. 'Frank's going to show me where we'll be playing. Can you tell me where I'll find him?'

'He'll be in the staffroom.' He wanted to say that if she could wait a few minutes he'd take her there, but he didn't feel able to ask her to wait in the cold, and as Johnny Mather came racing by he stopped him. 'Take Miss Heslop to the staffroom, Mather, she's come to see Mr Embleton.'

'Yes, sir.' Mather was panting, but he pulled himself together. 'This way, Miss—' He tried to remember.

'Miss Heslop,' said Margot, and then, to Steven, 'Thank you so much.'

He wanted to say, Not at all, or It's a pleasure. He said, 'That's all right,' and then a ball from another game shot suddenly past, and he turned to see where it had come from. When he turned back she and Mather were already on their way to the door, and then Turnbull from the Lower Sixth was ringing the bell, striding around the playground as if he owned it, and in moments they had disappeared inside.

'Sir? Sir, who was that?'

'A friend of Mr Embleton's.' He cleared his throat. 'One of the musicians.'

'What musicians, sir?'

Talking to one of the boys he could be like a man again, instead of a gormless youth. 'Do you not listen in Assembly, Wigham?'

'I try to, sir.'

'The Hepplewick Trio.' Not the kind of name which was often on his lips, though it tripped off Frank Embleton's tongue as if he'd been saying it since the cradle.

'Cor.'

'That'll do.'

As he stood at the door and watched all the boys pour in, he found himself wondering what the effect on them would have been if Diana Embleton had come dancing across the playground – somehow he imagined her dancing, perhaps in a fur hat – past the banked-up heaps of snow. He found himself imagining the effect upon the smoky staffroom.

'You're in a good mood today, sir.'

'You saw Margot,' Frank said at the end of the day, as they packed up their things in the staffroom, and he nodded.

'Did it go well, her visit?'

'I think she charmed Straughan completely.' Frank looked at his watch. 'I must go. See you tomorrow.' And he was gone, striding across the playground and out to the snow-lined Square, where his car stood with a little knot of boys around it.

'Sir? Sir, give me the starting handle.'

'Give it to me, sir!'

'Your turn, Atkins, I think.' In a few minutes, Atkins had triumphantly cranked up the engine, and the Imp was roaring away in the dusk.

Steven walked up to the bus stop. He made the journey out along darkening roads to the foot of the moor, and in the post box he found a damp letter from home. He read it indoors with his back to the range, the lamp on the mantelpiece lighting the small lined page, knowing what it would say.

Don't spend that sad day by yourself, love. Come home. We don't like to think of you alone . . .

Next day came another.

Andrew's coming down, but we don't want to be by ourselves. It would feel terrible without you. The road's not too bad, and the bus is running. You could stay the night . . .

He stood there thinking.

'What shall I do?' he asked the empty room. Would it hurt his parents' feelings if he went to the Ridleys? Would it hurt everyone if he spent the day here, as he wanted? And he wondered again if being an only child had got him too used to solitude. Stamp collecting. Bird-watching. Out walking with his dog too much, too often. Keeping things to himself.

Had he been lonely? A bit. A bit, and too shy to do much about it. It was Margaret who had dissolved him, turned him from hesitant man into ardent lover. At night he still took her into his arms.

He put down the letter. Without her, faced with the simplest encounter with a woman, he could barely conduct a conversation. He was lost. He was still lost and yearning.

Oh, my love.

He buried his face in his hands.

In the end, he asked Straughan for the afternoon off. It was the first time since his return to school last December that he had used the words 'My wife,' and almost no one after that first day back had even alluded to her death. It had happened: they'd said they were sorry. He had been away, now he was here again. This was how men did things: in many ways, it had been a relief.

Only Frank had stretched out a hand.

'I know it's hard for you, but—'

Evening sun slanted along the Shambles. They sat outside the Queen's Head, hearing the thud of darts from the snug, and Frank talked mostly about himself, and his childhood friends, and the sixth-form trip to Bavaria. Then he had drawn Steven into his world, with kindness, encouragement: Look, here's something different. Life lies ahead. I know it's hard for you, but—

'It must have been hard for you, Mr Coulter,' Straughan said now, leaning back in his seat behind the desk. The room stank of pipe smoke. Next door, Miss Aickman's office was hung with paper chains.

'I've been glad to be here, Mr Straughan,' said Steven, and it was true. 'It's helped. It's just this particular day to get through.'

'Of course.' Straughan reached for his pipe and lit up. It was hard to know which of them was finding this conversation more difficult. 'By all means take the time off – you'll have cleared it with Mr Embleton?'

'I thought I should see you first.'

'Very good. Well – I expect you'll feel better once the day is over.'

'Yes, sir. Thank you.'

He got to his feet. As he reached the door, Straughan said slowly: 'You've done very well, Mr Coulter. We all appreciate it.'

'Thank you, sir,' Steven said again, and then he was out in the corridor, the air thick with the smell of mutton stew. David Dunn was walking stiffly along with his book; they nodded to one another.

'Seen Embleton?' Steven asked, just for something to say, as they made their way down to the staffroom.

'Embleton?'' Dunn made meeting their head of department, a man they both saw every day, sound the most improbable thing in the world. He let Steven open the door for him. 'Thank you,' he said, and then, as they both saw Frank stuffing things into his pigeon hole, called out: 'Embleton! Mr Coulter would like a word.' He banged his books down on the table.

Frank turned. He and Steven exchanged glances, as so often where Dunn was concerned. They walked together down to the dining hall.

'Nothing to be Dunn,' said Frank wryly.

'He wept in the carol service,' Steven said. 'In Once in Royal.'

'Did he?' Frank shook his head. 'Poor fellow. Mind you – it's enough to set anyone off.'

They came to the roaring hall. 'I've just been to see Straughan,' said Steven, and explained why, trying to keep it light. 'I'll set work, of course. Put a prefect in charge.'

'That's fine.' Frank took his place in the queue. And then: 'I'm so sorry,' he said. 'You know I'll be thinking of you.' The look he gave him was so kind, so gentle and true, that for a moment Steven was almost taken aback. And the thought flashed again through his mind, as he thanked him, and picked up a chipped china plate: This is a man any girl could fall in love with.

The bus was almost empty as he travelled out to Cawbeck, just two or three women with baskets returning from their trip to town. Steven sat next to the window, half-listening to their talk across the aisle of Christmas shopping, and grandchildren, and the terrible price of things. It was comforting, until he thought that perhaps his parents were grieving not only on his behalf, and for Margaret, whose vitality had lit up their little house in Birley Bank, but for the grandchildren they'd so hoped for. Her parents, too, must feel this.

He looked out across the empty, snow-patterned fields. Plough land and grass land and dry stone walls. Hungry lapwing flew over them, crows stalked about. A vaporous pink sun streaked the clouds. The temperature had dropped again, and though the road was clear you could tell that by evening the heaped-up verges would begin to freeze once more. And he thought again – he couldn't stop thinking – of the bitter cold of the little room in which Margaret had fallen, and lain choking on the dusty floor, the small fire dying beside her, the snow at the window falling endlessly. He lowered his head.

'You all right, love?'

The bus had pulled up in the village.

'Yes, yes, I'm fine, thanks.'

And he got off with the women, clambering down with their baskets, and nodded to the driver refilling his ticket machine.

The street had a deep-winter quiet. Chimney smoke rose

into the misty air, firelight flickered behind lace curtains. He walked past the little school, which Margaret and Andrew had both attended as children, their father the headmaster. The single classroom was hung with paper chains; heads bobbed about.

He walked past the pub, where he and Andrew had often had a drink together in what, young as he was, he thought of now as the old days. And there Andrew was, suddenly appearing at the end of the street, raising his hand and walking down towards him. For a moment he looked so like his sister – taller, darker, but with that same clever look, that aquiline family nose – that Steven stopped dead in his tracks. Andrew lowered his hand: he understood, he hesitated. Then he walked on down the street, and reached him, and they embraced.

'Thank you. Thanks, Andrew.'

Together they turned off to Church Lane, the grass stiff with half-scraped-away snow, and walked beneath the trees. The quiet was broken only by rooks, and then the slow striking of the tower clock, the notes of the half-hour sounding in the still cold air. Half-past two on a winter afternoon. Then there was only the sound of Andrew lifting the latch of the lych gate, and their footsteps on the path through the churchyard, towards the grave where two people stood waiting.

'You don't mind?' Andrew's breath streamed out before him.

Steven shook his head. He had so wanted to be alone, to try one more struggling time to summon her presence within the empty cottage, to weep for her, shout for her, with no one to see or to know. But now it felt right as it was: to greet her mother with a kiss, to shake her father's hand, and for the four of them to stand together in silence, looking at the snow-trimmed head-stone, hearing the lapwing cry across the fields.

It was over. He'd done it. Next morning, catching the first bus back to Kirkhoughton, light breaking over the freezing fields, he thought it all through: the silence, the slow walk back to the house, and tea by the fire. The cat lay stretched out before it, as always.

'Come here, you.'

'Margaret loved that cat.'

The looking at photographs: the wedding, the picnics on the moor, Margaret and her first years, her second years, all lined up in the school garden, neat as pins, and she in a summer dress – 'I made that dress for her,' – smiling into the sun beside them.

'I wonder how they're all doing now. That Lizzie Lambert was trouble, remember her saying?'

Bringing her life back to life.

'More tea? Have another piece of cake, love. And you, Andrew. I don't know how you men manage on your own.'

Andrew cleared his throat. 'Not for much longer, Mother.'

A teacup set down in the saucer. 'What did you say?'

He said it again, suddenly looking quite different. He said he was getting engaged at Christmas, that she was a medical student, Rose MacBride, yes, funny, wasn't it. And yes, he did have a photograph, here – reaching into his breast pocket, pulling it out. A pretty dark-haired girl in glasses smiled at each of them in turn.

Kisses and handshakes and general excitement, the drinks cupboard opened, the day transformed. And then so poignant.

'I wish our Margaret was here to know this.' And then: 'But it's grand news, Andrew. Makes the future a bit brighter now.'

'Just so long as there's not a war,' Mr Ridley said suddenly.

'Oh, John, not now. Pour us another drink.'

The bus was slowing down as the early-morning lights of Kirkhoughton came into view. Tiny snowflakes began to blow against the windscreen. Steven thought of himself lying awake after supper, in the room which had been Margaret's when she was a girl, and which still had worn copies of *Peter Rabbit* and the others in a little white book case, and one or two dresses still hanging in the cupboard. It had felt both comforting and the saddest thing in the world.

They pulled up in Bridge Street; boys and girls clambered on, winter-pale beneath their caps and felt hats. The bus climbed the hill to the Square, the windscreen wipers going now. Everyone got off in a flurry of snow.

'Morning, Mr Coulter.'

'Morning, Potts.'

Already the lights of the school were coming on, the caretaker opening up. Steven and Potts walked together across the playground, as if it were any old day.

5

SIX O'CLOCK ON a winter evening, a time when the school was usually empty, shut up for the night. Tonight: a buzz. Staff had stayed on to do their marking in an empty classroom or in corners of the staffroom. In came Molly with tea and sandwiches, and out she went again, rattling down the corridor past the boys pouring back into school from tea at home.

'They're here,' said Frank, putting his books away at the sound of car doors slamming in the Square.

And if Margot Heslop had turned heads when she walked across the playground, the arrival of the Trio stopped people dead in their tracks.

The cars had pulled up at the gates. The headlamps, the running boards, the polish! The three musicians, in evening dress, got out and walked towards the main entrance. One, a slight young man, carried a violin case; another man, taller, older, carried a cello; and at the sight of them all, of tall straight elegance, of a soft fur hat – Steven had been right – on fair hair, and a dancing smile, something happened to everyone. Glamour was not a word you heard very often in Kirkhoughton Boys, but the atmosphere was utterly changed. Miss Aickman went out to greet them, stopped at the sight of the hat.

'This way,' she said after a moment. 'Follow me.' She was given a dazzling smile.

'They can leave their coats in here.' Frank was at the staffroom door, as they all came down the corridor. 'Thanks, Miss Aickman.' Handshakes, kisses on the cheek. 'Well done, everyone, come in.' They followed him into the battered room, with its smell of coal and pipe smoke, its pigeon holes, ash trays, scratched old table, and worn-out chairs by the fire.

'Gentlemen,' said Frank. 'The Hepplewick Trio.'

A general murmur, a getting to feet and moving of books on the table as cello and violin were laid carefully down. Frank made the introductions: Mr Heslop, of Hepplewick Hall; his daughter, the pianist Margot Heslop. 'My sister Diana, the cellist. Mr George Liddell, violinist and leader of the Trio.'

And he went round the room, fifteen or so staff, and everyone knowing that half these names would be forgotten. 'Mr Armstrong, Mr Gowens, Mr Dunn, a member of my department. Mr Coulter you know, of course.'

'Of course.' Margot was smiling at him, at everyone; Diana was radiant. George made a series of little bows. Steven, surprised at how drawn to them he felt, seeing them all again, was once more cloaked in shyness.

Still. Surely he could observe the courtesies.

'May I take your coat?'

He moved towards Margot, and she smiled again – not with Diana's lit-up expression, as if she were greeting the only person in the room, but with her own grace. That was how he thought of it, later.

'Thank you.'

He helped her slip off the coat, long, dark and heavy, beautifully lined, and laid it on the back of a chair. Thomas Heslop was helping Diana with hers; she carefully took off her hat. Out from beneath the soft fur came that mass of hair; out from a little bag came a hairbrush, a bottle of scent. In a moment the smoky room was full of a cloud of something heady, warm, alluring.

'I say,' said Armstrong, astonishingly, and everyone laughed.

Straughan suddenly appeared in his gown, dwarfing the room as usual.

'I see the entertainment has already begun. Good evening, everyone. Heslop.'

The two men shook hands. Then came more introductions.

'How do you do, sir.' Beside Straughan, thought Steven, George looked like a boy from the Upper Fourth. Lower Fourth, even, so small was he. Had he really commanded the room, that autumn evening?

'Very good to have you all here,' said Straughan. 'The boys are looking forward to the evening greatly. And when you are ready—'

A general air of readiness took hold. Out from their cases came violin and cello; Margot for a moment flexed her fingers. Straughan cleared his throat.

'Miss Aickman will show you the facilities.'

'Of course.' She appeared at his side. 'If you'd all follow me once more—'

Diana picked up her cello. Heslop stepped forward.

'Let me—'

She flashed him a smile. 'No, really, thank you. I can manage.'

'We're off!' George took his violin, flung up the other hand, and led them from the room.

As they entered the assembly hall, the noise of a hundred and fifty voices died away, and the boys rose to their feet. One or two programmes fell to the floor - Miss Aickman had run them off on the inky old Gestetner - and there was the usual scrabbling about. Staff took their places, Thomas Heslop sat down next to Frank, Straughan climbed the steps to the stage and stood waiting as the Trio followed.

It had taken four removal men to push the school piano up the ramp at the side, and the sight of it sitting up there, polished hard, but still a sad old ordinary thing, was extraordinary. More extraordinary still was the sight of Margot, who was accustomed, as Frank told Steven, to a grand in almost every house they ever played in, walking towards it, setting up her music and sitting down on a piano stool normally sat upon only by Miss Aickman. She adjusted the height, stretched out her hands. Her long dark dress brushed a floor scuffed and scratched from years of announcements, prize-givings, school shoes, chairs scraped back.

George and Diana were setting their scores on the music stands; Diana sat down. The midnight blue of her taffeta gown caught the light; her hair and her lovely face caught the light. Every eye in the school was upon her, you could feel it, as Straughan stepped forward.

'Good evening, boys.' He cleared his throat, thickened with thirty years of pipe smoke. He said that it gave him great pleasure to introduce the Hepplewick Trio; that as they would all see from their programmes, they were about to hear a fine concert of classical music; and that he would hand over now to the violinist and leader of the Trio, Mr Liddell, who would tell them all a little more of what they were about to hear.

George stepped forward. He was small, he was vitally present. In his light warm voice he introduced Margot and Diana, and told the boys they had known one another as children, and in fact their old governess was here tonight, he could see her, there in the middle. One or two boys turned round, and one or two prefects hissed at them not to be so rude. But Steven, too, though he did not turn, was curious to see someone whom Frank and Margot's conversations had made so important. Beside him, Frank murmured that he would introduce her.

George went on. He said that they had formed the Trio on his return from the Royal College in London in 1929, and that their repertoire encompassed some of the loveliest music in Europe. Tonight they were playing a trio by Mendelssohn, a nineteenth-century German composer he was sure they would all have heard of. As they knew – he used the generous phrase often used when the speaker knows that the listener probably knows nothing – Mendelssohn spent some time in England, and became a beloved guest in this country.

'He was one of those people so gifted it makes you feel rather faint.' You could almost feel the smiles amongst his audience. 'He wasn't only a great musician,' continued George, and spoke of his painting, his poetry, the languages he spoke, his athleticism.

'And his range was enormous: mighty things like *Elijah*; a sublime violin concerto, and lots of chamber music – music for three or four people to play in their own homes, or their friends' homes: a great European tradition, of course.'

He made it all interesting, individual and alive, had the tone for a school concert just right. Steven, watching his third years, could see that he had caught them, that they wanted, now, to hear what was to come.

'So,' said George, and his smile swept the darkened hall. 'Mendelssohn's Piano Trio No. 1 in D minor. It lasts for about thirty minutes, probably all we need on a cold winter night, with homes to get back to.' His smile deepened. 'Let us begin.'

He stepped back, they tuned up. Then he lifted his violin, and glanced at the others; once again Steven saw that swift little current run between them.

With the very first bars you could feel the whole hall sit up. And begin to swoon? Was that possible, with these boys? But Diana, on the cello, opened the piece with a phrase that caught you immediately. Margot was playing lightly alongside, then in came the violin, picking up that lovely tune. And as the three of them began to develop an utterly compelling relationship of parts, a deep, attentive silence settled over the hall. Now and then came a cough, or a shifting in a seat, but it quickly stopped.

Enraptured, thought Steven, that's what we are.

He was astonished to find himself thinking such a thing, here in a school hall usually filled with dutiful listening to announcements, hymns belted out, yawns and shuffling feet. And for the first time in a year, though he thought of Margaret with the same deep yearning, though he began to write to her once more – *Darling, I wish you were with me now to hear this* – he was conscious of feeling better, lifted and – yes – excited. He was watching all of them, but after a few minutes it was Margot who held his attention, playing so intently, going right into the music, as if it were a living thing.

Which it was, of course. How had he not known this, all these years?

The first movement ended. There was a cough or two. The second began, opened by the piano, tender and enquiring. And when cello and violin entered it was as if they spoke, saying, Yes – we hear you and we are with you. A couple of seats away he could hear jokey Donald Hindmarsh give a great sigh, and turned to see him lean back, and close his eyes. Steven closed his own, and let the music take him.

Gentleness and sadness gave way to something joyful and bright. By the fourth movement, as he opened his eyes once more, the playing was of such passionate intensity that he, like the boys around him, was almost on the edge of his seat. There was a wild, almost frantic race towards a crescendo, and suddenly, with a great triumphant uplifting of the bows, it was over.

The silence in the hall remained unbroken. Then came a roar of applause.

The musicians stood up, and bowed. They smiled briefly at one another, and bowed again. As the applause went on, they stood there smiling, gazing out over the audience with what was clearly both exhaustion and enormous pleasure. Steven looked from one to the other: at George's animation; Margot's slender self-possession, after all that outpouring; at Diana's mesmerising charm. And then he saw something he had seen before, and felt himself go very still.

George was raking the rows of boys and staff: clearly looking, as he had done on that rain-swept autumn night at Hepplewick, for particular approval. And this time there was no mistaking whose face he sought, and found, as he gave a smile which lit his whole being with elation, and bowed again.

PART FOUR

I

1938

HE CAME BACK. He was pale as a handkerchief, hollow-eyed, but he'd put on a bit of weight and here he was, walking slowly across the playground with McNulty in the teeth of a January wind, and arriving in class in time for Register.

'Moffat?'

'Here, sir.'

Steven looked up. 'Well done. Good to have you back.'

'Thanks, Mr Coulter.'

His pencil ran on, down the column of names. 'Potts.'

'Here, sir.'

He ticked them all off. Rigby. Stoker. Wanless. Wigham. 'Wilson.'

'Here, sir.'

He closed the book. The bell rang out along the corridors which stank of disinfectant; there was the usual clatter of desk lids as everyone got up and filed out for Assembly.

New Year. A new term, laughingly known as Spring.

It was marked by the fresh sound of the piano, used now not just for Miss A. to bang out the hymns in Assembly, but for individual lessons, once a week, from Miss Heslop.

Wednesday afternoons were for sport: out of the school and down the hill to the fields across from Bridge Street, football on grass stiff with frost or churned by winter rain into mud. Last autumn the rain had stopped play for a fortnight, and the burn almost burst its banks. Now it was no worse than the usual foul January days, and Out In All Weathers was almost the school motto. Down they all tramped with their kit.

But Wednesdays were also all at once for Music, scheduled into the timetable with Art, which no one had ever taken much notice of.

'What's that supposed to be, Wigham?'

'A still life. Apples in a dish.'

'They look like cricket balls.'

'You look like a cricket ball, Stoker. Go and stuff yourself.'

Powder paint and sugar paper; twigs in a vase.

'Like being back at Infants.'

So it went. And so, until the Christmas concert, had been the whole idea of music. Soppy stuff. Wets like Alfie Stote warbling away once a year. And anyway, if you learned an instrument you had to practise, and who had a piano at home?

Some did. Some had had lessons at home before. Some, now, just wanted to have a go.

'Morning, Miss Heslop.'

Footsteps over the worn scuffed floor.

'Good morning, Atkins. Come and sit down.'

Fiddling about with the handles on the piano stool, putting off the moment.

'I think that's fine, now, isn't it? Let's make a start.'

'Morning, Miss Heslop.'

Simple Pieces for Beginners open on the stand.

'Good morning, Sparke. Shall we begin with a few scales? Give me C Major, two octaves.'

'Morning, Miss Heslop.'

Dog-eared *Book Two*, riffled through for simple arrangements of Haydn and Grieg.

'It was this one, I think, wasn't it, Pearson? How have you been getting on?'

'Not too bad.'

Stumbling through, the left hand so difficult, suddenly sounding a chord with both hands and turning to beam.

'Well done! On you go.'

Wintry sun breaking through the cloud above the play-ground. The piano sounding, hesitant and slow. Joyful bursts of achievement. She'd been doing this for years: in private houses in Morpeth, in the villages around, in the drawing room at the Hall. This was different. For all sorts of reasons, this felt very different.

Clatter of plates in the dining hall, the smell of bubble-and-squeak.

'Third finger for that A-flat, I think.'

Leaning forward to pencil a 3 on the score. A bell ringing down the corridor.

'We'll have to stop now. Keep it up, Pearson, you're doing well.'

'Thanks, Miss Heslop. See you next week.'

Margot stacked up the music, pushed the stool back into place, took comb and mirror from her bag. The sun pouring in from high windows was brighter; dust motes spun in the air. Outside, the roar of dinner. In here, in the empty hall, with its dusty shafts of light, she stood for a moment full of the kind of nerves which might well precede a concert but not, surely, days at a hill-town boys' school. She bit her lip. Then she turned from the light, ran the comb through her hair, a finger over her eyebrows. There.

'Hello, Frank.'

'Margot. How are you getting on?'

'Quite well, I think. Hello, Mr Coulter. Steven.'

A stiff little nod, the corridor swarming.

'Joining us for lunch?'

'Yes. I was going to bring a sandwich, but—'

'A sandwich won't keep out the cold.'

That was nanny, buttoning up their coats for winter walks. Ice in the puddles along the lane, a red sun sinking in a freezing sky. 'You need something hot on a day like this, my ducks.'

'That's how our Nanny used to talk,' she said to Steven Coulter, and was given a fleeting smile. Of course – why should he care about nannies, the Hall, their past?

'How has your morning been?' she asked Frank, as boys poured by.

'Keep to the left!' he called out, and then: 'Tedious Acts of Parliament.'

They made their way to the dining hall, so noisy you could hardly hear yourself think.

Frank gestured for her to go ahead in the queue. She took a white plate, turned and passed it to Steven, behind her. The gesture was automatic, as if they were sitting next to one another at a dinner party, where you passed everything courteously to your neighbour before serving yourself. It also felt intimate: Please, let me do something for you.

'Thank you.' He smiled, more warmly, and she smiled back, turning to take her own plate and receive a dolloping ladle of bubble-and-squeak and a mountain of mashed potato.

'That's plenty!'

They scanned the hall for places. Frank nodded towards the top of the Fifth-form table; they made their way there and sat down. Staff duty at lunchtime rotated, he told her, pouring water for them all, as Steven passed bread. The boys saw enough of their form teacher; it was good to sit with other boys, keeping an eye on table manners and getting to know them outside class.

'Tuck in.'

They tucked. Watery, greasy, but hot.

'So,' said Frank. 'How are we getting on?'

'Pretty well, I think. They're nice boys.' One of them, Atkins, was on this table: she gave him a little wave, and he blushed.

'Have you done much teaching before?' Steven asked.

'Oh, yes.' She began to talk about the children coming to the Hall, some of them really quite talented, going up to Grade 7 or 8, and one, Lucy Gill, going on to the Royal College.

'I remember her,' said Frank. 'I remember her brother, at tennis. They lived out at Elswick Park. What was his name?'

They both tried to remember. And as they fixed on Jonathan, and what had become of him, they were all at once in a to and fro of names, families, houses where pupils had come from or where the Trio had played, at what weddings and parties—

Steven listened, eating his lunch, which for him, as for many of the boys, was often the most sustaining meal of the day. He envisaged, as Frank and Margot talked away, the great sweep of the drive to the Hall, seen only once in driving rain, but unforgotten, with that towering cedar on the lawn. He saw the candlelit drawing room, tried to imagine it on a summer day: a succession of children walking with their music across the rugs to the beautiful grand piano; brought there by their parents, from all the great houses which might lie round Morpeth and beyond: Hall and Park and Manor. Tennis lessons, music lessons, a governess, like the one who had come to the Christmas concert, who'd taught Frank and Margot before the War. Miss Renner?

How easy and animated were these two with one another now: he watched the way Frank leaned towards Margot, her laugh. He knew that the boys had been knocked sideways by Diana Embleton, had overheard a corridor conversation after the concert.

'Wouldn't mind learning the cello.'

'Me neither.'

'She was—'

'She blimming was.'

And he had understood it. Had he, for a moment, felt the same, as Diana radiantly took the applause? But now, observing Margot's bright dark eyes, her poised and attentive air, remembering her passion and delicacy at the piano, he thought there was something about her which – well, he didn't know how to finish the thought.

'I'm so sorry,' said Frank, turning to him at last. 'We're running away with ourselves, how very rude.'

'Not at all.' He smiled, finishing his plate, but beyond the banality of 'It sounds very interesting', he didn't know what to say next. And watching him flounder, Margot felt herself go hot with embarrassment.

Please, she had thought, passing that old white plate, let me do something for you. And now here she was excluding him from a conversation about people he didn't know from Adam.

She wanted to say: Tell me about your family, but she knew it would only sound patronising. And besides – Frank had told her what had happened. Death wasn't something to talk about over lunch.

Boys were getting up with their plates, going up to queue for steamed pudding and custard. I've made a mess of this moment, she thought, pushing her chair back, and she said: 'I don't think I've got room for pudding – I'll just have a bit of a walk-about before the next lessons.' And she gave them both a smile which felt utterly forced, and picked up her things. 'Have a good afternoon.' In moments she had returned the plate to the counter and was walking from the hall.

Where should she go? Too cold outside. She walked along the corridors, empty for once, and saw the staffroom door. A bolt hole, just for a little while.

The room was empty. It stank of sweat and coal and

cigarette smoke. She dropped her bags, crossed to open a casement window, stood for a moment looking out at the hills. Plover and crow flew over them, sun came and went in the clouds. Behind her, on the other side of the table, she could feel the warmth of the fire on her legs. She thought: I will sit beside it, and it will calm me, and she went across, and sank into a brown moquette chair with varnished arms – like a nursing chair, she thought, with another little pulse of memory.

'Where's Mummy?'

'She's resting. You come and sit on my lap, my duck. That's it.'

From the end of the room, by the pigeon holes, there came a cough.

It startled her so much she almost leapt. There came the sound of a striking match.

Margot got up. She walked towards the end of the room, saw a dark, thin-faced man leaning up against the wall, inhaling deeply from a cigarette, his eyes closed. She'd met him with all the other staff at the concert, and she'd seen him since about the place, though she couldn't remember his name. Then it came to her: Mr Dunn. David Dunn, as Frank referred to him. Shell-shock. Shell-shock and shrapnel, and invalided out of the trenches. Out of the Somme, where Miss Renner's fiancé had been – she imagined – blown to pieces. Such a long time ago now. Had Miss Renner ever recovered?

And here Dunn was, away from the crush of the dining hall, away from everyone, the cigarette held in his long thin fingers, which shook a little. He opened his eyes, and saw her.

'Mr Dunn. I'm so sorry, you startled me.'

But she had startled him, she could see, and she wasn't even sure if he knew who she was.

'Margot Heslop. I'm teaching piano here now.'

He nodded. 'I hope I'm not in your way.'

'Of course not.' The words were meaningless. And she

turned and left him, as he drew on his cigarette. She returned to the fire, and the chair which looked like a nursing chair, but wasn't. She sat there, thinking of each of them, retreated from lunch, where you had to be sociable and easy, something clearly impossible for him, and becoming difficult all at once for her, too, though she usually found it so natural.

The term went by.

'Afternoon, Miss Heslop.'

'Good afternoon, Turnbull. How have you been getting on?'

''Fraid I haven't had much time for practice.'

'Well, we'll start with scales, shall we? C Major. Off you go. No, change from the third to the first finger, remember. That's it. And now with the left hand. And again. Good. Now let's try C Minor. Can you hear how different it sounds?'

'It's a bit sad, isn't it?'

'It is, you're quite right. But rather lovely? Try it again.'

Tender melancholy, in fits and starts. There was an awful lot of this: hunched shoulders, heavy breathing, tongue sticking out, as one after another they stumbled through. The right hand, the left hand, the great leap to both together.

'Play those first three bars again. And once more.'

'Don't think I'll ever be much good, Miss Heslop.'

'The more you can practise, the better you'll get. See you next week.'

But there was also—

'Good afternoon, Miss Heslop.'

'Good afternoon, Herron. How have you been getting on?'

'A bit better, I think.'

Tall and dark, Tom Herron, with a voice quite thoroughly broken, and an easy but respectful manner. And he could play.

'Scales and arpeggios first.'

Up and down the keyboard, confident and good to hear.

'Good! Very good. Let's hear the Bach now.'

Pages turned, an intake of breath. Away. The light at the windows darkening, lights going on through the school. The sound of the football players returning, tramping through the gates. And in here: what a lovely thing.

'Well done! Let's just take it again from the middle, try the left hand again from here—'

'I find those two bars really hard.'

'They are hard. Try again. Good. And again.' She got up to turn the lights on. The windows on to the playground were suddenly black. 'Now let's go through it all once more before we finish.'

And he went through it all once more and the shabby old hall was filled with something beautiful and strong. She could hear people going past outside stop to listen. The bell for the end of the day rang out.

'Very good. Thank you.'

'Thank you, Miss Heslop.'

'Mr Embleton tells me you've won a place at Oxford. Reading History? Congratulations. I hope you'll manage to keep up your music.'

'I'll try. See you next week, Miss Heslop.'

And then it began: the packing up of the scores, the walk through the milling, dimly-lit corridors to the staffroom for her coat. Masters coming out with their bags of books, as eager to get home as the boys.

'Goodnight, Miss Heslop. That sounded rather good.'

'Thank you, Mr Armstrong. Goodnight.'

'Goodnight, Miss Heslop.'

'Goodnight, Mr Gowens.'

Goodnight, Mr Duggan, Mr Dunn, limping along. Out they all came.

'Goodnight, Steven.'

There he was, in his scarf and greatcoat, carrying his hat and his bag, coming towards her through the throng, and did she imagine it, or did his easy smile and manner with the boys change when he saw her? Did he look somehow embarrassed?

'Goodnight, Miss Heslop. Margot.'

And he was past her, calling out to one of his class, and gone. Sometimes he'd be gone by the time she got into the staffroom. Frank had often left by then.

'Meetings,' he said, when she asked him once why he was always in such a rush at the end of the day, but he didn't explain and she didn't ask. Frank had always had a life away from all of them. Friends in London. Dreary political friends, probably.

Inside the staffroom she took down her long winter coat from the peg and settled her hat on her head. Gloves, music bag. Handbag. Another week done. And another whole week to go.

She walked out of the school, to where her car stood waiting beneath the leafless trees in the Square. A bus was standing at the top, the engine running. She saw Steven at the lit-up window, talking to a boy across the aisle. Could he see her?

The sky above the ring of hills round the town was dark. Perhaps just a little lighter, for a little longer, as the winter ebbed away. The bus began its slow descent, passing the shops and the war memorial, passing her. She lifted her hand in a wave. Half-lifted it.

SPRING ON THE moor. Just the first hint of it, tough little shoots of moorland flowers here and there, the first brush of green on the thorn tree. March winds, spring rain, sudden sun lighting the fresh new grass and the sailing clouds, the rise and fall of birds. The water-butt brimmed and shone. Then the first lambs began to call from the farm below.

It was still dark in the evenings, but the days were growing longer, perceptibly longer, as he got off the bus and crossed to the foot of the track. His torchlight flashed over the letter box. Often nothing there. A letter from Andrew Ridley once – *You must come up to Edinburgh. Rose wants to meet you.* Then nothing, for days at a time. Then suddenly a hand he didn't recognise, in a good cream envelope. He tucked it into his pocket, climbed the track as the first stars appeared, the torchlight dancing before him.

Fresh wood into the range, lamps lit, kettle on, a stab of curiosity as he slit open the envelope, with its graceful hand and smudged postmark.

And what was this? Margot Heslop was inviting him for tea.

Spring at Hepplewick. Just the first hint of it, still early March, but the buds on the shaggy forsythia at the door were a sharp fresh green. Rain in the night, in pools on the flagstones, gleaming; the first pale sun filtered through the dense wet branches of the cedar into the shady drawing room, striking marble mantelpiece, brass fender, upraised piano lid.

Chanson du Matin, the kind of thing her father loved her to play. 'It reminds me of your mother, darling – she loved Elgar.'

Do it now, do it before breakfast, still in your dressing gown, the door to the hall flung wide, and a window open at last.

Morning! A soft spring morning in March.

Wet grass glistening all the way down to the ha-ha. The cows out last week from their long winter months in the gloomy sheds; everything so quiet now you could almost hear them grazing. Wet gravel, where her father's footsteps came crunching in from the lane, back from a walk at dawn. Then came the pattering dog.

Chanson du Matin – light, sprightly, joyful. She sang the bright tune as she played, and the footsteps stopped on the flags, where the dog stopped too, for a drink. In the hall the grandfather clock was striking the half-hour – Dah-dah-dah-dah, dah-dah-dah-dah! – perhaps one of the first musical sounds she had ever been aware of, even before her mother's playing. Half-past seven. Boots pulled off in the porch, the front door pushed open, footsteps in the hall.

She finished as he came into the room with the dog, bringing the smell of grass, damp tweed and animal, morning air.

'Lovely, Margot. You're feeling better.'

She turned on the piano stool. The dog padded over to greet her and she bent to stroke his head.

'Was I feeling worse?'

'You've been looking a bit pale.'

'"A bit peaky, my duck. A senna pod, that's what you need."'

He laughed. 'Oh, dear. And what are you doing, now it's half-term?'

She got up. 'Just an ordinary day – practice with everyone this afternoon. For the concert at Easter.'

'Very good. Practising here, I hope.'

'Yes. And then—' she was walking to the door. 'Tomorrow Steven Coulter is coming to tea.'

'Steven Coulter—' He frowned, trying to remember. 'The History teacher. In Frank's department.'

'Yes. I'll go and have my bath now.'

Out to the hall, and up the curving staircase. *Chanson du Matin* hummed all along the landing. She lay in the bath and swished the shining water.

Her letter had hoped he was well, that it was not too cold up on Hencote Moor. Frank had given her his address – she hoped he didn't mind. *It's always so busy, we don't have a chance to talk.* And she'd ask Frank to bring him over to Hepplewick, but Frank always had so much on out of school, and he'd said he was going to London for half-term. She thought there were buses.

There were. Steven took the usual hourly one into Kirk-houghton, and then the bus to Morpeth, a good twenty miles, so he'd had to leave straight after an early lunch, bread and cheese.

He was spending the half-term mornings in the garden again, digging and sowing, feeling the sun and wind on his face, a good feeling. Birds flew by, and with the high mournful pipe of the lapwing he thought again of the walks he and Margaret had taken, down to the river, across springy grass to the fort. The wind carried the cries of the lambs with their ewes, all out now, speckling the moor with white.

Darling, it's just as it was . . .

But today was different.

The bus followed the Wansbeck, stopping in riverside villages where washing blew and children played on the banks. It drew up in Morpeth, outside the town hall. A lovely old town, the county town, with a medieval bridge, and places to see properly one day: a castle, a court house, the church where Emily Davison lay buried. The streets were crowded with shoppers, grand cars parked outside the bank and a big department store. When he found that the bus to Hepplewick and beyond wasn't due for another half-hour, he took out the map and began to walk.

She'd invited him for three o'clock – *so there'll still be some light, and I can show you around* – and as he set out the town clock was chiming the hour. Within a mile or so he was out in open country, and it felt prosperous, ploughed fields greening up with early wheat, cattle grazing in parkland. He passed a lodge, an avenue, glimpsed creeper, a pillared portico. Was that the Hall? No – he remembered the village where Frank had slowed down in the pouring rain, and now he came to it, houses clustered round the green, a little shop, a church. A lane stretched out of it, bordered with oak and elm.

The sky was streaked with red, the sun beginning to sink. And now he was suddenly nervous. He ran his finger over the map. Hepplewick Hall. Within fifteen minutes, he was at the open gates.

He stopped, seeing the place in daylight for the first time, remembering almost nothing of the outside, only the driving rain, the dash from the car towards the porch, the welcome and his crippling shyness. Then music and candlelight and his aching grief.

Darling, I need you beside me—

But she hadn't been, and she wasn't here now. She never would be.

With this thought, suddenly slammed into him as if for the first time, he stood very still, looking ahead at the house, the light just beginning to fade. Smoke rose from tall chimneys into the gathering cloud. The huge cedar he now remembered darkened the lawn on the right, and an old swing hung there, moving just a little in the raw spring air.

He took a breath, folded the map, put it back in his pocket.

It was cold, and he couldn't go on standing here. He walked up the curving drive. The long stately lawn ran down to the right, past a sundial and on to a ha-ha, with cattle beyond, huge and dark in the failing light. His feet crunched on the gravel. No one about. He went on, noting a little summer house across the garden, the pele tower on to which the house had been grafted, and the arch to a stable yard beyond. Then the gravel became flagstones, and he saw the dog's dish set by the porch, and knew that the dog would steady him, as the door inside the porch swung open.

'You found it!'

'I did, thanks.'

He lifted his hat, and as they smiled at one another he felt some of his nervousness evaporate. Behind her he could see the glow of the fire in the hall.

'It's so nice of you to come all this way.'

'It was nice of you to ask me.'

'Well – everything's always such a rush at school, isn't it? Would you like to look round a bit? Before tea?' She took down a coat from a hook in the porch, not waiting for him to answer. 'My father's out with the dog – he'll join us later.'

'Let me help you.' He took the coat from her, held it out so she could slip into the sleeves. She was almost as tall as he was.

'Thank you.' She moved quickly away, turned up the collar beneath her dark bob. The coat was a worn old tweed, quite different from the long lined elegance of the one she had worn for the concert, and not unlike Margaret's, still hanging by the kitchen door in the cottage. Would it ever not hang there? For months, he had thought of it as waiting for her return.

Margot pulled on her gloves. 'So – off we go.'

She led him to the left, towards the stable-yard where he recognised her little car, and along to the kitchen garden, with

127

a tennis court alongside. She clicked open the wicket gate of the garden and beckoned him through. It was big: he looked round at greenhouse and potting shed and tilled beds just beginning to sprout: onions and broad beans and tight spring cabbage. A light wind was getting up, and the air smelt of smoke from the house and of freshly dug earth. Everything was immaculate.

'It's a lot of work.'

'It is. We have a man who does it all, we're very fortunate. Mr Barrow – I know, it's funny, isn't it? His wife helps in the house.' They walked along the paths. 'Do you – do you garden at all?'

'I do.' And he told her about the patch he had dug up on Hencote, windswept but surviving, though nothing as far on as here, sheltered by stone walling. 'I fenced it in from the sheep,' he said, as they came out through the gate again.

Now they could see the pele tower properly, and for a moment he stopped, and stood looking up at it, a mighty thing adjoining the main house, with its high narrow windows and a weathered door which he guessed Margot's grandfather might have had made.

'My boys would like that tower. They like hearing about border raids and battles.'

'Do they? I'm afraid it's just where my father keeps his guns: he belongs to the local shoot. Mostly it's full of Barrow's tools and things.'

'His barrow.'

'Yes.' She gave a little laugh, and for a moment he felt so easy with her that he almost put her arm through his as they walked on, over the flag-stoned terrace.

'And you grew up here?' he asked. 'You were born here?'

'Yes. Heslops have lived in this house for over two hundred years.' They turned to walk over the darkening lawn. 'We're a mining family, originally, my father's still a director – it's just a small mine outside Morpeth now. He can tell you more about it, if you're interested.'

'I'm a historian – of course I'm interested.' He thought perhaps that sounded as if his curiosity was only professional, was perhaps a bit curt. And he said, as they walked slowly down past the sundial, 'And you grew up with your friends – with Frank and everyone.'

'Just for a couple of years, but we stayed very close, we were lucky.' They came to the edge of the ha-ha, deep and grassy. 'We used to race down here,' she said, looking out at the cattle.

'And Frank always won?'

'Almost always. He's one of those people, isn't he?'

'I think he is.'

The wind blew over the field, and the light was almost gone. She put her arms about her.

'Come on – let's go and have tea.'

They turned and walked back, past the little summer house standing before a line of trees, and up towards the Hall. The cedar overshadowing it was so dense and dark, and the swing beneath it such a fragile thing.

'We used to love that swing,' said Margot, seeing Steven turn to look at it. 'Frank used to make us go higher and higher.'

Two little girls and a skinny little boy – a trio – and the other boy tall and strong and fair and full of energy, then as now: Steven thought that was how it must have been. And as they came to the terrace he remembered, as he had often done since the Christmas concert, that search across a packed school hall for one especial face.

'Diana and I still swing on it sometimes, in summer,' said Margot, as they reached the porch. 'It's very restful.' She hung up her coat, pushed open the heavy front door. Inside, in the fire-lit hall, the grandfather clock ticked steadily.

'Let me take your things.'

'Thank you.' He gave her his hat and scarf, shrugged off the heavy winter coat. 'Let me—'

'No, no, it's fine.' She took the weight of it, crossed to hang it on the stand, his hat and scarf on the hook above. 'There. I thought we'd have tea by the fire. Come through.'

He followed her into the drawing room. Rugs, pictures, a table piled with books and magazines, another with scores. A couple of music stands were folded against the wall. No longer a concert salon but a great, airy, comfortable room, tea laid on a lamp-lit fireside table, two wing chairs on either side of the hearth.

'Do sit down – I'll be back in a minute.'

She went, her shoes clicking over the floorboards, and he crossed to the fire, taking the chair on the right. It was good to sit down; it felt good to sit here, in this calm old room. He stretched out his feet by the flames and looked across at the piano. Might he ask her to play, or did she not like to be asked? He hardly knew her at all.

And though he no longer felt ill at ease, he wondered, as he had done when he first read her letter, that she should do this, that someone with a life of concerts and parties and good close friends should bother with coming into a school to teach awkward boys, or seek out the company of a teacher who until now had been pretty awkward himself.

Photographs stood here and there about the room: studio portraits in silver frames and some more informal. He didn't like to go picking them up and looking at them, but one on the far side of the mantelpiece showed a woman in profile, dark-haired, with a glimpse of pretty earring, gazing out of the frame in the misty halo photographers liked to use to give their subjects depth and meaning. There was a photograph like that of Margaret at her parents' house, taken for her twenty-first.

She hadn't needed such a background, and neither did this woman, with her bright expressive face. He knew who it must be.

The clock in the hall struck the three-quarter hour. What a good sound. And here was Margot, bringing a tray: silver teapot and hot water, a silver muffin dish. He got to his feet.

'Let me help you.'

'It's fine,' she said again, and carried it over to the table, sitting down opposite him, asking if he took milk.

'Please.'

The last women to pour him tea were his mother, Margaret's mother, and Margaret herself, from the big brown teapot bought at the auction where they'd bought their bed. Both items had made them feel very married.

Margot lifted the lid of the muffin dish. Hot buttered muffins, strawberry jam, pretty china: he noted a third cup and saucer.

'Where does your father go walking?' He took a soft muffin dripping with butter.

'Everywhere. Sometimes just along the lanes, sometimes quite far afield.'

'And your mother?' He nodded towards the photograph. 'That's her?'

'Yes.'

It felt too personal to say that he thought her lovely-looking. He just said:

'She won't be joining us?'

Margot put down her cup. 'Frank didn't tell you?'

He shook his head.

'She died when I was eight.'

The muffin was halfway to his mouth. He almost dropped it.

'Oh, Margot.'

Was that the first time he had used her name? It felt as if

it was. And the look he gave her across the hearth was as if something had been unmasked.

'I'm so sorry.'

'It's all right,' she said, as she always said: so much sealed over, for so many years. 'I'm surprised Frank didn't tell you, but perhaps he just takes it for granted, it's so long ago.' She saw Steven hesitate. 'Can I remember her? Yes, a little. I think we were very close. And she played the piano- I can remember that, and her teaching me. Starting me off.'

His smile made her want to get up, cross the hearth and kiss him. 'She did very well,' he said.

'Thank you.' And now it was she who was hesitant. 'But you - you've lost your wife. Frank did tell me that.'

'Yes.'

And then, leaning back in his chair, he found that he couldn't speak.

'Forgive me,' she said, and he made no answer.

Firelight played over the hearth, the light at the windows deepened. Footsteps came up the drive: a man and a dog, out walking, as every day. For the first time she thought of her father and the man sitting silently opposite her as two widowers, and she wondered at the length of her father's time alone. Perhaps, like Frank, she had taken something for granted.

The front door banged.

'I'm sorry to be so—' Steven struggled to collect himself. 'I think of my wife all the time, but I hardly talk of her.' To say this to someone he barely knew, to reveal how much Margaret still lived within him - it felt very strange. Especially, perhaps, because, as he'd stood at the open gates, he had felt her leave him completely.

Footsteps came into the room.

'Hello, Father.'

'Hello, darling. Afternoon, Coulter, good to see you.'

Steven got to his feet. His fingers were covered in butter, and he pulled out his handkerchief.

'Here.' Margot passed him a napkin.

'What am I doing?' he said, taking it from her. 'You must think I'm—' He wiped butter away with worn linen. 'Good afternoon, sir.' They shook hands. 'How was your walk?'

'Very good, thanks. Bit of a wind now.'

And there was the dog, nosing up to him, and he bent to greet and pat him.

'Good dog, good dog. How was *your* walk?'

'He put up a rabbit or two.' Heslop moved to the sofa, and took his cup from Margot. 'And how are you, Coulter? Enjoying your half-term?'

'Yes, thank you. It's very nice to be here.' The dog made his way to the hearth, and Steven went back to his chair, and stretched out a hand as he sank down before the fire. Margot gave him a smile, and he returned it, recovering himself, feeling the complicity which two people who like one another – and unexpectedly, improbably, even, it seemed that they did – always feel when they're joined by a third. Especially if they have been making disclosures.

He glanced across again at the photograph of her mother – surely, like Margaret, much too young to die. And taking fresh tea, passing the muffin dish to her father, he felt his picture of Margot begin to change: behind the accomplished musician, the confident young woman on the concert platform, with a background of friends and comfort, he saw a little dark-haired girl, alone with her father in this enormous house.

The dog yawned and stretched on the hearthrug. He bent to pat him once more, stroked the warm dark coat. The paws twitched.

'He's dreaming of those rabbits,' said Heslop.

Steven gave the dog another pat, and looked up to see Margot's eyes upon him. She smiled again, quickly, and poured fresh hot water into the pot.

The conversation turned to the house, its history, generations of Heslops, coal. Coal, and the mine outside Morpeth which Heslop still managed, now in decline, like so much industry. Unemployment, and the march from Jarrow two years ago, said Steven, thinking of his class.

'Me uncle's on National Assistance, now.'

'Of course,' said Heslop, 'If there's a war—'

Margot was pouring the last of the tea. 'I don't want to think about that.'

Would she play for him, before he left? She would. Was there anything in particular he might like to hear? He shook his head: he knew so little – she should choose.

'Father?'

'You know I always like to hear Elgar. Or Chopin. But do what you feel like, Margot.'

She got up, crossed to the piano, leafed through the music there.

'Mendelssohn,' she said, after a moment or two, and began to play. Outside, all was darkness, the rising wind in the cedar the only sound. In here, something gentle and quiet began – the kind of thing, thought Steven, which if you hadn't been listening to music for very long, you could enter and appreciate at once. But as Margot played on, the tone of it deepened, became grave and thoughtful, more complex. He settled back in his chair.

What an interesting choice. He was glad of it: had she played something bright, or sad, he would not have known how to respond. But this – this was music of the mind. And as it gradually increased in vigour and intensity, building towards a climax, he closed his eyes in utter concentration.

It lasted just a few minutes, ending almost as gently as it began. No one spoke. Steven went on sitting there, hearing the sough of the wind, the sigh of the sleeping dog, logs falling apart in the grate.

'Very nice, darling,' Heslop said at last.

Steven opened his eyes. 'What was it?'

'A fugue,' Margot turned on the piano stool, and once again he thought how graceful she was. And how pale – did she always look so pale? 'Did you like it?'

'I did, very much. Thank you: it was just what I needed. Tell me about it.'

'It's just one of a sequence: *Seven Characteristic Pieces*. That was Number Five. I think they were written for friends.'

'Like Elgar and the *Enigma Variations*,' said Heslop, and gave a yawn.

The grandfather clock in the hall began to strike, and Steven looked at his watch. Six o'clock. He mustn't outstay his welcome. The windows were pitch black and he had a journey of perhaps two hours.

He rose from the chair. 'I must be off.'

'Won't you stay for a drink?' Heslop was getting up stiffly, and the dog thumped his tail. 'Or supper – stay for supper, why don't you? I'm sure we can rustle something up.'

He shook his head. 'That's very kind, but I've a long way to go.'

'I'll run you into Morpeth,' said Margot, and then, more hesitantly: 'May I?'

'No, thanks, really – I mustn't trouble you – the walk will do me good. If I could just—' He gave Heslop a glance.

'Let me show you.' The dog followed them out as he led him back to the hall and pointed to a passage door. 'In there. But do let one of us give you a lift.'

'No, no, it's all right, thanks.'

Why didn't he just say yes?

Too much on your own, love, he heard his mother say, and it was true. He went into the capacious lavatory, and saw in the mirror someone too much on his own, who didn't know how to break out of it. When he came out he could hear Heslop clattering about in the kitchen at the end of the passage. Margot was playing again, something very gentle, like a nursery rhyme.

She stopped as he came into the room.

'What was that?'

'Just something my mother used to play. I haven't thought of it for years.' She got up, and came towards him. 'You're sure I can't drive you?'

'Quite sure, thanks.'

'I'll get you your things.' And she was in the hall in a moment, up at the stand, saying that her father was feeding the dog, and passing his coat and scarf. He wound it round his neck, took his hat.

'Well – thank you, Margot.' He put out his free hand. 'I've really enjoyed it – especially hearing you play.'

She took the hand, and released it. 'Do come again.' But now it was hostess talk, he could feel it. Then her father was coming up the passage, saying the same thing, and he felt the waters close over the afternoon: he wouldn't accept their kindness – very well, goodbye. And perhaps he had embarrassed Margot, with his sudden flood of emotion, that long silence, when she spoke of Margaret. Or did he imagine all that? They stood in the porch as he thanked them again, and walked away down the drive. Stars were rising. The door closed firmly behind him.

Had she upset him? Should she not have asked about his wife, whom he thought about all the time? And couldn't talk about. He'd closed quite off from her again, just had all that talk with

136

her father. She bit her lip. Then she went slowly back to the
piano, and played the sweet tune from the past.

Now the day is over,
Night is drawing nigh;
Shadows of the evening
Steal across the sky. . . .

She was on her mother's lap, she was singing with her,
watching the fingers move over the keyboard, as dusk fell over
the garden. Such a long time ago.

Out in the hall she could hear her father throwing more logs
on the fire, then standing still, listening. She could sense him
doing this. Then he went into the library and closed the door.

How had he endured so many years alone?

How had she?

Now the day is over . . .

She played it once more, and then she got up and began to
clear away the tea things. A napkin had fallen to the floor beside
Steven's chair: she went over, bent down. No – not a napkin.
His handkerchief. She picked it up, and pressed it to her lips.

'Margot? Darling?' She was getting supper, heard her father
open the library door and call her. She could hear the murmur
of the wireless as he walked down the passage to the kitchen.
'I've just heard the news.' She turned, saw his troubled face.
'Hitler has entered Austria. It seems they've welcomed him.'

3

PRIMROSES STARRED THE grassy verges in the lane from Hepplewick. Daffodils blew in a fresh April wind all the way down the garden and sprang up in the ha-ha. On the terrace, in the far corner of the house, the forsythia was in full bloom: such an ordinary old thing, but Barrow kept it cut back so it grew more vigorously, and she could not remember a time when it had not been there, when it had not greeted her on her return from school in the Easter holidays, bright against grey stone, yellow flowers floating in dark rain pools on the flags.

It was the Easter holidays now, and, as every year, the Trio was giving a concert in St Mary's, Hepplewick, whose window ledges were full of spring flowers in jam jars.

'Lovely,' said George, pushing open the door for a morning rehearsal. Diana and Margot had parked their little cars on the roadside outside the churchyard wall; he'd left his bicycle in the porch. He walked down the aisle with his violin case and stood in the middle, breathing in the scent of primroses and prayer books, candle wax and cold stone. 'Gorgeous. If you could bottle Anglicanism you'd make a fortune. I don't believe a word of it, but oh, how it soothes the soul.'

'My soul needs soothing,' said Diana, setting down the cello beside him and breathing deeply. 'All anyone can talk about at home is *politics*. Frank at breakfast – he goes on and on. My father doesn't seem so worried, but he's always talking about some Mosley man, do you know who he is? Daddy seems to think he's a good thing, but Frank gets so upset.' She put her head on one side. 'What do you think?'

'I'd put my money on Frank, if I were you,' said George lightly. 'He generally knows what's what.' And then: 'Mosley's a thug.'

'That's what Father says.' Margot walked past them with her music case. 'Oh, I hate it all, don't you?' She went up to the piano. Like the one at Kirkhoughton, it was old and worn, but kept well in tune and in truth made a sound rather better than the dilapidated organ, rarely used, for which the vicar was always fund-raising. She lifted the lid, and ran her hands over the keyboard.

'How's that?'

'Fine,' said George. 'I suppose Frank's coming to the concert,' he added to Diana, as she picked up the cello again. They walked up towards the chancel.

'You never know what he's going to do these days. He's always off to some meeting or other. Mummy never knows if he's going to be there for supper or anything.'

'Shocking.'

'Well, it is a bit *inconsiderate*.'

Their voices rang out in the clear acoustic.

'That's not like Frank.' Margot finished a couple of scales and looked up. 'What are all these meetings he goes to?'

'I don't know.'

'What about his friend?' asked George, setting the violin case in the front pew and opening it up. 'That tall quiet chap – Steven Whatnot. Will he come, do you think?'

Margot studied the keys. 'He might. I've sent him an invitation.'

'I see.'

'No, you don't.' She picked up her music case, pulled out a score. 'Come on, let's make a start.'

❧

In the ebbing spring light of the afternoon, Steven was back from Birley Bank, his knapsack stuffed with clean shirts, a fruit cake and a pie; as the bus went on up the hill he crossed the road, and lifted the lid of the letter box. There had been nothing for days, and he was expecting nothing. But here - a little package. He took it out, saw the Morpeth postmark, and her hand. How curious: what could this be? Whatever it was, he was glad to hear from her, he realised, and he dropped it into his pocket, and set off up the track.

As he climbed he thought once again about his visit, and the stiff little letter he had written afterwards. *Thank you for a very nice afternoon, and for showing me round . . . I did enjoy talking to your father, and hearing you play . . . I expect I shall see you at school again before too long. Until then, best wishes . . .*

Of her mother's death, of his own bereavement, he said nothing: it felt too intimate, in the kind of thank-you letter he had been taught to write. And that sudden flood of emotion, his utter silence - it must have embarrassed her. But as soon as he'd posted it, he wondered once more if he had offended her with his determination to leave on his own. When they saw one another at school she just gave a nod and a smile.

The cold April wind blew over the moor. Climbing, he thought, too, of today's visit home, of the mixture of guilt and tenderness he always felt on leaving his parents. They wanted him home, he knew they did, though they never said.

'Goodbye, Mother.' He lifted the knapsack in the tiny hall. 'Thanks again for all this.'

'Goodbye, Steven, love.' She stood on tiptoe for his kiss. 'Come again soon.'

'I will. Chin up.'

Out to the workshop, with its fresh smell of sawdust and timber.

'Bye, Dad.'

A chair leg was clamped in a turner. There was sawdust on his overall, and some in his hair, going grey.

'Bye, lad. You're doing well.'

'See you again soon.'

'That'll be grand.'

Waiting for the bus in the village, everything known and familiar since childhood, he tried to imagine returning, living at home again, and knew it would be impossible. Leaving the cottage, the moor, would be a final goodbye to his marriage: it would feel like a dream, and he couldn't bear that.

Something else felt like a dream, hearing the quacking of ducks on the river, watching a little boy spin by on a tricycle in the peaceful street: events in Europe.

At school they felt more real: it wasn't only Frank, flinging down a copy of *The Times* in the staffroom, open to show a grainy photograph of Vienna with swastikas fluttering all along the Ringstrasse; it wasn't only David Dunn's set face as he unfolded his own *Morning Post*. There was quite a lot of talk about the uncertain future now, and not just in the staffroom.

'Me Dad says there'd be call-up.'

'Me Mam says I'm too young.'

He came to the top of the track, where packed earth became grass, springy underfoot again now. The ewes and their lambs were spread out everywhere, their questioning and answering cries carried far on the wind. There was another sound, too, a shouting he at first put down to the farmer calling his dog, but it wasn't that. He stopped, trying to make it out, but he couldn't, and he crossed to the cottage, where the daffodils Margaret had planted in the first autumn of their marriage nodded by the door.

Inside, he set down the knapsack, topped up the range and set the kettle on top.

Then he pulled out the little brown-paper package, and slit it open with his penknife.

He put his hand inside, felt an envelope, and the rustle of tissue paper. For a moment he had a child's excitement. Then he withdrew it, a small white square, and unwrapped his handkerchief, beautifully washed and ironed.

Well.

How stupid of him to have dropped it. But astonishing, how pleased and touched he felt.

He opened the envelope.

Dear Steven,

Thank you so much for your letter. We loved having you here, and I hope you reached home easily. I found this by the fire! One other thing – we're giving our annual Eastertide concert at St Mary's in Hepplewick soon. I enclose a little advertisement – it would be lovely if you could come.

With all good wishes,

Margot

He read the advertisement, he sniffed the handkerchief. It smelled of some pretty kind of soap, quite different from the smell of the shirts and handkerchiefs his mother laundered for him.

Well.

But how strange, really. She could have given it to him at school. She could simply have said: You dropped this, and by the way there's a concert. Or she could have put it in a paper bag, and put it in his pigeon hole with a note. But since term had begun again they'd only spoken in passing, and now she'd gone to all this trouble—

Wind rattled the door, and then the shouting he'd heard a few minutes ago came closer, and now he could hear the words.

'Left, right, *left*, right!'

Feet were tramping over the moor, somewhere behind the

cottage: he went outside, and walked round. In the last of the light he made out the bottle-green of the Northumberland Fusiliers, perhaps thirty men marching down towards the track. He saw their heavy backpacks, the flash of red on their caps, and then, on their shoulders, the silhouetted guns.

4

THE CHURCH WAS almost full when he arrived, and he was almost late, the bus to Kirkhoughton delayed for once, so he'd missed the connection to Morpeth. He slipped into a pew at the back, next to two elderly ladies, and picked up the programme before him. He remembered the composers from the advertisement Margot had sent: Dvořák of course he knew of, but he'd never heard of the *Dumky* Trios. And he'd never heard of Frank Bridge, opening the concert. Something modern, which he might not like. He glanced at the programme notes, signed with George Liddell's initials: Benjamin Britten had been Bridge's pupil once, apparently. He knew nothing of Britten, either.

He looked round, saw that the audience was more mixed than the one at the Hall last autumn: fewer grand cars were parked outside, and this felt more like a village affair, more old suits, print frocks and cotton hats than linen and tweed. Did he recognise anyone? Yes, he could see Thomas Heslop up at the front, next to a couple he remembered from the autumn: the Embleton parents. But no Frank – he hadn't heard from him since the end of term, when he'd said he was going down to London.

'What will you do there?'

'Browse in the bookshops, I expect. See friends. And I've got one or two meetings.'

Steven didn't like to ask what they were, guessed they might be political.

'The Fusiliers are out on the moor in manoeuvres now – I see them quite a bit. It looks pretty serious.'

'It is serious,' said Frank, picking up stuff from the table. 'You know it is. I wish I could get my family to see.' He piled papers into his bag and closed it. 'Still – have a good Easter, Steven.' And with that ravishing smile, and a gentle clap-clap on the shoulder, he was gone, swinging his briefcase, the boys outside swarming round the little red Imp as usual.

The tower clock was striking the half-hour. Early evening sunlight streamed serenely through stained glass, candles burned palely in the chancel. A concert in a country church: it all felt at such a distance from the possibility of war – except for one of the windows which Steven, looking around him, now noticed on the far side of the north aisle. A fallen knight in armour lay beneath the unfurled red and white flag of the George Cross, gazing up at the cream-robed figure of Christ, whose hand was outstretched towards him. Beneath the leaded frame ran a legend, but from here he couldn't read it.

Sentimental? He thought it was, and he suspected that someone like Frank would dislike the whole idea of it, religion and patriotism intermingled, and yet it was hard not to be moved by the looks of love and compassion that passed between those figures.

'Good evening, ladies and gentlemen.'

As the audience fell silent, a cheery young vicar welcomed them all to the annual concert at Eastertide. The Hepplewick Trio – their very own trio, you might say – needed no introduction, but they went from strength to strength. Under the leadership of George Liddell, who of course had studied at the Royal College in London, they were always adding to their repertoire, and tonight were opening with a composer who would bring everyone up to date with modern times. Frank Bridge. Super. So now please welcome them.

Out they filed from the vestry. Bow tie, midnight-blue taffeta, black silk. Steven thought it was silk, as they bowed to the applause, and took their places. Whatever it was, Margot looked poised, graceful – always that – and, sitting down at the piano, marvellously remote. They tuned up. Then that magical swift glance ran between the three of them – *Ready? Yes!*

Even from here, at the back of the church, he could feel her entire concentration as they began to play, and he thought of the dark spring evening when she had played just for him and her father, of the grave quiet beauty of that fugue. Had he thought himself unmusical? It wasn't true. He was learning to take pleasure in music, wanting to understand it, feeling musicality begin to unfurl within him.

The Dvořák was full of contrasts. He looked at the programme notes again. *Dumka* – a Ukrainian folk song. 'Sometimes of elegiac and meditative character, sometimes exuberant' – and what he was listening to now was certainly that, sprightly and uplifting. But as they played on, each movement kept changing, now dancing, now singing wistfully.

The applause at the end was enthusiastic, though he noticed, as the Trio took their bows, that the smiles they gave were perhaps less radiant than usual. Certainly George was less radiant. Had he hoped, until the last minute, that someone in particular would be here?

They bowed for the last time, stood upright once again. Did he imagine it, or was Margot giving one swift look across the pews? *I'm here*, he wanted to tell her, suddenly full of a nervous excitement, as the clapping died away. *I'm here, right at the back.*

The interval was noisy with talk: everyone knew one another. Should he go up to the front, and greet Thomas Heslop? Looking across at him through the throng, deep in conversation with the Embletons, he decided against it: he'd say hello afterwards, not interrupt. And there was something about Embleton he couldn't warm to on sight: fair-haired like his wife and children, he perhaps had been handsome when he was young. But now he was beefy, a little too red in the face, and a bit complacent. Even at this distance, he gave off the air of someone who had never had to struggle, or ask many questions about his place in the world, and now he was holding forth, you could tell, and his pretty wife – surely it was from her that Frank and Diana had inherited their charm and good looks – had stopped listening, and was waving to a friend. Embleton and Heslop were left up against one another, in some kind of disagreement.

Steven got up. What he really wanted was to do was go to the vestry, to tell them all how good they were; to tell Margot. He saw her face turn to his, their eyes meeting. But he couldn't do that: it felt presumptuous. He'd stretch his legs, have a look round the church until the second half – the kind of thing he encouraged his boys to do when they trooped up to St Peter's, or went on school trips, learning history: not just from castles and bridges and battle sites, but from a Norman arch, or Gothic vaulting, from window and plaque and effigy.

'Sir? Sir, is it time for our sandwiches yet?'

He walked across the north transept, where the loops of bell-pulls hung, ghostly in the fading light. What was there to see? In the north aisle, a couple of elaborate marble plaques. He went to have a look.

And of course: they were Heslop plaques. Heslops must have worshipped here for over two hundred years, clip-clopping down from the Hall in carriage or trap, taking their places in the family pew – probably the one where Thomas Heslop was sitting now, at the front; buried out in the churchyard when their time had come. He'd noticed a couple of tombs, and stone angels, when he'd hurried through.

Sacred to the memory of Sir Thomas Heslop, Bart . . .

He thought suddenly: There must be a plaque to Margot's

mother, and he walked on down the aisle, where one or two other people on their own were looking at things.

Here. An elegant little brass plate, set beneath a window ledge.

To the memory of Evelyn Margot Heslop, 1884-1916
Beloved wife of Thomas Geoffrey, and mother of Margot Evelyn

How strange: Margot's father and his father shared a name. Geoffrey John Coulter, cabinet maker. Thomas Geoffrey Heslop, land owner. Descendant of the founder of a coal mine, and now a director. Such a huge social gulf. Yet son and daughter were getting to know one another.

Modern times.

He stood there, thinking, and another inscription came back to haunt him:

In loving memory of Margaret Coulter, née Ridley . . .

He must put spring flowers there on Easter Day. Primroses, picked in grassy Church Lane.

Oh, darling—

Should he feel guilty, now, that interest in someone else was beginning to quicken?

He walked slowly on. Light was fading behind the memorial window, but now he could read the legend beneath that fallen soldier.

Sacred to the memory of Captain Edward Gibson, 1893-1916
Dulce et decorum est pro patria mori.

He must have been killed at the Somme. Steven had a sudden flash of David Dunn, limping down corridors and into his class; twitching in meetings, weeping in the Christmas carol service. And he thought: I teach all this history, I reel off all these battles, and I know nothing, not really. Not as Dunn knows.

Footsteps came up towards him. Someone else was coming to look at this window, a tall, stiff, grey-haired woman in coat and hat. Someone he recognised, though he couldn't think from where he knew that handsome face. She must have been beautiful once. Then—

'Miss Renner?'

She gave a little frown.

'Forgive me—' Something in her solitary dignity compelled him. 'Steven Coulter,' he said diffidently. 'You won't remember me, but I teach at Kirkhoughton Boys. You were there for the concert at Christmas, I think - Frank Embleton introduced us at the reception afterwards.'

'Oh, yes.' She gave a smile which changed her features entirely. 'A very good evening. And you teach—'

'History. I'm in Frank's department. He's talked about you - so has Margot Heslop. You obviously meant a lot to them all.'

'I was fortunate to teach them. A very nice group of children - I'm pleased that they've all done so well. It's a pity Frank isn't here tonight. It never feels quite right without him.'

A bell was ringing for the second half. She turned to look up at the window, and fell silent.

'It's very striking, isn't it?' he said. 'Do you know anything about it?'

'Captain Gibson was my fiancé,' said Miss Renner, looking back at him, calm and direct. 'His parents commissioned that window.' And then, as a hand bell began to ring, 'You never forget, you know.'

The Frank Bridge was delightful: he hadn't expected that. *Miniatures for Violin, Cello and Piano*, amiable, pleasing, unemotional. And he was glad of that for once, to be offered order and calm. As he closed his eyes and listened, he thought of Miss Renner, and her shining knight, dying in that bloodbath more than twenty years ago. No one, it seemed, had taken his place. Well - there must be women like her all over the country, half a generation of young men gone, and those who had loved them

149

living on alone. But what a distinctive air she had: no wonder her pupils had thought so much of her, and their time together.

The last bars sounded, there was a silence, the sense of a sigh. Then the applause began, and he opened his eyes. The windows of the church had darkened completely now, and the candlelit Trio in the chancel looked like something from Rembrandt. They took their bows. And as he joined in the applause he knew that his life was being enriched by all of this: he was clapping hard and wanting, like everyone else, an encore.

Which the Trio gave them. 'It's the last movement of a Haydn trio,' George announced, giving his bow a flourish. 'But often played alone. You'll see why. It's called "Gypsy Rondo"'. He smiled. 'You'll see why.' He had recovered himself, it was clear, was buoyant and vital again. And what a dancing, joyful piece this was, the violin like a mad thing.

More applause at the end, and then it was over, everyone gathering up their things and talking, making their way towards the west door. Someone had opened it wide; it was suddenly very cold. Pulling his coat on, Steven looked out and saw the first pale stars.

'Here we are, here we are!' George was leading the others up the nave, a coat round his shoulders, an opera scarf flung round his neck. The violin at his side, he looked every inch the musician. He could be – perhaps he should be – famous. Behind him, Margot and Diana were in wraps, Diana shivering exaggeratedly. Where was the cello? Heslop was carrying it. It seemed he always did.

'Well now, what did we think?' George demanded of Steven, as if he'd known him for years. Impossible not to warm to him.

'We thought it was rather good,' came a light dry voice.

'Miss Renner! You're here!'

'Of course.'

'You're coming back for supper?'

'If I'm asked.'

'You're asked! Of course you are. And you, too, Mr History Teacher. Master, perhaps I should say.'

For a wild moment, as Steven laughed, he thought: Are you flirting with me? And then, as Margot put out a hand and said lightly, 'Oh, yes, do come,' he forgot everything, and took her hand in his. 'Thank you. That was really lovely.'

There were other people gathering in the kitchen: people he'd seen at the autumn concert, and who introduced themselves now. Jonathan Gill. Hugo and Imogen Raeburn. The Lindsays. Used as he was to learning new names every year, with every fresh intake of boys, he struggled now to keep hold of all these as everyone talked away. Was it Jonathan, whom people seemed to call Jonty, pouring Diana a drink?

'Super, sweetie. Just what I need.'

'You look gorgeous, Di.'

Was Hugo the one whose sister had gone to the Royal College? She wasn't here now, was she?

Margot had run him up to the Hall. 'May I?' she'd asked, as they crossed the starlit churchyard. The moon had risen: the shadows of Heslop tombs lay over the grass.

'That's very kind. Thank you.'

Ahead of them, Heslop was putting the cello into the back of the Model T, Miss Renner already in the front. Diana and George and the violin were cramming into her little two-seater. Doors slammed around them, headlamps came on.

'Look!' called a voice. 'Look at that owl!'

'Diana's parents aren't coming?' Steven ventured, seeing Embleton tug open the door of what must be a Bentley, wondering once again at the wealth behind Frank, who surely could do anything he wanted, but had chosen to come home and teach.

Margot shook her head as they got in the car. 'Mr Embleton

and my father don't really get on nowadays. It's a shame, when we're all so close.'

'You children, you mean.' He shifted his legs, too long for this little car. 'You young things. That's how George would put it, isn't it?'

She smiled, turning on the ignition. 'You're getting to know us all. I'm so glad you enjoyed the concert.'

'I loved it,' he said, and as they pulled out from the verge, and he saw her smile deepen, he felt their closeness in this tiny space. The headlamps came on; they sped after the others, fast down the darkening lane.

Now, in the warmth of the kitchen, everyone drinking and talking, and he needing a role, he said: 'Let me help you,' as she bent to take plates from an oven, and found himself piling them on to the table, putting out knives and forks with Imogen Raeburn, and carrying dishes of baked potatoes to the table, where people had taken their places.

'This is what I like to see,' said George, leaning dangerously back in his chair, waving his drink. 'People at work.'

'One day you'll break your back, George Liddell,' said Miss Renner, from her seat at the head of the table, and he tipped it forward again, grabbing the edge. Everything shook. Everyone laughed.

'It's only simple supper, I'm afraid,' said Margot, as Jonty Gill came over to help with the stew.

'A Mrs Barrow supper,' said Heslop, pouring more drinks. 'Diana, my dear, your glass is empty.'

She passed it, she flashed him a smile. 'You *mustn't* make me drink too much!'

'I won't, I promise.' He poured carefully. 'There, how's that?'

'Perfect.' She raised the glass to him, to her lips. 'Thank you.'

The candlelight lit her lovely face, the cloud of fair hair and the milky white skin of her neck. Heslop turned back to the others.

'Who else would like another glass?'

'Please!'

'Emily?'

Miss Renner shook her head. 'Not for me, thank you.'

Jonty was bearing the stew across from the range – 'Mind out, everyone, clear a space!' The dog took a keen interest in this procedure, nosing about hopefully.

'Good dog, good dog.'

Steven bent to fondle his ears. 'Not for you, I don't think.'

'Basket!' said Heslop. 'Basket!'

The dog padded over to the corner, sank in with a sigh. Margot sat down next to Steven. For a moment their arms brushed.

'Now, then,' said George, getting to his feet. He reached for the ladle and gave it a flourish. 'Pass your plates, dear people.'

'But where's Frank?' asked Imogen, reaching for a baked potato. 'We never see him these days.'

'Frank has other fish to fry,' said someone, and Steven, reaching to take his plate, saw the ladle above it go still.

Then: 'He's mad about *politics*,' said Diana. 'We do find it all such a bore.'

A ripple of sympathetic smiles ran round, but then:

'My dear,' said Miss Renner, shaking out her napkin. 'When will you ever grow up?'

Despite the endearment, her tone was sharp, and Diana flushed. There was a sudden silence. At the other end of the table, Heslop said quickly: 'I'm sure Miss Renner didn't mean to upset you, Diana.'

Miss Renner did not respond to this, and Diana bit her lip.

'I just think—'

But whatever she thought was unspoken. She reached for her glass.

'At school—,' said Steven, surprising himself by addressing the table, '—at school we admire Frank a lot.' He picked up his knife and fork.

'We all admire him,' George said brightly. 'Now then, who's next?'

'Yes, do get a move on,' said Margot, patting his arm. 'We're all starving.'

Supper was over, everyone gathered in the drawing room, curled up in armchairs or sprawling on the sofa. A few little concert chairs took up the overspill. Candle and cigarette smoke drifted through the room, Imogen and Diana brought in tinkling trays, and went round offering coffee in tiny cups. Outside the un-shuttered windows the garden was lit by stars and moonlight.

'Cream? Do help yourself.' Diana had recovered herself. She stood before Steven, perching on one of the bentwood concert chairs, and bent down with the tray. 'You look rather uncomfortable on that thing.'

'I'm all right.' Her scent wafted over him as he lifted the cream jug. 'Thank you.'

'You must think me an awful fool,' she said suddenly.

He was taken aback. 'Why do you say that?' He put the jug down again. She straightened up, and the taffeta rustled.

'Miss Renner ticked me off, didn't she?' She bit her pretty lip again. Then: 'She used to tick me off when I was little, always telling me to pay attention. I think she thought I was the dim one. Perhaps she was right, I don't know – I don't care about politics and things. But I am a serious person.' She looked down at him gravely. 'I'm serious about my music.'

If the candlelit Trio in the darkened church had made him

think of Rembrandt, Steven thought now that Diana was a Botticelli nymph or angel: that halo of spun-gold hair, that skin, that dreamy gaze.

'I know you are,' he said.

'Thank you.' She gave him a smile which made him think of Frank: ravishing, meant only for you. 'I mean – we all hardly know you, but you seem so nice. I'm glad Frank introduced you.'

She was utterly beguiling. And then she was moving away, offering coffee to the Lindsays, and as his eyes followed her he saw someone else watching her intently: a man with his back to the fire, as always, the dog at his feet, as always.

Margot was up at the piano, turning over scores. She found something, put it up on the stand and began to play. Steven didn't know what it was, but then he knew so little. But as a tender, elegiac theme wove in and out of the murmuring talk, the chink of coffee cups, he saw Heslop close his eyes.

Margot played on. At length it ended; there was a scattering of applause.

'Lovely, Margot, thank you.'

'What is it?'

She turned on the piano stool. 'Guess.'

Nobody could.

'It's Elgar.'

'Good heavens.'

Margot looked over to the fireplace. 'You like it, don't you, Father?'

'I do,' he said slowly.

'I always think of Elgar as mighty, don't you?' said Hugo Raeburn. 'Great big symphonies and things. What's it called?'

'*Dream Children.*' Margot got up, and George, rising from his chair, said: 'Ah, yes, that was us.'

'You were a nightmare at times, George Liddell,' said Miss Renner from across the room, and everyone laughed.

'A nightmare? Me?' He sat down at the piano, started to play. And now something quite different filled the room, romantic and yearning.

'Blue Moon . . .' sang Imogen, and then: 'Oh, I do love this.'

Cigarettes lit up, people began to hum. George played on, moving from romance to ragtime, everyone happy and relaxed. Steven saw Jonty Gill move a little closer to Diana on the sofa, saw her move away with her dreamy smile. Then the clock in the hall struck ten, and people began to get up.

'Time we were off.'

Coats, hats, car keys. Thomas Heslop out to the stable yard: he'd run Miss Renner home. Affectionate goodbyes. George, at the piano, called out: 'Goodnight, everyone!' and Steven got to his feet: if he left now, he'd just catch the last bus from Morpeth. He could walk from Kirkhoughton, if he had to. Should he ask Margot for a lift? Should he ask someone else? Or might he, perhaps, stay on for a little? Might they both like that?

Voices came and went in the hall.

'*What* a good evening.'

'When's the next concert? You must let us know.'

'Bye!'

Out through the porch, dashing across the terrace in the cold night air. Car doors slamming in the drive, engines started up with a crank shaft. He went to the window and watched. The garden was bright with moonlight.

'There she goes! Jump in!'

'Bye! Bye everyone!'

And suddenly the place was empty. There was only the cedar, casting its great dark shadow over the lawn, and the moonlit outline of the swing. He went out to the hall. Where was she? Behind him, in the drawing room, George was playing something sleepy and slow. The hall fire was sinking, candles burning low. From the kitchen he could hear the clatter of dishes. It must be Diana clearing up, for here was Margot, coming in from the porch, closing the front door behind her. He stepped forward.

'There you are.'

'Here I am.'

It felt such an intimate, natural exchange, as if between two people who had wanted one another for a long time. And as she turned to draw the long green curtain across the door the words flooded up from the past—

'Here I *am*.'

In bed with him, starlight over the moor at the open window, kneeling up before him, pulling off her nightgown—

'*My love . . .*'

He was shocked. It was as if a door had been pushed open by the wind: she had gone, she was returning, the door swung to and fro. Perhaps it would always be like this, and how was he to live?

The curtain rings rattled, the long folds brushed the floor.

'Steven?' Margot turned to look at him, all at once so hesitant. And the door to the past swung to, and again he saw that little girl here in the hall, the sweep of the staircase above her leading to a shadowy landing, the clock beginning to strike above her, as it struck the quarter-hour now: deep and sonorous, the pale moon's profile rising high, trailing those dusky clouds.

She said: 'You're thinking about your wife.'

'I was,' he said slowly. 'And now I'm thinking about you.'

She stood very still. He stepped forward, put out his hand. She took it.

He drew her into his arms, brushed her lips with his. Once, twice.

A car turned into the drive and went slowly across to the stable yard.

'Your father,' he said, releasing her, as the dog came at once up the passage from the kitchen, and stood by the fire, waiting.

157

'Yes,' said Margot, and he felt her tremble. 'I wasn't thinking straight.' And she went to the curtain to draw it back again. He was trembling, too, flooded with feeling and desire.

Behind them, the music ended. George's footsteps sounded across the drawing room floor, and stopped abruptly.

'I must go,' said Steven, as the car door slammed in the yard, for how could he stay here in this state, with everyone around, and her father about to come in? He kissed her quickly again, saw her eyes close. 'I'll write to you,' he said, releasing her, and then George was all at once asking about cocoa, and the front door banged. In came Heslop, bringing a draught of cold air.

'Coulter, you're still here, I'm so sorry. Let me run you into Morpeth.'

PART FIVE

I

AND NOW, EACH morning: the watch for the post. Margot ran down the stairs, opened the front door on to the dewy garden, greeted old Barrow as he trudged in from the lane, pushed up the heavy sash windows - let the house be wide open! Let her hear the crunch of gravel, the postman's wheeling bicycle—

'Morning, Miss Heslop.'

'Good morning!'

She took in her father's letters, often foolscap, often from the bank, and set them beside his place at the dining room table. She took the plain white envelope, with its Kirkhoughton postmark, up to her bedroom; she sat at the desk her father had given her, so many summers ago, and picked up her mother's slender paperknife.

Dear Margot . . .

My dear Margot . . .

She looked out over the glistening lawn. Birds sang their hearts out. As Emily Renner had done, many more summers ago, she pressed a white page to her lips.

And Steven, getting off the bus each May afternoon, the days longer and lighter now, crossed the road and lifted the lid of the wooden letter box. No longer just family letters, though those still came between his visits to Cawbeck and Birley Bank. Not just a letter from Andrew, now and then, in Edinburgh. Heavy cream envelopes waited for him, day after day. He slipped them into his jacket pocket, climbed the track, saw the sheep and fat lambs spread out everywhere, grazing contentedly; smelled the heather, warm from the sun. Once, at a distance, he saw the Fusiliers again, tramping down towards the river.

Dear Steven . . .

My dear Steven . . .

He read sitting outside on a hard kitchen chair by the door, as Margaret had used to sit, sewing curtains and a tiny quilt, while he sawed away in the woodshed. The call of the curlew came bubbling up, the sun began to slip down the limitless moorland sky. The view went on for miles.

Come and see me! wrote Margot.

Should he invite her here? It was something he still could not contemplate. But could he go on visiting the Hall without giving something in return?

It grew cooler; he went inside, tried to imagine her moving about the kitchen. It didn't feel right.

I'll come, he wrote, sitting at the table with the door still open to the evening air. Last summer he had written to Margaret, over and over, aching for her. Now, he was writing to a living woman – living and wanting him. And he wanted her – he was astonished by how much she lived in his thoughts. *Tell me when I should come . . .*

He lit the lamp, and moths came in through the door. He made supper, got out his marking. At school, everyone was preparing for the summer exams: the big ones and the-end-of-year ones. And at school, where Margot still came in once a week to teach, she and he hardly spoke to each other. They smiled, and sometimes his guts turned to water. They went past; sometimes they lunched with Frank, who'd returned full of energy, but no one would ever have guessed they were anything more than distant colleagues.

I hope you don't mind – I just don't feel ready for that . . .

Would it hurt her? Was he being too hesitant?

I do understand. But just come! Come on Saturday. Can you do that?

I can, he wrote, putting away his books. Moths bumped against the glass shade of the lamp, seeking and frantic. He scooped them up with jam jar and envelope, and shook them out into the night.

Books were heaped up on the staffroom table. It was always a muddle in here: people coming and going from classes, flinging stuff down before lighting a pipe or cigarette, or taking tea from the trolley. Then they got out their books for the next lesson, bunged the last lot into pigeonholes.

The windows were wide open on to the hills. The talk was of cricket – the Test Match at Lord's, where Duggan and Gowens had booked seats for July, and Northumberland County. Events in Europe featured less: Chamberlain was in talks with Hitler, and he'd keep this country out of a war, said Armstrong, lighting up.

But Steven, coming in one break-time, dumping his things on the table, saw something which brought him up short. A book lay on a pile in the corner, half-hidden by a text book, but the jacket's image leapt. Outlined in thick black ink, a great fist smashed through to the foreground. Behind were bombed-out buildings. He made to see the title, the author, but Frank was suddenly there, scooping everything up as the tea girl came rattling in, and turning to greet her.

'Good morning, Molly!'

'Morning, Mr Embleton. Morning, everyone.' She pushed the trolley into its corner. People swarmed round.

Steven took his place in the queue and watched Frank go over to the pigeonholes. What was he reading? What bookshops had he visited in London? What was the meaning of that fist, those half-glimpsed ruins?

163

'Frank?'

'Steven.' Frank gave him his easy, beautiful smile. Was it too easy? Was it a mask?

'How was London?'

Steven had asked this before, on the first day of term, just had the reply, 'Very good, thanks. And how was your Easter? You went to the concert?'

'I did. Everyone missed you.'

Someone in particular had missed him, but he couldn't bring himself to touch on that. Was Frank even aware of how much he was searched for at the end of every concert, how much he meant? If he wasn't, it was not for Steven to tell him.

'I missed everyone, too,' said Frank. 'Remind me what they played.'

And then they were talking about the music – how quickly the conversation had been diverted – and about Miss Renner at the memorial window.

'Poor Miss Renner. There are so many women like her.'

Should he tell Frank about how much she'd upset Diana? It almost felt like breaking a confidence, though surely he must remember those long-ago days in the classroom, have heard those reproaches to his beautiful, half-attentive sister.

The bell rang down the corridor, Frank got to his feet. 'We'd better go.'

Since then they'd talked only about classes, exam timetables, Straughan's summer-term meeting – all the usual stuff.

Now: 'How was London?' Steven asked again. 'You haven't really said much about it.'

They were moving up in the queue; clouds of steam rose from the tea urn, drifting with cigarette smoke into the crowded room.

'I saw some good people,' said Frank, and reached for the teacup Molly was passing. He gave it to David Dunn, limping up alongside. 'How was your class?' he asked him, and in moments was drawn into conversation about a boy called Makin, who could be difficult, and had been difficult today.

'I'm sorry to hear that.' Frank took his own cup, and Steven took his, and a bun, and gave up. He couldn't bring himself to ask: Who are you seeing? What are you reading? Why, these days, do you never talk about yourself?

But as he went back across the room and stood drinking his tea by the window, away from all the smoke, he acknowledged that he, too, was concealing things. If Frank had asked him about going back to the Hall after the concert he would have talked about the supper, and perhaps mentioned the pretty piece by Elgar which Margot had played, and which, it seemed, so haunted her father. Would he have asked Frank about that? About why? There were criss-cross currents running everywhere, it seemed, in that little group of people.

And he had his own secret, now. He wouldn't have mentioned the brief moments he and Margot had had alone together, nor those fleeting kisses in the empty hall. He wouldn't say that they were writing to one another, almost every day, nor that he longed to be with her.

Elgar on a summer afternoon. As he turned into the gates he could hear it, the windows of the drawing room pushed up high, the music floating out into the golden air. When he looked back on this day, that was how it seemed: that the mellow sun was lighting not only the trees and garden, but the very air itself. Even the summer house, even the cedar, and the worn old swing, were outlined with gold.

Midges danced before him as he walked up the drive, a dragonfly suddenly hung there, its wings translucent. Then it darted away. High on a chimney pot a blackbird was singing as only blackbirds sing. Steven stopped on the flags, and stood taking everything in: the deep rich light and the stretch of shadows which intensified it; the scent of grass and roses, and of the lavender planted all along the terrace, humming with bees; the music dancing into the quietude, weaving in and out of the blackbird's song.

And he felt then something he had not felt for years – the long years of illness, anxiety and grief – nor had expected ever to feel again: happiness, pure and simple.

It was so quiet that he thought he could hear her turn the page. Was she playing to welcome him? Had she heard his footsteps? He walked slowly up towards the window, and waited for the piece to end, watching that intent, absorbed face, those slender fingers. He'd heard this piece only once, at the supper party, but he remembered it, as he had not expected to be able to remember music. Perhaps, now, everything she did would be charged, and unforgettable.

She stopped, he waited. Then she looked up, and visibly jumped.

'Oh, I'm so sorry.' He moved closer to the window. 'I didn't mean to frighten you.'

'It's all right.' She got up, and came towards him. The sun struck the floorboards, dust danced everywhere. The window was pushed up so high he could climb through into the room. He made to do so, and she laughed.

'Come on.'

He thought it was the kind of thing which perhaps the children had done long ago: clambering up and scrambling in, getting told off by Miss Renner. But if Heslop saw him now—

'Where's your father?'

'He's having supper with the Lindsays.'

'Is the dog having supper there too?'

She laughed, and nodded, but Steven knew it must be so – if the dog were anywhere about he'd have come racing out at the first footfall. And he ducked down a little, climbed through the window. It felt like the freest and most spontaneous thing he had done for years.

'Hello.'

'Hello.'

They stood before one another as they'd done in the fire-lit hall, and still, for a moment, there was shyness between them. Then he stepped forward, and held out his arms, and she came into them, swift and sure. He held her close, he stroked her head as she leaned on his shoulder. They were so much of a height. And it felt as if they had all the time in the world, that for as long as they wanted there was no need for anything more than this: just holding each other at last.

He might have murmured any number of romantic things; he might have kissed her. But at length he held her a little away from him, and said: 'We have nothing in common.'

She looked at him, half laughing. 'Does it matter?'

'I don't think so. We feel so easy together, don't we?'

'We do now.' She lifted her hand to his cheek, began to stroke it. And she thought: Now I can be myself with him. After all this hesitation and doubt. And now – life can begin.

Life can begin! She wanted to dance across the room.

He took her hand away from his cheek and kissed it. 'Tell me why you were playing that piece.'

'Just because it was the last thing you heard me play.'

'Thank you. It's lovely.' He kissed her hand again. 'Well, now – what shall we do?'

She raised a dark eyebrow, and he laughed, seeing then not the lost little girl who had haunted him, but a young woman at ease in the world, as he had first sensed her to be.

'May I get you a drink?'

'That would be wonderful – just something cold. Shall I come and help?'

'No, wait here. Draw breath after your journey.'

He brushed her lips with his, released her. 'Come back soon.'

'I will.' And she walked from the room; he heard her quick footsteps down the passage to the kitchen. Out in the hall, the grandfather clock struck three. For a moment he simply stood there, taking in the warmth of the room, the space of it, wondering that he should be here, with everything about to happen. He had a look at the tables with their piles of *The Field* and *Country Life*. Then he walked slowly over to the piano, and let himself try the keys. What a sound they made, on this great instrument: he thought of Miss Aickman, gallantly bashing out hymns at Assembly. How grand it must be, to play.

The music stood open before him on the stand: he picked it up, and turned the pages back to the beginning.

Dream Children. He had a sudden memory of Heslop, at the supper party, standing before the fire. A tapestry fire screen stood there now, put in place for the summer, but he remembered the leaping flames of a cold spring evening, and the way Heslop had closed his eyes as Margot began to play. Perhaps it was just because he loved the piece, but it had felt much more significant.

And what was this? Opposite the first page of the score was a quotation; he began to read.

'And while I stood gazing, both the children gradually grew fainter to my view, receding, and still receding till nothing at last but two mournful features were seen in the uttermost distance, which, without speech, strangely impressed upon me the effects of speech: "We are not of Alice, nor of thee, nor are we children at all . . . We are nothing, less than nothing, and dreams. *We are only what might have been . . .* "'

Steven frowned. What could this be about? Beneath ran the source of the lines: 'From *Dream Children; a Reverie*, by Charles Lamb.'

He knew nothing of Elgar, not really. Was he still alive? He knew nothing of Lamb, except for a dim memory of reading *Tales from Shakespeare* at school. This must be from an essay, but what did it mean? And what might it mean to Heslop?

He turned to look out of the window: at the long lawn stretching down to the ha-ha, where the children would have played, and run about; at the swing, now so still in the late afternoon sunlight, but on which they had swung so often. And he thought of Heslop, lonely and bereaved, standing here too, or perhaps at an upper window, looking down on them all; looking down in particular, perhaps, at one of them.

Footsteps came along the dark passage from the kitchen, there was the chink of glasses.

'Here we are.' In she came, with a tray – a tall jug, two tumblers – and set it down on the table by the far window, pushing books aside. She was wearing a green linen dress he thought he had seen before – was it the one she had worn when they first met last summer, she and Frank walking down through the leafy square in Kirkhoughton, Frank so easily introducing her? He had been so immersed in his grief and longing, walking and walking over the moor, writing to Margaret almost every day. To meet a sophisticated young woman whose name so nearly echoed hers: it had left him stupid and tongue-tied. And now—

He turned back to the piano, replaced the score. One day perhaps he might ask her about it; today it felt far too intrusive. And today, after all, was for them, and them alone.

'I heard you play,' she said, pouring a glass.

'I'd hardly call it playing.'

'Have you ever?' She handed him the glass, turned to pour her own.

'Never.'

'Well—' She came to stand beside him. 'If Donald Hind-

marsh can stumble through his scales I'm sure we can do something with you. Cheers.'

'Cheers.' They chinked glasses, he smelled the sharp tang
of lemonade. 'Delicious,' he said, at the first sip. 'Thank you.'
Then: 'He's a good lad, Hindmarsh. The class joker, but he
does his best.'

'I know.' She gestured to the sofa. 'Shall we sit down?'

They sat, they drank.

'I was so thirsty after that walk.'

'This is Mrs Barrow's finest.'

'Thank her from me.'

Everything felt easy and known. And charged with excitement and desire.

He said, turning to look at her: 'You've been very bold, I
think.'

'Bold?'

'Writing. Inviting. Bold moves. Is that right?'

'I'd say brave,' said Margot. '"Bold" sounds – I don't know
– did you think me too forward?'

'Not at all. I don't think I quite realised what was going on.'
He shook his head. 'What a fool.'

'Inside, I was trembling.'

'Oh, Margot.'

He put down his glass. She put down hers. His arm went
round her, she put her head on his shoulder. For a long moment
they sat there in silence, listening through the open windows
to the buzz of bees in the lavender, the blackbird's endless
song.

'You never hear that on the moor.'

She nestled further into him. 'What do you hear?'

'Curlew. It's the most glorious sound, like bubbling water.'
He tried to imitate it, and she laughed.

'What else?'

'Lapwing, mostly. They look so pretty, and they sound so sad.'

She turned to look up at him, turned his face towards her. 'You've been sad for a long time, haven't you?'

He shut his eyes, thinking, and trying not to think. For a moment Margaret's dear bright face came floating up before him. Night after night without her came back to haunt him. He felt Margot go very still in the curve of his arm.

'It's all right,' he murmured, and tightened his embrace. Then he drew her face up to his, and then they were kissing unstoppably.

At last they drew apart. He reached for her hand.

'My love.' He had never thought he would say those words again, nor ever want to say them. He stroked her hand, gently, from wrist to finger. She shut her eyes. 'My love.'

She lay back, feeling his touch. 'That's so lovely. Go on, go on—'

He went on stroking, drew her to him again.

'May I ask you something?'

'Anything.'

'Have you ever—'

She shook her head.

'Nor wanted to? Do you mind my asking you that?'

Out in the hall the grandfather clock struck the three-quarter hour. She was silent. The chimes had been with her all her life, marking lessons, mealtimes, bedtimes, concerts. Now they were marking this breathless moment, a new life beginning: could it really be so?

But up from the past came the end of a summer day, the end of a game of tennis; of walking back to the house as the shadows lengthened. Frank had pulled her to him, he had kissed her hard.

'Stop it! You're like my brother—'

171

'You're not like my sister. Please, Margot. Please.'

'No!'

She broke away, ran into the hall as the clock struck six, as if it were waiting, saying to her steadily: here you are. This is where you belong. She stood there trembling. With fear? With longing? She heard a racquet flung into the porch. Then he was gone.

'Margot?' Steven's hand went on stroking hers, over and over, gentle and thrilling.

'I don't know how to answer,' she said slowly. 'A long time ago, I couldn't decide if I wanted someone or not. I decided I didn't - it didn't feel right. We managed to stay friends, we're still very good friends.'

She stopped. Should she tell him who it was? Might it make things difficult between him and Frank at school? More powerful was the thought that she would be betraying Frank, who surely must have had a million girls at Oxford, and long since forgotten that distant kiss, but with whom she felt now - oh, such a bond!

'Since then,' she said, into the quiet of the sunlit room, where she had spent countless hours of practice, playing, performing, 'music has been everything. It's filled my whole life. I know lots of people, I've been out with lots of people, but—' She turned to kiss him. 'No one has touched me. I've never felt about anyone as I feel about you.'

'Astonishing.'

'Astonishing that you should care for me,' she said, and turned to kiss him again.

The sun began slowly to slip down the sky, but at the front of the house the warmth of the day was everywhere: in this room; in the hall, where sun poured in from the open door; on the flagstones where the bees still droned in the lavender. The one cool place was the kitchen, where they went to make a little meal – late lunch, early supper.

'Scrambled eggs?'

'Grand.'

This was the first time he had been in here without a crowd of people. As he watched her slice bread, break the eggs, fetch a jug of milk from the pantry, he remembered those sudden sharp words across the table from Miss Renner, and Diana's flushed distress. How quickly Heslop had come to her rescue.

'Margot?' And then he stopped himself. This was their first meal together, this was not the time. He went up behind her, put his arms round her as she stirred the pan on the range.

'What can I do?'

She showed him the china cupboard. They carried an old wooden tray into the dining room, where the sun lit the polished mahogany of the table and the candelabra on the dark oak sideboard, the candles half burned down. Did she and her father eat here every evening? Steven wondered. Or were there endless dinner guests? There was so much he didn't know.

'Our first meal together,' she said, putting down the tray.

'My love.'

He looked about him as she laid mats, silver, glasses and water jug. Everything in here was old, well-made, well cared-for: how his father would like it all. Everything should be well made, he thought, pulling out his chair: furniture, an essay, music. A life between two people. She sat down opposite him, reached a hand across the table.

'What are you thinking?'

He held her hand. 'How pleasing all this is. How my father would appreciate it – he'd like everything in this house. That staircase – what a piece of work.'

'Tell me about him.'

He kissed her hand, released it. They began to eat, and

he told her: about his father's apprenticeship at fourteen, his knowledge of old furniture, his skill at making new - the Art Deco things everyone was after now, the workshop in Birley Bank.

'He's been on his own for a long time, he has quite a name, I think.' He put down his knife and fork. 'And your father?' he asked her, reaching for her hand again. 'You've always lived with him?'

'Always.' She raised his hand to her lips. This will be one of our gestures, she thought, kissing his fingers, feeling her heart lift again. 'I mean - Diana and I went away to school, but apart from that - George went down to London, to the Royal College, but - I just couldn't leave here. My father needed me so much. I suppose I needed him.'

'And—' he hesitated. 'He's never wanted to remarry?'

'Not as far as I know. Of course, lots of people were interested in him, but—' She got up, came round to his side of the table. 'I want to sit in your lap.'

'Come on.' He was filled with longing, all other thoughts flown away. And he took her on to his lap and pulled her to him. How long did they sit there, kissing and kissing? The clock struck a half-hour, but which one he had no idea. At length he held her a little away from him, aching with desire.

'Margot? Would you come to bed with me? My darling?'

She covered her face, awash with feeling. The house stretched all around her, empty and waiting. She thought of her bedroom, where she had wept as a child, overawed and lonely, and of how she had grown to love it, to love looking out at the cedar, the great stretch of lawn, the distant ambling cattle. She thought of how every morning she woke in her bed to the sound of a dog whistled up, a walk beginning, come rain, come shine, and of the return: footsteps over the flags, boots wiped on the scraper, the dog lapping from his bowl, the ragged forsythia shaking in the wind. Bang of the front door, bang of the porch door, into the hall.

'Hello, *darling? Are you up?*'

What was she thinking now? That he could come home and find them? Or that it might break his heart to lose her?

'Margot?' Steven was drawing her hands away from her face. 'It's too soon,' he said gently. 'Isn't it? It doesn't matter.' And he lifted her from his lap. 'Let's get some air.'

'You're cross with me?' She could hardly speak.

'Never. Perhaps – well, perhaps it's too soon for me, too.'

'Oh, Steven.'

'Sssh.' He took her hand, and led her out through the hall, glancing at the clock. Almost six o'clock: well, well. He stopped and looked up at the face, the pale profile of the moon just beginning to rise, with its sleepy, secret smile, its clouds. Another thing beautifully made.

Margot said: 'I used to adore that clock. When I was little, I mean.'

'I can see why.'

They went out through the porch to the garden. He stood still. 'Listen to that bird.' It was still singing, up on the topmost chimney.

'It must be another one,' said Margot, beginning to recover herself. 'Surely no one bird could sing that long.'

'I don't know. Blackbirds are tough old things.'

The terrace was sun-warmed, the lavender a symphony of bees. The shadow of the cedar fell deep on the grass, the evening sun glancing through the dense full branches. Against that depth, that darkness, the swing was so fragile and light. He'd thought this before, on the March afternoon when Margot had shown him round. How they had misunderstood one another then. Now—

He led her towards it. He touched the rope, let the swing

move back and forth just a little. Then he eased himself on to the narrow seat, and pulled her on to his lap.

'Yes? It's all right to do this? It won't break, with two of us?'

'I don't think so.' She leaned back against him, and he put his arms round the ropes, and then round her waist. For a little while they just sat there like that, listening to the blackbird. After a while, he said:

'You remember you said I'd been sad for a long time. When we were having our drink.'

'Yes.'

His arms tightened around her. 'That's what I thought about you – when we were getting to know one another. That you'd lost your mother so young, that it must have haunted you. I saw a lonely little girl, in this great big house.' He kissed the back of her neck. 'Is that right? Do you mind my saying that?'

She hesitated.

'It was true. Often it was true. And you know – a lot of the things in the house you like: they came from her. She chose so many things. I remember her dressing table, everything so pretty. *She* was so pretty.'

He thought of the photograph, the glimpse of earring. 'She was.'

'But I had the others,' Margot said. 'Diana and everyone. We stayed close in the holidays and they meant everything. And then I had music. And my father, always.'

And another distant day came floating up from the past: cold, autumnal, leaves blowing about, Barrow waiting in the trap.

'*Please don't cry.*'

'*Don't you cry, Daddy.*'

'How will he feel about us?' Steven asked her.

'I don't know. Let's not talk about it now.'

He kissed her again, and then he began to push back with

his feet on the ground, with its scattering of cones and needles, until their legs were stretched taut, and they were standing. Then, tall as they were, they began to swing. The rope creaked, the branches of the cedar, rising so vast and old above them, released their cedar smell: pungent, resinous, unforgettable. Everything was shadowy, as the sun slipped further down. They swung back and forth, back and forth, their feet – oh, so lightly – just brushing the grass.

2

'WELL NOW,' SAID George, parking his bicycle against the window, and peering in. It was morning, dewy and fresh, the drawing room barred with shadow. 'How are things?'

'Things are fine, thank you.' Margot was looking through scores. She went on looking. George lowered his violin through the window on to the floor, and climbed in after it.

'Which tells me precisely nothing.' He straightened up, brushed dust off his trousers.

'Who said I should tell you anything?'

'I did. Where's Diana?'

'On her way, I imagine.' Margot riffled through Beethoven trios. 'What do you think? The *Archduke*? The *Ghost*?'

'The *Archduke* gets everyone going, of course. But then it's done so often.'

Outside, Barrow was trundling the mower out of the pele tower, bending to adjust the clippings box at the front. George turned to watch.

'Marvellous. You come here and all's well with the world. Feels almost Edwardian, doesn't it, old Barrow keeping everything in trim, just as usual, that blackbird singing away. You'd never think that war was in the air.'

'Oh, don't say that.' Margot propped up the score on the stand. 'Father thinks it's less likely now.'

'I'm glad to hear it.' He spun across the room. 'And what does Mr History Teacher think? Does he have a view?'

'Stop it.' She flattened the pages. George put his arms round her waist.

'Don't be like that. I want to know *everything*.'

'What makes you think there's anything to tell?'

'Margot dear, I'm not stupid. I saw you both spring apart in the hall.'

'Spring apart?' But she was laughing now. 'I don't think we sprang, exactly.'

'Oh, yes you did. Like a couple of antelopes.' He leapt across the room. 'Or gazelles, possibly.' He made a gazelle face, huge-eyed and doleful, and bounded towards the door. She was helpless.

Out in the garden the mower had started up. Petrol fumes rose into the air.

'Oh, how that takes me back.' George stopped bounding. 'And here's Miss Embleton,' he said, as a sports car slowed down in the lane. 'Perhaps she should decide about the Beethoven. The cello's rather gorgeous in both, of course.' He stood at the open window, drinking in the scent of petrol and cut grass, and for a moment Margot saw all playfulness evaporate, and with that lost, intent expression felt a wave of warmth and affection.

But then, she loved everyone now.

The car pulled in at the gates, and George lifted his hand. Then he turned back to the room.

'The main thing is, are you happy? That's all I want to know.'

'I am,' she said, and then: 'Oh, I am!'

'Good. Long may it last.'

'Don't sound so doubtful.'

'I'm not. Not for a moment. But on the face of it – not a huge amount in common.'

'That's what he says.'

'Then he has more wit than I gave him credit for. Anyway—' he bent to pick up the violin. 'Since when did "having things in common" have anything to do with love?' The car door slammed, and he leaned out of the window. 'Good morning, Miss Embleton!'

In the end, they decided on the *Ghost*.

'It's just so heavenly,' said Diana, and no one could disagree. And this was their big summer concert: they needed to make an impact. With two or three weddings before then, there were lots of little pieces to rehearse as well.

'We're going to be busy,' said George over lunch in the kitchen. He tipped back his chair, and tipped it forward again as Mrs Barrow stirred soup on the range and turned to tut-tut at him. 'Sorry, Mrs B. You're quite right.' He reached for the breadboard and began to slice the loaf. 'Is your father joining us?' he asked Margot.

'If he's back in time. He's gone to a Directors' meeting.'

'And what about Mr History Teacher? Can he get away from school?'

'Don't be ridiculous. Of course he can't.'

Diana was pouring water. She stopped, and put down the jug.

'Goodness,' she said, looking at Margot across the table. 'Are you – is it – I mean—'

'Try again,' said George. He shook out his napkin as Mrs Barrow came over with pan and ladle and gave her a dazzling smile. 'Thank you so much.'

'You haven't said a *word*,' Diana said to Margot. 'You haven't told me a *thing*.'

'I know.' Margot reached for the butter dish.

'But why?'

'I don't know.'

'She knows, and she doesn't know,' said George, picking up his soup spoon.

Both women turned on him. 'Oh, do stop it!'

He stopped it. He drank his soup.

Then: 'You're my dearest friend,' Diana said sadly to Margot. 'How could you not tell me something like this?'

'I'm so sorry.'

'How long—'

'A little while. A few weeks.'

Diana was silent. Mrs Barrow went round with the soup and took sandwiches out to share with Mr Barrow, as usual. George remarked on how touching that was.

'Steven Coulter's nice,' Diana said at last. 'You're lucky.' She gave a sigh. 'I don't know why I never seem to get involved with anyone.'

'Do you want to?' asked George, wiping his mouth. He reached for the breadboard again.

'Of course I do. Give me a slice.'

'You're too gorgeous, that's your trouble,' he said, passing one with his fingers. 'Frighten them off. Though Jonty Gill seems pretty keen still.'

'Oh, Jonty Gill.' She raised her eyes to the heavens.

'No?'

'No, George.'

'Whereas I,' said Margot, laughing, and mopping up crumbs, 'I'm just so plain and ordinary that no one was ever remotely interested.'

'Frank was,' said Diana. 'You know he was.'

'That was a long time ago.'

'I think he still carries a candle.'

'I don't.' Margot reached for the cheese. 'How is he, anyway? Still at mysterious meetings?'

'I don't think so. All that political talk seems to have died down. He's gone awfully *quiet*, now I come to think about it.'

'Pass the mousetrap, there's a good girl,' said George. 'And tell him to come to the concert.'

'What about you?' Diana asked suddenly.

'What about me?'

'Love. Romance. Lots of girls like you, I know they do.'

'I'm dedicated to my art, don't you know.'

'We all are.' She frowned. 'But even so – why are you always so *happy?*'

There was an infinitesimal pause. Then:

'Queer, isn't it? Do pass that cheese, dear girl.'

'Revise! Revise, my boys!' Straughan, at Assembly, spoke as if mustering his troops for a charge. His gown almost billowed as he flung his arms wide. One or two boys sniggered, and stopped quickly at a look from prefect or teacher. But a lot of them were fired up: you could tell, as they got to their feet for the hymn, that they were putting their hearts into it.

'I vow to thee, my country,

All earthly things above,

Entire and whole and perfect

The service of my love . . .'

Gowens said that Straughan had been choosing that one at exam time since before the Flood, that it always got them going, as if they were vowing to do well for old Straughan's sake. It felt different singing it now: news of Hitler taking troops to the border with Czechoslovakia, Anglo-French talks in London. And last month Alicante had been bombed to pieces. Over three hundred dead.

But to hell with it, said Armstrong, lighting up at break-time. England had declared 658 for 8 v Australia at Trent Bridge, the sun was out, and Norris, always a bit of a bonehead, seemed finally to be getting to grips with the square root. He blew out a stream of smoke in the trolley queue, and Steven coughed, and took his tea to the window.

It was very hot. On the hills, sheep in need of shearing were moving down to the cool of the bracken. After break he was taking the fourth years through the Civil War again: Cromwell's New Model Army, the battles of Edgehill, Marston Moor and Naseby, five thousand Royalists taken prisoner. Charles's flight in disguise, his capture and eventual execution.

Thirtieth of January 1649. Everyone's mind was always working towards that freezing day: the scaffold in Whitehall, the king in two shirts so he would not be seen to shiver, his last defiant words, 'A subject and a sovereign are clean different things.' Then the horrible fall of the axe.

By the time they got to the fourth year the boys had many a beheading under their belts, as well as gruesome deaths on the battlefield. They'd had burnings at the stake – Tyndale, Cranmer – and any number of hangings. Boys were boys, and they lapped it up. But the death of a king still awed them, as it had awed him at school, even though by instinct most were on Cromwell's side.

'Sir? Sir, do you think kings are appointed by God?'

'No, Todd, I don't.'

But still – Charles's end, and Cromwell's character, meant that the Civil War was generally popular, something they could get their teeth into.

As for the threat of war now – like Armstrong, like most of them, they were pushing it aside, swotting up. And, as for Armstrong, cricket was the great diversion from everything: in the news, and down on the playing fields, where Frank and Duggan, or Gowens and McLaughlin and sometimes Steven, walked them down on exam-free afternoons, or supervised net practice at the end of the day. As the huge summer clouds sailed slowly over the hills, and a ball flew into the deep with a mighty thwack, it wasn't hard to think that this peaceful scene could go on for ever.

Then it was pens filled, papers given out by tight-lipped

invigilators, Quiet Please notices put up by Miss Aickman all down the corridors. Heads down, a swallow as they turned the papers over, a rush to the teachers afterwards.

'Sir, sir, we never did that bit!'

'Oh, yes, we did.'

The whole school was in the grip of all this, and Steven was, too, you couldn't help it, though for much of the time he was in such a haze of delight that his own concentration wavered.

Darling Steven . . .

My darling Margot . . .

Their letters flew back and forth. Last week he'd found one in his pigeonhole at the end of the day, when she'd been teaching here for the last time before the exams began – the exam hush couldn't be disturbed by scales and pretty little arrangements of Tchaikovsky. No one, after all, was taking Music. But on that last day he'd heard the piano through lesson after lesson, floating out of the hall, and then, though they'd only greeted each other with a surreptitious smile, after she'd gone he'd found the cream envelope slipped in on top of a textbook.

My love, my sweetheart . . .

Next weekend, they were going to the coast, their first trip together.

Everything these days had such markers: first kiss, first meal together, first trip to watch seabirds and seals. And walk out to Lindisfarne, perhaps. The last time he'd gone had been with Margaret, and at first, when Margot suggested it – 'I haven't been to Lindisfarne since I was little' – he'd had a sliver of doubt: could he do this again? Then he looked at her happy face, and kissed it, and began to feel happy himself at the prospect. Absurdly happy.

Was someone calling his name? He turned from the window. They were. Something was happening across the room. In this crowded, noisy place, it wasn't always easy to hear when boys knocked at the door, and they weren't made very welcome when they did: this was a sanctum, the one place where you could draw breath—

'Coulter?'

Duggan had turned from the open door. Steven could see McNulty, grown six inches in the Easter holidays, standing like a telegraph pole beyond it, very white.

Moffat, he thought, putting his cup on the sill. It's Moffat, and he pushed his way through the throng and the smoke, and out into the corridor.

'Where is he?'

'In Miss Aickman's office, sir. She's phoning Dr Maguire.'

No one was allowed to run in the corridors, ever. They ran.

In her poky little office, Miss A. had put three chairs together, side by side, and Moffat was lying along them, his head on his folded blazer, his feet dangling. He was so thin you could see his ribs through the worn white shirt, and his eyes, fixed on the ceiling, were huge and sunken. He was gasping.

'Hello, young lad.'

Beside him, as he took Moffat's feather-light hand in his, Steven could feel McNulty's tension turn to relief: Mr Coulter was here, he'd make things better.

But how could I not have seen? he asked himself, squatting down in the gap between desk and chairs. How could I not have noticed? It must have half-killed this boy to come into school each day, to sit in his place at the back and try to take notes, to keep up, to turn in those skimpy essays.

He knew why he hadn't noticed, or had chosen not to see, and everything else fell away. And as Moffat tried to turn towards him, and tried to smile, another face turned towards him from her pillow, and he felt himself go cold.

'You're a good lad,' he said at last. 'Soon have you right.'

'Sir.' It was a whisper.

'Dr Maguire's called the ambulance,' said Miss Aickman, hovering at her desk behind them. 'It should be here soon.'

He could hear her trying to sound ordinary and calm. 'That's good.' He could hear himself doing the same. 'Where's Mr Straughan?'

'He's with an invigilator, I think.'

Out in the corridor the bell for the end of break began to ring. The Civil War was waiting. He told McNulty to go to Form Four and tell them he'd be there in a little while, to get out their books and read quietly.

'And then you'd better get back to your form,' he said, as Moffat's gasping breath went on and on. 'What do you have now?'

'Maths, sir.'

The bell stopped ringing. 'Off you go.'

'Sir – sir, can I stay? Till the ambulance gets here?'

Steven felt Moffat's hand in his give the lightest pressure.

'You'd like McNulty to stay?'

A nod, another gasp.

'Come back, then,' he told McNulty, and got awkwardly to his feet, banging his back on the desk behind him. The open door was suddenly filled with Straughan, his black gown all at once a terrible thing, as if to tell them what they already knew.

By lunchtime it was all around the school. By the end of the day, it was over.

Straughan came to the staffroom as the three-thirty bell rang out, everyone in there getting their things together, the door banging open and shut as staff from the last class, the last examination, came in with a sigh of relief, and stopped short at the sight of him, towering and sombre. The call had come from the cottage hospital. Tomorrow, at Assembly, he would tell the boys.

Out in the Square they were letting off steam, as usual. Steven stood at the bus stop, watching them tussle, throw punches, loosen their ties, though they weren't supposed to do that until they got home. He saw the usual knot of boys gather round Frank's oh-so-cheerful red Imp, saw Frank shake his head, drop in his bag, drive away. Unheard of. No 'Hop in!' No toot-toot on the horn. They stood gazing after him.

'Sir?' Hindmarsh and Wigham were walking up beneath the trees. 'Sir, how's Moffat?'

'I expect we'll hear tomorrow.' That was the truth, after all.

He could see McNulty walking slowly down the hill with Mather, saw Mather's arm go round him. McNulty would guess, surely. Surely they'd all guess. The bus pulled up, and he got on, his limbs like lead, and no boy came to sit near him, as he gazed out over the sunlit hills, and the clouds sailed calmly by.

The long track up the moor felt endless. Not since the days after Margaret's death had he felt himself walk more slowly, even in snow, even in mud. Above him skylarks soared to the limitless sky, their song an ecstasy. On other afternoons this summer he'd heard and rejoiced in it, alight with happiness himself. Now he could hardly bear it.

Oh, the indifferent world. Margaret had died, and in spring the birds sang on. Now it was the turn of a boy not yet fifteen. Who else might tuberculosis claim? Could there not be some kind of test, some warning?

In his pocket, today's letter, picked up from the box when he got off the bus, offered the prospect of comfort, but also, for the first time, filled him with anxiety.

He could tell Margot of Moffat's death – if she hadn't already heard of it from Frank – and he knew she would be sad, gentle and kind. But how could he tell her of the feelings it stirred in him: the pity and sorrow for that lost young life, but also the echoes, the terrible surge of old grief?

Not so old, not really. What was a year and a half?

Perhaps she would guess. Perhaps he need explain nothing. Perhaps he could lie in her arms. Or would she be hurt, and draw away? Then what would he do?

He came to the top of the track. Ahead stood the cottage, its small square windows shining in the sun. Distantly, on the clear summer air, he could hear the shouts: 'Quick *march!*' but he couldn't see the men, and all around him the sheep were cropping the turf, as always.

Saturday afternoon, the sun high and the sky most ardently blue. For a long time they drove along the coast in silence.

'I'm sorry,' Steven said at last, and put out a hand. 'Just can't stop thinking.'

'I know. He was the nicest boy.'

'And the bravest. McNulty, too – he's very cut up. But still—' He let his hand rest on her lap. How good that felt. 'We're together. We're going to have a good day.'

'We are.' She put her hand on his, then slowed down as they came to Bamburgh village. Ahead stood a church on a rise.

'St Aidan's,' he said. 'Grace Darling is buried there.' And he began to feel a bit better, in command of facts again. Home ground.

'I know,' said Margot, changing gear. 'Everyone knows about Grace Darling, don't they?' She remembered a picture in one of Miss Renner's school books: a stormy night sky, a girl and her father rowing like mad towards a shipwreck, the beam of the lighthouse sweeping across the waves. That was when they were doing heroines. Grace Darling, Florence Nightingale, Marie Curie. Who else? There'd been an awful lot of heroes: Frank had been mad about Robin Hood.

'Shall we stop for a minute?' Steven said, as they came to the church, and she drew up alongside. They got out, walked up the long sloping path through the churchyard, stood looking about them. Gulls flew over the tower. 'This church,' he said, putting his arm round her, 'was founded on the site of the Saxon church where St Aidan died. Did you know that?'

'I didn't.'

'Do you know about St Aidan?'

'Not much. Go on.' She pulled her straw hat from her bag. 'Mr History Teacher, as George would say.'

And he put on his teacher's voice, up at the blackboard, chalk in hand, eyes in the back of his head.

Oh, poor Moffat.

'He was an Irish missionary, but lived on Iona, I can't re-member why. King Oswald invited him over in 635, and he lived on the Farne Islands.'

'Surely it's only sea birds.'

'He had a little place there in 635. A little hut or something.' He drew her to him. 'On Inner Farne. Anyway, he was a good man, I think, gentle and kind. He used to walk everywhere, just getting to know the farmers and labourers. Christian civilisation in northern England really began with him. And St Cuthbert, of course.'

'Of course.' She kissed his cheek.

'And do you know where he died?'

'Where?'

'Leaning against the wall of that Saxon church.'

'Like an old sheep.'

'Exactly.' He drew her closer. 'Do you want to look inside?'

'Have we got time?'

'Probably not. Not if you want to get out to Lindisfarne and back.'

'I do. Kiss me.'

People were walking up the path behind them. His lips brushed hers. 'Shall we drive on? Have a look at the castle on our way?'

Bamburgh's great stone keep and mighty walls towered on the promontory over everything: sea, sand dunes, village and farmland.

'The capital seat of the Kings of Northumbria,' he said, as they drove slowly past. 'Founded by King Ida in 547. Most of what you see now is eighteenth and nineteenth-century. But if you go inside, you can see the medieval dungeons.'

'Have you brought your boys here?'

'I have. They loved it. One day I'll take you properly.'

They had wound down the windows, and the hot sea breeze blew in. Out at sea the sun glinted off the lighthouse Grace Darling's father had kept, and a million birds wheeled over the Farne Islands, shrieking.

'Let's stop.' Margot pulled into a verge, and they walked down to the harbour.

A motor boat just back from a trip was easing its way up to the wall, and the salty air was full of petrol fumes. They shaded their eyes, looked out at the towering rocks, every ledge crammed with birds, more ever circling above the waves.

'Herring gulls, black-backed gulls, kittiwake and cormorant,' Steven recited. 'Guillemot and puffin.'

'You know everything.' Margot slipped her hand into his.

'I know almost nothing,' he said. How good it felt to have the sea air on his face. He squeezed her hand. 'Dates and birds and moths and things. That's it, really. I know nothing about music at all.'

'It's all I know about. I spent my whole youth practising scales and arpeggios. Great swathes of ignorance hang about me. George and Frank soaked up facts - especially Frank - but we—'

The motor boat was being tied up, the ferryman helping passengers clamber out.

'That were grand!'

'I want to see a puffin,' she said. 'A puffin and a seal.'

'I'll try and arrange it.'

They went back to the car, baking in the sun. The leather seats were almost too hot to touch.

'Go, go!'

Down came the windows, in came the salty breeze.

The tide was far out, and the level sands stretched for miles towards the island. They parked on the sea front, one of only a handful of cars, for how many people could afford them? Most people came to this stretch of the coast - this beauty spot, as Steven's mother called it - by bus. That was what he and Margaret had done, years ago, holding hands as they rattled along. Now, Margot's sleek little sports car stood out amongst the few Austin Sevens.

'We've got about six hours to get there and back,' Steven said, shading his eyes against the glare. 'Will we try?'

'We will.' Margot pulled her straw hat down further, shading her neck. 'You need something to protect you, too,' she said, as they walked down on to the shore.

He pulled off his jacket and slung it over his head. 'How's that?' He peered down at her from beneath it, feeling a trickle of sweat run down beneath his collar.

'You look like an animal in a cave.'

'I am an animal in a cave. Come here.'

They stood against one another on the sand and he tugged the jacket over her head, too, enclosing them both in darkness.

Their mouths sought each other, his hand went round her neck, drawing her closer, closer, and then her hat slipped down and the whole thing became hot and impossible, and they laughed and drew apart.

'My darling one.'

Children ran past them. Hand in hot hand they set forth.

For a long time they walked in silence, watching the gulls wheel by, or bob on the distant waves, watching the little fishing vessels out near the horizon. There were other people walking – a summer Saturday, everyone carefree, in sun hats and frocks and rolled-up trousers. Far ahead, the rocky island waited, a grassy slope rising steeply to the castle, a little picture-book thing, after mighty Bamburgh. The sun beat down.

Nothing in all this could be further from the image of a boy stretched out on a few wooden chairs, gasping for breath, but in the darkness of the jacket draped over his head and shoulders, it was what Steven thought of, as they walked. He couldn't help it. And then – here was Margaret beside him, her long hair blown by the breeze, on another summer's day.

'Go on,' said Margot, after a while.

'What?'

'Tell me about the castle?' She stopped, tugged the jacket aside. 'You're miles away. Aren't you?'

'A bit. I'm sorry.' He took a breath, kissed her. 'Well. The castle was just a fort, originally, built to keep an eye on the Scots in the sixteenth century. When it fell into ruin they used stones from the Priory to rebuild it – Henry VIII, Dissolution of the Monasteries. Did you do that at school?' He lifted her hand to his lips. 'Henry and Elizabeth I and James all had a hand in it, but then – what do you think?'

'I don't know.' She was serious and sad. 'I don't care, really. I just wonder—'

'Don't. I'm a bit cut up, it'll pass. Now, if you leap forward a few centuries, as we historians like to do, you'll find the owner of *Country Life* commissioning Lutyens to turn the whole thing into a family home.'

Margot smiled. 'Darling Steven.' She stroked his face. 'Darling Steven,' she said again. 'I'm so sorry. Poor Moffat. Poor you.' And then they walked slowly on.

'My father loves *Country Life*,' she said after a while, and they both began to laugh.

'I know – I saw all those piles. Have you told him about us?'

'I think he's guessed. If you say you're going to spend the day on the coast with someone—'

'And?'

'I think he's glad. I think so.'

At last they came to the island, and walked across to the shore. The stones were lovely enough to take home: round, smooth, washed and washed by the tide. Steven slipped a small one into his pocket. Then they climbed the endless steep slope to the castle, panting by the time they got to the top. Margot pulled out a little flask of water from her bag and they drank and drank.

'Let's go inside, let's get cool.'

Quite a few other people had the same idea: they queued for their tickets and plan and went into the hall.

'Goodness. It's like a church.'

Stone pillars, stone floor, whitewash. Everything, as they walked through, was simple and plain: stone, brick, slate. Every now and then a wall was gloriously painted: green, Prussian blue. They wandered from room to room, soothed and uplifted. Cupboards, chairs, tables and a huge four-poster bed were all dark wood, oak, mahogany, polished and bright.

'The best possible Arts and Crafts,' said Steven. 'My father

193

would love it.' They climbed stairs, looked out of traceried windows to the sea, walked into a gallery.

'This is the music room,' said Margot, taking the plan. Like everything, it was airy and beautifully kept: pictures, an oak wall cupboard, a little stage set on a patterned carpet.

'But no piano.'

'No, but Suggia's played concerts here.'

'Who?'

'Guilhermina Suggia – a cellist, Portuguese. She's old now, but Diana's heard her, I think. I think my father took her. Ages ago.'

'You didn't go?'

'Not that time. Shall we go down?'

They descended the stairs, and then more stairs, right down to the dining room. A huge fireplace, a bread oven, an iron range polished to within an inch of its life, Windsor chairs.

'But this is the remnants of the fort,' said Steven. 'See those vaults? They're supporting the gun batteries.'

In the scullery a tiny window over the sink was overhung by some kind of contraption.

'What's that?'

'That's where they operated the portcullis.' He made a gesture. 'Down it comes. Bang.'

'You should be a guide.'

'I'm your guide.'

They brushed lips as a family came in through the door.

'I'm hungry.'

'Me, too. Let's have tea.'

Outside, they walked into the village, found a crowded little café, sank on to hard wooden chairs.

'That waitress looks like Grace Barrow.'

Steven couldn't remember what Grace Barrow looked like.

'She and Nellie did the supper at that autumn concert.'

He took her hand across the table, remembering the rain, the mass of people he didn't know, the beauty and power of the music, moving him almost to tears.

'Who would have thought it?' he said, as her dark eyes gazed back at him. 'Who would have imagined that you and I—'

'I would,' said Margot, as the waitress came up with her pad.

'But why?' he asked, when they'd given their order. 'I mean, on the face of it—'

'Something in you just moved me. That's all I can say.'

And she thought of him then, tall and pale and shy, with that flop of light brown hair and a smile, when it came, which changed everything.

'Margot.' He lifted her hand to his lips. A little girl at the next table was told not to point.

After tea they followed the path to the ruined Priory. The sea wind blew through broken arches, and rippled the grass. They walked through the spaces of cells and cloisters.

'Tell me things,' said Margot, her hand in his.

'The Lindisfarne Gospels,' said Steven, and remembered how Margaret had loved them, and once had her girls copying initial letters in powder paint. 'You know about them, you must have seen pictures.'

Had Miss Renner talked about them? Shown a book? Or had that been at school?

'Tell me.'

And as they walked on in the sun he tried to describe them – the illuminated manuscripts, eighth century, exquisitely done, using Anglo-Saxon jewellery designs, pigments from local vegetables and animals. All written and painted by just one man, Eadrith, Bishop of Lindisfarne.

'I suppose Eadrith gave his life to them, the Gospels, and he created the most beautiful thing. But he died before he could finish it all.' He put his arm round her. 'When I was at Durham we heard a lot about them – they were housed there until the Dissolution. Now they're in the British Museum.'

They came to the long grassy space of the refectory. The sun was slipping down, and the shadows of the ruins began to deepen.

He drew Margot closer. 'End of lesson. No more lessons now.'

They stopped, and looked out over the shoreline: one or two fishermen's cottages, boats here and there. It was growing much cooler now, clouds beginning to gather. And with this change in atmosphere, this sense of the long summer day beginning to ebb away, Steven all at once felt sadness and sorrow well up once more, and could do nothing to stop it.

Beside him, Margot said again, 'You know everything.' She leaned her head on his shoulder.

'Except how to live a life.' He couldn't stop himself.

She lifted her head and looked at him.

'Don't say that.'

'I'm sorry.' He looked away.

'But why do you say it?'

'Just—' He spread his hands. 'Moffat has set something off in me, that's all.'

Her look was so searching and deep, but she didn't ask anything further, and he could sense her pulling back, not wanting to say: 'About your wife? About Margaret?' And he thought: Am I going to hurt her? When we've only just found such happiness? Or perhaps she'll hurt me – she might grow tired of all this. Then he remembered something.

'Here.' He reached in his pocket, pulled out the stone he'd picked up from the shore, small and smooth and perfect. 'This is for you. A keepsake.'

'Thank you.' She turned it over, held it between finger

and thumb. 'It's lovely.' But he could sense her caution, as she slipped it into her bag.

'That little song,' he said gently.

'What little song?'

'The one you said your mother used to sing – about the day ending. Remember?'

She remembered. Such sweet poignant lines. And that he had remembered it, after hearing it only once, that he understood what it meant to her – she was filled with tenderness again.

'We are close, you and I,' she said slowly. 'Whatever happened – whatever is making you sad – I think we're very close, really.'

He drew her to him. 'I think so, too. Forgive me?'

She kissed him. She was warm and loving and alive, and his misery began to dissolve. He gave a great sigh.

'Oh, that's better. Sing the little song?'

And she sang it as they made their way back to the long stretch of sand leading across to the mainland, where mighty Bamburgh Castle, miles down the coast, stood silhouetted against the sinking sun.

'Now the day is over,
Night is drawing nigh;
Shadows of the evening
Steal across the sky . . .'

Seabirds wheeled above them; slowly the waves began to come in and retreat, to and fro, to and fro, as always.

3

THE EXAMS WERE over. The exams were over! Down came the Quiet Please notices, Miss Aickman picking away at the sticky tape; up came the usual roar of noise in corridor and playground. There was a sudden burst of summer rain, washing away the dust on the trees and pavements of the Square; next morning, it felt as if a whole new world were beginning, the air fresh, the sun shining bright as anything. And Northumberland beat Yorkshire Second XI. Murray was 104 not out!

'Sir, sir, that's grand, isn't it?'

'Splendid. Straighten that tie.'

Only the absence of a thin white coughing boy cast a shadow over the general jubilation. His name was crossed out in the register: Steven felt it the hardest mark he had ever made on paper since he came to the school. And everyone felt it, the first morning when he went down the line of names.

'McNulty?'

'Here, sir.'

A pause. 'Potts?'

Potts was here, Potts was filling the gap. It might be something he remembered all his life, thought Steven, as he went on.

'Wigham.'

'Here, sir.'

He closed the register. At break, Potts and McNulty went out together, two boys who'd never had much to do with each other before.

The exams were behind them; then came the results. Not for the upper school, taking the School Certificate and Higher levels: those would come in the holidays, though everyone had a pretty good idea of who was going to do well, and who might be leaving at the end of the Upper Fifth. Tom Herron and Jack Halpin were bound for Oxford, a first for the school.

'Thanks to you, Mr Embleton,' Straughan said in the termly meeting. Frank shook his head. 'They're bright, hard-working boys, I'm sure they'd have done it anyway.' Beside him, Dunn dropped a book.

But now, for the lower school, it was marking, marking, smoke and swearing filling the staffroom, people lugging boxes home. Within a couple of weeks the results, and the places, were pinned up on the boards, the boys crowding round. The usual whoops, the crestfallen walking away. And then the wretched re-sits.

Out on playground duty, Steven tried to console.

'Never mind, Hindmarsh, you did your best.'

'Not good enough, though, was it, sir?'

'Not as bad as all that. And cricket this afternoon.'

'I'm not that good at cricket, either.'

It was true. Steven let his arm go briefly round beefy shoulders.

'You're a good lad.'

'Thank you, sir.'

And no one could fail to be cheered by the walk to the playing fields, down the hill and across the sparkling burn, the sun on the hills, the sight of the nets and pavilion.

'Sir, sir, who's taking us?'

'Duggan and me.'

'And Mr Embleton?'

'I think he's on tomorrow, with Mr Gowens.'

'Where's his car?'

Steven looked across to the railings. No bright gleam of red, but sometimes Frank parked further down. And no Frank at lunch, now he came to think of it, but sometimes he went out at lunchtime, everyone did now and then, when they weren't on duty, just to have a breather, buy cigarettes or tobacco.

As they all trooped out with their kit he looked up and down along the Square. No Imp beneath the trees.

'Where's Embleton?' Gowens, at break time next morning, checking the cricket list.

'Anyone seen Embleton?' David Dunn, tight-lipped at the tea trolley.

'Sir, sir, have you seen Mr Embleton?' Todd, from the Upper Fifth, knocking at the staffroom door.

'Has anyone seen Mr Embleton?' Miss Aickman, coming in as the bell rang.

No one had seen him. No one had seen him since yesterday morning, now they came to think of it. No one had a clue where he was, and in the sunlit staffroom Steven felt himself suddenly go cold.

And then the letters came.

Great Whitton
30th June 1938

Dear Mr Straughan,

The office, with its ancient smell of musty textbooks and pipe smoke, had the windows wide open to the morning air. Out on the hills the sheep had been taken for shearing, and it was unusually quiet. Straughan read on.

I know that this letter will come as a shock, and I must apologise. I have waited as long as I could: now that the examinations

are over, I hope you will not think that what I am doing is too
irresponsible . . .

He read on to the end. He read through it again, put his
head in his hands.

Dear Dunn,
I want to thank you for all your good work this term, and in the
past. I know it has not always been easy . . .

In the crowded noisy staffroom, standing in the corner by
the pigeon holes, David Dunn gave his mad harsh laugh. At
first, no one took any notice.

My dear Steven,
I know that this letter will come as a shock. I have often wanted
to confide in you – indeed, there were times when I wanted to
suggest that you joined me in what I'm about to do, but I knew
that it wasn't right. I know you will magnificently fulfil the
duties which I hope old Straughan will give you now. I have
decided . . .

No sheep on the hills, steady and eternal. No Frank. Perhaps
no Frank ever again. Steven read on, and the image of a fist
smashing into the foreground, of devastated buildings, leapt
suddenly out from a bright spring morning. He knew who had
written that book, and why: of course he did.

You might think it all futile now, but there's going to be one
last push . . .

He read on, and his hands were shaking.

Dearest Mother and Father . . .
I hope you can forgive me. By the time you read this . . .

Sun poured into the breakfast room at Great Whitton,
winking off the cut-glass jar of marmalade. At one end of the
table, the letter was crumpled into a ball and hurled across the

room. At the other, Priscilla Embleton pushed back her chair and ran sobbing into the hall. Behind her, her husband roared out, 'And where's that silly girl?'

But Diana had got up early, and driven over to Hepplewick for breakfast in her nippy little car, singing *Happy Days Are Here Again* as she sped away over the hills.

Dearest Margot . . .

At first, she had thought it was a letter from Steven, and her heart leapt. Then she saw the handwriting, and frowned, standing there in the porch in the morning sun, the dog beside her, as the postman cycled away.

Wait until the others are with you before you read this, and give them both my love. I give you my love, dearest Margot, as I have always done, though I always knew it was hopeless. Now put this back in the envelope. Go on, darling – I shall never call you that again. Go and have breakfast now.

She was trembling from head to foot.

'Father?' She walked slowly, unsteadily, into the hall. 'Father?' Then she remembered: a meeting in Morpeth, back for lunch. Beside her, the dog put his nose in her hand.

The post came early at Coquet Bridge. In the shady hall, wisteria stirring at the leaded windows, George, in his dressing gown, bent to pick up the letters. He leafed through them, most for his parents, as usual: he could hear his mother moving about in the kitchen, and smell the toast; from the dining room, he could hear his father turning the pages of *The Times*. Then he saw the one for him, saw that distinctive, beloved hand.

His parents' letters fell to the floor. Slowly he opened the envelope.

My dear George,

I ask you to forgive me, and to understand. I know it will be hard . . .

He read on, standing absolutely still, feeling the blood drain out of him.

Diana turned into the drive and drew up. George's bicycle was flung against the porch: everyone must be up early today – that was what summer did to you. She turned off the ignition, sat for a moment listening to the birds. Sometimes through the open drawing room window you'd hear the other two tuning up, or playing a little duet. Not today. She picked up her music, got out, reached for the cello. As she walked towards the house she could see the outline of the two of them through the open drawing room windows, just sitting there.

'Morning!'

No answer.

She turned into the porch, walked through the hall as the grandfather clock struck nine.

'Bong! Bong!'

Margot and George just looked at her, Margot now standing there in the middle of the room, he flung into the wing chair looking – well, very strange.

'What's up?' Diana set down the cello. 'What on earth is the matter?'

'You haven't heard,' said Margot. 'You haven't had a letter.'

'A letter? Who from? The post hadn't come—'

'From Frank,' Margot said slowly. 'He's gone to Spain.'

'Spain? Why? What on earth's he going to do there?'

And what would he do? Look at pictures in Madrid? Visit the Alhambra?

'I don't understand.'

'He's gone to fight, you dolt.' George was ashen. He got to his feet. 'He's gone to *fight* – there's a war there, remember?

Do you never think of anything beyond your own silly nose?'

She burst into tears.

'Oh, George, don't.' Margot began to cry too.

'Don't what? Don't be angry? Don't be upset?' He paced the room, and the girls ran into each other's arms. 'Don't *feel?*'

'George, please! I've never seen you like this—'

'No,' he said, shaking. 'You haven't. You haven't seen a bloody thing.' He clamped his hand to his mouth. And then he too began to weep. 'What am I going to do?' He paced up and down like a mad thing. 'What am I going to do?'

'Come here,' said Margot, breaking away from Diana. 'Let me – let me—'

'No!'

He turned and ran from the room, out through the hall, out from the porch, into the tranquil garden, and the dog got up from his basket and followed. Everything glistened, and the air was full of song. For a moment or two George just stood on the flags, sobbing. Then he began to run, the dog running joyously after, down the dewy lawn towards the ha-ha. Margot and Diana watched him, tight in each other's arms.

'He doesn't know what to do with himself.'

'I know.'

It was one of Nanny's expressions. 'You don't know what to do with yourself, do you, my duck? You come to me.'

But George did not come to them. At the brink of the ha-ha he stopped, and they saw him fling out his arms, in a gesture of utter despair. Then he turned, and raced back, the dog racing with him.

'Go away!'

He ran, gasping, into the shade of the cedar, and grabbed at the swing. He got on, and pushed himself back on the worn dark grass, still weeping, till his feet left the ground and he was away, swinging and swinging, flinging his feet back and forth until he was higher than you would think possible, though he was so light that it seemed he could fly to the moon.

'Frank!' His sobs rent the air. 'Frank!'

Above him the cedar spread its enormous arms; above him, the bough where the rope had been fastened all those years ago began to creak, and the rope, worn and frayed now, out in all weathers, year after year, began to give a little.

George swung higher, his legs like pistons, pulled under, then flung out before him, up and down, up and down, and then there came a sound which no one had ever heard before in this lovely old garden – a bough finally beginning to break, twisting the swing, ready to fling him unstoppably into the air and down to the ground far below, until Barrow, working in the kitchen garden, looked up for a moment at a sudden wild barking, dropped his hoe, and went haring towards the gate, and Margot and Diana, screaming George's name, went flying out of the house, and managed, just, to save him.

4

I T WAS LIKE an earthquake. The suddenness of Frank's departure, the shock of it, the enormity of the realisation that he might never return – it was like rocks hurled into the air, like plates shifting within the earth. Nothing could ever be the same, and anything could happen. In a strange way, it gave permission for anything to happen.

And for weeks, fragments of the letters came back to haunt them all.

All my life, I have had such a burning desire to do more . . . I cannot live the life I was brought up to lead . . . We are on the brink of catastrophe, and we have to act . . .

Up at her dressing table, Priscilla Embleton gazed at her pretty face unseeingly.

I thank you both for all you have given me . . .

From the dressing room came the sound of clothes swept violently along the rail, and a roar of irritation. Priscilla turned from the mirror and looked at her wedding photograph, in its silver frame. She picked it up, and turned it over, face down on the kidney-shaped glass, with such a lovely print beneath. Roses. Roses and phlox. Then she went quietly across to the wardrobe, with its heap of hat boxes, and pulled down a little suitcase, lined with oyster silk.

Don't cry, dearest Di, I'm as sure as I can be that I'll be back. Until then, look after Mother, keep close to George and Margot, with whom you play so wonderfully, and try not to think too badly of me . . .

She stood at her bedroom window, looking out over the Great Whitton parkland towards the lake, the boating house, the island. She saw picnics and parties and lots of people. She saw herself leaning back on a cushion as Frank rowed out across the water, ducks quacking quietly in the reeds. She heard him talk, on and on, when it was just the two of them – home from school, home from Oxford, all through the holidays from Kirkhoughton.

'Why would you want to teach *there*?'

What answer had he given? When had she ever listened? When had she ever thought about him at all, really, and what he was trying to say? He was just always there, laughing and clever and kind and beloved.

Now he wasn't. Now she wondered if anyone had ever meant as much.

And what have I done with my life? she asked herself, pulling her silky dressing gown closer in the cool morning air. I've played the cello, that's all. Is that enough?

It's what makes me real, that's all I know.

She turned from the window, and went to run her bath. Sitting on the old cane chair beside it, watching the steam begin to rise, she saw, as she saw every day, and sometimes every hour, Barrow haring over the grass, and George falling into her arms, sending her and Margot thudding to the ground as the swing tore loose and flung him away. He was white, deathly white, he was bruised and winded, but he was alive.

I know it will be hard, but I'm acting as I believe I must, and I pray that you'll understand. Please understand too that although I cannot return your feelings in the way that I know you would wish, I love and admire you, as my oldest and my dearest friend . . .

George lay on his bed in the room of his childhood, and

the creeper stirred at the window. He could hear his mother, getting lunch in the kitchen, the clatter of plates, the pulling out of a tray from the wooden rack. He could hear, just, the music of the Coquet, babbling over the great flat stones of the river bed, through the little village and out towards the Tyne. Those sounds, this shady house, this room: they were a part of him, like the picture books, the bricks and trains and soldiers of his boyhood: gradually, over the years, packed away, put into labelled boxes, put up in the loft.

'One day you'll have children, darling. We'll keep them safe till then.'

Gradually, the room had filled with other things.

More than any other composer, Beethoven deserves to be called the Shakespeare of music, for he reaches to the heights and plumbs the depths of the human spirit as no other composer has done . . .

The books, the scores, the gramophone records: they were part of the texture of his adult life, always here, like his parents, always waiting: on his return from London in the holidays, his return from a concert or party.

They were a part of him, but they were not what had made him who he was.

What had made him – what, inextricably intertwined with music, had given his whole life meaning – was a laughing fair-haired boy, running like the wind down the lawn of another house altogether, where an only child had been sent to make friends, and have lessons with others, and had fallen in love. Lying now beneath the leaded window, watching the creeper brush gently against the pane, he saw himself panting, a shrimp of a boy, catching up at last with a boy of his own age, but taller, stronger, cleverer, turning from the edge of the ha-ha to smile – oh, that smile – and fling his arm around him.

'*We've beaten the girls! Race you back.*'

Pelting up the endless lawn again, leaping on to the swing.

'*Push! Push me harder!*'

He saw the cricket ball hurled towards the wicket, batted out in an arc through the summer air, and he saw the rainy afternoons indoors, Miss Renner at the piano, all of them marching round the room. He saw Margot slide on to the piano stool, her feet barely touching the floor, and pick out a tune, her face intent and happy, and Diana dancing across the rugs, while he and Frank sprawled on the floor side by side, marshalling their troops.

'*Well done, that's a good idea.*'

He was alight with love.

And he saw, when all of this came to an end, the two of them sent off to prep school, crammed into the railway carriage, pressing their faces to the sooty glass to wave at their waving parents. His mother was weeping, and trying to pretend she wasn't: he swallowed hard, and an arm went round him.

'*We'll be all right.*'

Lessons were harder. Life was harder. Then he had his first lessons on the violin. A revelation. But up in the dark of the dorm, a musical shrimp of a boy could get bullied, and was.

'*Stop that!*'

All through his childhood, and boyhood, Frank had been there, his friend and protector. He was at the centre of everything, always, admired by everyone: dorm captain, cricket captain, first eleven and head boy – there would always be people like this, in every generation, and Frank was one of them, at prep school and public school, shining.

And then it was time to part. Off to Oxford. Off to the Royal College.

Footsteps were moving through the hall below; he could smell soup. As his mother climbed the stairs with a chinking tray, George shifted his bruised and aching body, and saw the great plume of steam begin to gather as the train pulled out for

London, and Frank, with all the others, waving and still waving from the platform, wishing him well.

'You're gifted, you're really good. You're going to be such a success!'

He saw himself standing in the middle of his fourth-floor student room in Kensington, looking out at the Albert Hall, sick with longing.

'You'll meet lots of girls, my darling – you must bring them home!'

An omnibus rumbled along Exhibition Road. In the middle of his room, with its narrow bed and grimy window, he said aloud: 'I have to face it. This is who I am.' Then he pulled on his coat, and picked up his violin, and went down to walk to his class.

His mother was coming along the landing.

'Here we are!' An innocent anxious face at the bedroom door. 'Feeling better, darling?'

All my life I have had such a burning hatred of injustice and inequality . . . Orwell opened my eyes to action . . . He's not just a writer, he lives out his beliefs. He's prepared to wash dishes, to sleep in a filthy doss house. He's prepared to fight. Read him! And if you read Homage to Catalonia *– I know you caught sight of it, Steven, but I had to hide it from you that day, or tell you everything – then you will ask yourself why, when it's almost all over, I should leave now – but I have to. One last battle, and who knows if it might not turn the tide . . . I have to play my part. Please tell the boys that I care for them so much . . .*

The timeless life of the moor went on: the slow-moving sheep beneath that enormous sky; the cries of lark and lapwing, the scent of the sun-warmed heather.

On these clear high days you could see right out towards

the distant town, make out the tower of St Peter's, make out the school.

It was almost the end of term.

'I must ask you to serve as Acting Head of Department.' The pipe smoke in Straughan's office had never been thicker. 'I take it you're prepared to do that, Mr Coulter.'

'Yes, sir. I'll do my best.'

'There won't be a great deal to do now, of course. As for next term – I shall have to think. There'll be a great deal then. We shall have to see.'

What they had to see was whether Frank Embleton would be back: slamming the door of the little red sports car, striding across the playground with his bag, greeting them all with that smile.

'Sir! Sir! Sir, what was it like, in Spain?'

What it was like in Spain was hunger and filth and endless boredom before the battle. It was not enough weapons, and those they had, old and rusty; frostbite at night, unspeakable mud after rain. It was lice, and rats in the trenches; blood in the trenches, body parts scattered, the battle raging. It was mules bounding shrieking away from the bursts of shrapnel, men stumbling with stretchers over the ravaged ground. 'Out of the way! *Move!*' It was fighting in the streets of Barcelona, slogans scrawled on bombed-out buildings, red flags flying high – *Obreros a la Victoria!* It was factions, and inter-factions; treachery, betrayal and torture. You died in a trench, or a god-forsaken dressing station, or screaming in a prison cell.

Or, like Orwell, you survived. You were wounded, you were in agony, but survived to tell the tale. He had told the tale.

This war, in which I played so ineffectual a part, has left me with memories that are mostly evil, and yet I do not wish that I had missed it . . .

Dusk was falling once more. Steven, reading outside the

kitchen door, got up, and went inside. Once again, he lit the lamp, and the small plain room was illuminated, the little flame burning bright. It shone on the dresser, and the rows of cups and plates; on the smoky old range and the saucepans on the shelf above. It shone on the bookcase, where the letters he had written to Margaret last summer were still tucked away, and on her coat, still hanging on its hook by the door, just in case she came back, and needed it.

Everything was just the same, and everything looked completely different. The letters from Margot were heaped up on the table, the letter from Frank was propped against a pile of textbooks. Eighteen months ago, neither of these people had meant a thing: Frank had been a respected colleague, Margot barely a name. Margaret had died, and that had been all he could think of. Now—

Now his whole life had changed – Frank had seen to that. He had introduced him to music, and another world; he had introduced him – how deliberately? – to another woman. Now both filled his mind with love and apprehension. What could he do for them? What lay ahead?

In came the moths, making blindly for the flame. He sat down at the table, while his supper heated, and picked up the book again. That fist smashing into the foreground of the cover, those bombed-out buildings, looked outlandish in this quiet place. He turned the pages, re-read Orwell's last lines, written of the journey home, puffing at last on the train through southern England.

Down here it was still the England I had known in my childhood: the railway cuttings smothered in wild flowers, the deep meadows where the great shining horses browse and meditate, the slow-moving streams ... and then the huge peaceful wilderness of outer London, the barges on the miry river, the familiar streets,

*the posters telling of cricket matches and Royal weddings, the men
in bowler hats, the pigeons in Trafalgar Square, the red buses,
the blue policemen – all sleeping the deep, deep sleep of England,
from which I sometimes fear that we shall never wake till we are
jerked out of it by the roar of bombs.*

*I have always loved you . . . There are some things one can't have,
and you are mine . . .*

*Do you remember our only kiss? Oh, how I wanted you. I
want you still . . .*

She sat at the piano, and she tried to play. In three weeks
time they'd be playing the summer concert at Great Whitton,
and never had they been more under-rehearsed. But George
wouldn't think of cancelling.

'Of course I'll be better, of course I will.' And then, not
looking at her: 'He'd want us to do it, you know he would.'
He walked stiffly across the room and lowered himself into the
wing chair, wincing.

'You shouldn't be cycling.'

'Yes I should. But what about you, poor Margot? I sent you
both flying – are you still hurt?'

'It's easing.' She ran her fingers over the keys. 'Just my right
arm, a little.'

'Let Mr History Teacher kiss it better.'

She turned on the stool and looked at him.

'George – you don't have to be flippant and silly.'

'Yes I do.' And then a shadow passed over his face: just for a
moment, but she saw it, and he saw that she had. 'I have to,' he
said quietly. 'You saw how I really am. If I let my guard down
again – I'm done for.' He gave her a look, then, which tore at her.
'Help me get through.' And the look was gone. 'Now then—'
He clapped his hands, and winced horribly. 'How about tea?'

That was a week ago, and tomorrow afternoon was a full

rehearsal for the first time. She turned the page of the score. The piano part of the *Ghost* was such a gentle thing at first, but then it became impassioned. She went back to the beginning, checked the fingering, went through the second page for what felt like the twentieth time. Oh, so beautiful.

Don't misunderstand me, darling: I'm not going to Spain to try to forget you – I'm going because I must. Ask Steven: I've told him to read a book which means so much to me . . . Perhaps you'll read it one day . . .

She tried again, running over the keyboard, trying to concentrate. What a blessed gift was practice: focus your mind and forget all else. For years it had sustained her.

But in some ways your not loving me makes it easier. There are so many things I want to do with my life, but – well, if I lose it, I might not care too much . . .

She fumbled, and stumbled, and gave up, weeping.

5

E ACH OF THEM, in their different ways, was struggling to come to terms with it all, to hold on to what they had. What they had was mostly each other.

'Mummy? Where are you going?'

Walking quietly over the great tiled hall with her suitcase, Priscilla Embleton froze.

'Darling. I thought you were out.'

'Where are you going?'

'Don't you have a rehearsal?'

'It's tomorrow.' Diana closed the front door behind her. 'I've just been for a walk.'

'That's not like you.'

'Nothing's like me any more. What are you doing with that suitcase?'

'Oh, darling. I'm just—' What was she just doing? Leaving a marriage of thirty-one years. At last. She dropped the suitcase, dropped down to the foot of the stairs, and told her.

'You can't.' Diana was scarlet. 'You can't! Oh, Mummy, I don't know what I'd do if you weren't here - I'd go mad without you.' She flung out her hands.

'Sssh, darling, sssh!'

'I can't sssh! And listen! There's the concert - it's *here*!' Her voice was rising wildly. 'You know it's here, and we're doing it for Frank, George says we must - you've *got* to be with us, you've *got* to.'

'Darling, come here.' Priscilla held out her arms, and Diana ran into them. Side by side on the broad shallow stair they rocked one another, holding tight.

'Please don't go, Mummy, please.' And then: 'Suppose he came back, and you weren't here?'

Priscilla was silent. Distantly, there came the sound of a car driving slowly up from the gates. She shut her eyes.

'I was hoping—'

'I'm sorry, I'm sorry – but please stay. Look at me, *look* at me! I'll look after you, promise.'

'Sweetheart.' She opened her eyes upon her lovely, frivolous daughter. 'When have you ever—'

Diana looked back at her, steady for once. 'I've looked after Margot. We've looked after each other, always. And also—' She gazed at her. 'I've just saved a life, remember? Well, me and Margot saved him.'

'Margot and I,' Priscilla said automatically, stroking her hand. 'Miss Renner would be shocked.'

The car was approaching the house, in a spray of gravel.

'There are more important things to be shocked about now,' said Diana. 'I feel – oh, Mummy – I feel so shaken, don't you?'

'You know I do.'

And then, as the car pulled up outside, she got to her feet, and picked up her pretty suitcase, and slowly re-climbed the stairs.

Almost the end of term. Letters between him and Margot flew back and forth.

My love, I'm so very sorry, I think of you all the time . . .

Oh, Steven! If we hadn't got there, if Barrow hadn't got there – I can hardly bear to think of it . . .

They still hadn't met.

I just can't face coming in to give classes, pretending to the boys that all is well . . .

And although Straughan had said there wasn't much for Steven to do, there was. Cover Frank's classes for one thing.

'Miss Aickman? Can I have a word?'

She pulled out a file labelled Substitute Teachers, ran down the list of names: retired teachers, working as examiners, invigilators, substitutes in a crisis. They were elderly men, and the boys were liable to rag about. He had to keep an ear out.

'Quiet, boys! What do you think you're doing, when Mr Pringle has kindly come in all the way from Hexham?'

'Sorry, sir. Sorry, Mr Coulter.'

'Sir, when's Mr Embleton coming back?'

Straughan had decided not to tell them, or not to tell them yet. Mr Embleton was unwell, it was unfortunate, but he knew the boys would do their best in his absence.

'He'll be back when he can,' said Steven, addressing the dusty blackboard. 'He sends you his warmest good wishes.'

Sometimes Dunn took a class, irritably forsaking a free period; sometimes he did so himself. With the exams over, he let the lower school relax a bit: quizzes and things. With Frank on his mind almost all the time it was a relief to whizz round a class, firing questions, have a laugh all together at wild guesses. At the end of the Upper Fifth there was always an exodus: those boys who'd done poorly in School Certificate, or failed it, didn't come back in the autumn.

What were they destined for, with unemployment still at a record high? The Army, that was more than likely, and who knew when they'd be called up? The Fusiliers were out on the moor most weekends and some evenings, tramping over the heather, scattering the sheep. And in June the RAF had had a recruitment drive: Armstrong, reading the paper at lunch-time, said there'd been a thousand new recruits on the first day.

'Sir? Sir, I'd love to fly, wouldn't you?'

The next week, the government announced the doubling of anti-aircraft forces.

'Sir, does that mean we'll be shooting planes down?'

Scanning the stately clouds above the Square, so still in the summer heat, it was hard to imagine such things.

. . . sleeping the deep, deep sleep of England, from which I sometimes fear we shall never wake . . .

Taking a class in the Sixth it was different: he knew Frank had liked to discuss things, to open up questions, get them to form their own views. He'd never taught the Sixth before: it felt something of a privilege, to be with these bright, hard-working boys. Already, they knew almost as much as he did.

As Acting Head, the other thing he had to do was check his staff's reports, as Frank had done. *'It's just a matter of form, I know they'll be impeccable.'* Now, he would have to check Dunn's.

'Mr Dunn? Would you mind?'

They sat side by side at the staffroom table, the papers spread out before them. He ran his finger down the list of marks, as Frank had done.

'I see Makin has done poorly again.'

'Makin is a troublesome boy.' Dunn lit a cigarette and blew a stream of smoke out over the table. His fingers shook, as always. 'You'll see that Ingham has done quite well. I'm pleased with Ingham.'

'Yes, that's splendid.' Steven skimmed over each boy's Remarks. *'Pays insufficient attention . . . Needs to revise much more thoroughly . . . A disappointing term . . . Very weak . . .'*

He hesitated. 'I know that Embleton always tried to begin with something positive . . . Do you think that's a good idea?'

Dunn drew on his cigarette, and coughed unpleasantly. 'If there is something positive to say, Coulter, I will say it. Most of these boys – well, you don't need me to amplify.'

For a moment Steven felt a wave of irritation. Dunn had a job, and was lucky to have it. He was lucky that the staff – and the boys – put up with him: his awkwardness, his temper, his complaints and strange solitary ways. Then he felt ashamed: the man had been through hell. He deserved to have a job. And he thought of him, all of a sudden, weeping in the Christmas carol service, and of what the Christmas holidays, and the summer, must be like for such a man – weeks stretching ahead, with few friends, and perhaps no family. He remembered his own dreadful loneliness last summer, and on impulse – making the kind of gesture Frank would make, he realised – he invited him to the Trio's summer concert.

George insists we must do it for Frank, Margot had written, *and I suppose we feel the same . . .*

'Do come. It's out at the Embleton place at Great Whitton.' He stacked up the heap of reports. 'Miss Heslop will be playing, of course, and Embleton's sister – you remember her?'

He smiled as Dunn flushed a little, and stammered out that he'd think about it, the Christmas concert had been rather good. Even Dunn would remember Diana.

When he got home, a letter was waiting in the wooden box. He tucked it into his pocket and walked up the track, spring mud turned into hard-packed ruts by the summer heat. A newly -sheared ewe was sunning herself by the cottage door: she got up at his approach, and trotted away. He dropped his bag, pulled out the creamy envelope, kissed it, sat down on the grass.

Darling Steven,

Thank you so much for your last letter. I do understand how much you're having to do in the wake of Frank's departure, but please come and see me soon. Everything still feels – oh, so shaken up and dreadful. That Frank could be killed, that George almost was: I can't stop thinking about it. I suppose I never thought that such things could happen to us – how blinkered we've all been. Now we're trying to keep steady and rehearse, but I need you – don't you need me? And I feel I must tell you something about Frank which has upset me so much . . . Please come . . .

Far below in the valley, the grey stone farm buildings lay so solidly in the tranqil afternoon. He could make out the farmer crossing the yard, and his dog padding after him, as always. These things – these timeless English things: like Orwell's great shining horses, and slow-moving streams; like the boys filing into Assembly, or ragging about in the Square – they brought comfort, connection, meaning: to him, and to generations stretching away behind him. Were they, as Orwell predicted, all about to be blown apart by bombs?

Everything still feels – oh, so shaken up and dreadful . . .

While he, at school, was caught up and distracted by things that just had to be done, Margot was weeping, he could sense it in every line. And what did she need to tell him?

He got up, went indoors, and wrote to her.

Forgive me, forgive me, my darling. Term ends on Wednesday: I'll come the next day.

A baking afternoon. The trees in the lane approaching the Hall were motionless, the field cattle standing close together in the shade, swishing away the flies. The air was full of the smell of cowpats, and grass turning slowly to hay. The birds had stopped singing – no need for song now, their courtship and endless feeding over, the fledglings gone – and only his footsteps sounded as he turned the last bend in the lane. Already, yesterday's rush and roar was fading.

'Praise my soul, the King of Heaven,
To His feet thy footsteps bring . . .'

Straughan always chose that one for the last day of the summer term, and no one doubted that he knew quite well that the lusty singing of both staff and boys was as much about the end of lessons, confinement, homework, marking, exams, the whole exhausting business of it, as gratitude for the intervention in their lives of saints, angels and God Almighty.

'Praise Him! Praise Him!

Praise the everlasting King.'

It rang, you might say, to the rafters.

'Have a very good summer, boys.' Straughan stood towering on the stage in his gown, and the wave of mingled relief, respect and affection was almost palpable in the chorus of 'And you, sir,' which ran around the hall.

Then it was all packing up books, clearing desks, prefects checking the cloakrooms for the last bit of cricket kit, the last unmatched sock, and out in ragged order across the playground.

'Have a good summer, Mr Coulter.'

'Thank you, Hindmarsh. And you.'

What did the weeks ahead hold for most of these boys? Fishing in the Burn, walking in the hills, mooching about. A trip to the coast if they were lucky. Helping out at home: what was that like?

'Me Dad's still on National Assistance.'

'Me Dad's joining up with the RAF. Ground work, he says.'

In the roar of bombs there was employment at last: an uneasy thought.

'Sir, do you think Mr Embleton will be back next term?'

'Let's hope so, Todd.'

'Goodbye, Mr Coulter, sir.'

'Goodbye, Herron. The very best of luck.'

'Thank you, sir.'

Off to Oxford. Frank's world. And where was Frank now? Had the last push begun?

There were the gates of the Hall. When he reached them, he

stopped, and listened for music, realising that he longed to hear it, that it was a part of him now – and yes, she was playing to welcome him, that was how it felt, something plangent and melodic which he knew he had heard before. It came floating out of the open windows, and his thirst and fatigue were forgotten. He walked through to the drive, his jacket slung over his shoulder, saw the dog flopped down in the corner shadow of the porch. He looked up at his approach, and his tail thumped, but he didn't get up: this wasn't a stranger, and he was too hot to move.

Steven went on, stopped, and stood listening for a moment to the sound of the piano, looking about him. Was something different? Something felt missing. He frowned, then realised. Of course: the swing. The cedar stretched emptily over the grass, and now he could see that the branch had been sawn away. That would be Barrow – Barrow, who had raced out of the kitchen garden to save a distraught young man quite beyond his ken, but whom he had known since childhood.

If we hadn't got there, he might have been just in time. Might. I can still hardly bear to think of it . . .

Walking slowly on towards the terrace, he tried once again to imagine it all, shrinking, as everyone did, from that 'might'. And then there came a sound from far across the garden, and he froze. Someone was weeping, weeping in the most terrible way, as if shocked beyond measure. He looked quickly across the lawn, saw the door of the little summer house burst open, and Diana come flying out over the grass, her hands to her face and her hair streaming out behind her. In the house, the music stopped abruptly.

For a second he thought: Frank's been killed. Frank's been killed, she's just heard. Oh, Jesus. And then, just as suddenly, he saw the tall figure of Thomas Heslop come out after her. For a moment he stood stock-still beneath the trees, and in the same moment Steven realised what Margot – quite by chance? – had been playing, and he knew.

Dream Children . . . And while I stood gazing, both the children gradually grew fainter to my view, receding and still receding . . .

Heslop had stood gazing. For years he had watched a beautiful little girl grow into an entrancing young woman. He had watched her, and longed for her: an exquisitely desirable thing a generation younger, young enough to be his daughter; his daughter's dearest friend, surely beyond his reach. Now, with Frank gone, with everyone in turmoil, he had reached for her.

'Diana—' Steven stepped forward as she flew towards the house.

She stopped dead, and looked at him wildly. Then: 'Leave me alone!' And she ran on, past the sleeping dog and in through the open porch door.

Into the hush which followed, the grandfather clock began to strike. Three o'clock on a summer afternoon: such deep steady sounds striking through the heat, as if everything, eternally, would stay the same.

Steven stood on the terrace. What should he do? Bees droned in the lavender, the dog's long sighs of sleep went on and on. Across the lawn, Heslop still stood beneath the trees, and even from here, as he dared to look at him, Steven could see he was utterly changed. He was grey, all the life drained out of him. For a moment their eyes met, and then he turned and walked down the great length of the garden, still keeping to the shade. He had acted, and now his heart was breaking: it was visible in every step he took.

The hall was empty, the drawing room was empty, a score lying on the floor by the piano. Swept aside as Margot leapt to her feet, hearing that wild weeping? Steven walked over, past the great slabs of sunlight falling in at the windows, and picked it up. And as he stood there in the silence, reading the mysterious, aching lines of the epigraph once more, it felt as if the whole house were suspended in time, that ghosts and dreams and longings haunted it, even on a summer afternoon.

We are nothing; less than nothing, and dreams. We are only what might have been . . .

Out in the hall, the clock struck the quarter hour: a quarter of a phrase which longed for its completion – unmusical though he had always felt himself to be, Steven could feel that as clearly as if a garden gate had clicked open, and were waiting to be closed.

And now? What completion could there be? What could fill the great absence that Frank had left behind him? What could follow that passionate outpouring of love and desire, so pent up for so long?

He walked out into the hall again, stood listening. He could not hear the murmur of Margot's and Diana's voices, but he knew that they must be up there, in a bedroom with the door shut tight.

A tiny sound behind him: he turned to see the dog walking slowly through the porch, dazed with heat and sleep.

'Come on, boy.'

Together they walked down the long cool passage to the kitchen, where he drank and drank from the stone sink tap, then pulled out a chair and sat waiting, the dog at his feet. And because they were right at the back of the house, at some distance from the garden, he couldn't hear the footsteps of a broken man walking fast and deliberately back up the lawn and towards the pele tower, nor the creaking open of the old oak door. But he did hear it slam behind him, and then, after a frowning few moments, the echoing, unmistakable blast of a gun.

6

AFTERNOON SUN SPREAD in the deepest tranquil-
lity over the grounds of Great Whitton. The parkland
bordering the avenue of beech, the reed-fringed lake, the island:
all were bathed in mellow light. Deer rested in the shade. In the
boat house, the dinghies lay side by side on the dappled water.
In the fields beyond, and up on the hills, sheep grazed unceasingly beneath the summer sky. It was all as it had ever been.

Inside the house, beyond the cream-painted double doors
which opened off the hall, a little group of people were setting
up music stands before a grand piano.

A stranger arriving now might at first glance have thought
simply: preparations for a country-house concert: how charm-
ing. Three young musicians: how delightful. Had such a
stranger crossed that serenely sunlit hall and walked further
into the room – so spacious, so airy, with its plasterwork ceiling,
long windows at the back overlooking a terrace; had he sat down
on one of the elegant little hired chairs set out in rows, he would
have seen that each of the musicians was as pale as the scores
opened out upon the stands, as the ivory of the piano keys. He
would have seen that they moved very slowly, as if in shock, and
barely spoke, and soon he might have guessed that something
had happened, something had marked them indelibly, so much
so that it was extraordinary that they should now, in silence,
get out a violin, a cello, go to the piano, sit down, and prepare,
in rehearsal, to play.

Steven, who was anything but a stranger, saw all this.

They were tuning up. Haydn, they'd decided, should open

the programme: something formal and calming, before the great emotion of Beethoven, and the *Ghost*. Steven knew neither piece, had heard only snatches in rehearsal, but as he took a seat – near the back, to test the acoustic, as George had asked him to do – he wondered, indeed, that the Trio could even contemplate this concert. Surely it could be, should be, cancelled. The merest weeks had passed: everyone, unquestionably, would understand.

But then, as they looked at one another – that infinitesimal glance of accord – and began to play, he closed his eyes and saw not the horrible, relentless re-running of the past few weeks, but himself in a snowy playground, eighteen months ago, walking towards the gates at the end of the afternoon.

'Sir! Sir, you forgot this!'

Johnny Mather, missing an icy patch and racing after him with his textbook.

'*Wouldn't have been able to do your marking, would you, sir?*'

'Thanks, Mather.'

Barely a week since the funeral – the freezing Cawbeck churchyard, that terrible descent onto snow-speckled earth – and he had gone back to teaching.

'Stop a moment.' George was tapping his bow, and Steven opened his eyes. 'Can we do those last six bars again? Diana, I can't really hear you.'

'Sorry.' They began again. And now he could hear and see, as they repeated that last little passage, that Diana's playing was stronger, and more confident: she was recovering herself a little, getting into her stride. This, after all, was her home: she had spent years practising here.

Had Frank come to listen to her scales, her going over and over the cello part alone?

My sister and a couple of friends play in a trio – I'd love you to come and hear them . . .

Why? Why would Frank love that? Had he just been taking

226

pity on him in his loneliness and grief? Perhaps: kindness coursed through every cell in his body. Yet to introduce him to the woman whom Steven now knew he had loved unrequitedly all his life – had he guessed what might happen? Even wanted it? Had he, in the ultimate sacrifice, simply wanted her to be happy?

But then, as Diana bent low over the cello, drawing the bow across with sudden energy, it came to him.

Not Margot. Not Margot at all.

'This is my sister, Diana . . .'

A rain-swept autumn night, a concert, interval drinks. A beautiful, unattached sister: had it really been she whom Frank wanted him to meet? Had he honestly thought that a young woman of such a background, such head-turning loveliness, might be interested in a shy, bereaved teacher from a local school? If so, thought Steven, he must have seen something in me that I cannot see myself.

The piano stopped abruptly. Now it was Margot wanting to try a passage once again. 'I just can't seem to get it right. Can we go from Bar 34?'

Oh, how pale she was – paper-white, and thin. Much too thin. And as they ran through again, and then again, Steven stretched his legs out beneath the chair in front, closed his eyes once more on all that frailty, and waited for everything – yet again – to well up before him. That baking afternoon, Diana flying over the grass in tears, the tall dark figure beneath the trees: a man who for decades had longed and longed in secret, who had finally spoken, and been most consummately reject-ed. He heard the slam of the pele tower door, saw the dog's head jerk up. Animals know before humans when something is wrong, or about to happen – had Steven himself guessed, in those uneasy few moments, what Heslop was about to do?

'My father keeps his guns in there . . .'

'And Barrow keeps his barrow . . .'

They had laughed, walking over the flagstones on a cold March afternoon, the light beginning to go, the air smelling of freshly-dug earth and smoke; he had wanted to put her arm through his. Had he begun to love her then?

The music was dancing – absurdly, defiantly – out across the room. How could they do it? How could they play like this?

He heard that shocking, echoing, unmistakable shot, saw himself running like the wind down the corridor to the hall, heard the bedroom door upstairs flung open, and the first wild question.

'What was that?'

'Stay there!'

He went on running, out through the porch, the dog behind him, turning on the terrace, with its drone of bees, racing to the pele tower, wrenching the oak door open wide and almost fainting. Then the dog ran in, and he had to haul him back.

And he saw them all gathered in the kitchen, after the funeral in the little church at Hepplewick: another Heslop gone, and gone most terribly, so terribly that he could not be buried within the churchyard walls. The mourners had left – the Embletons, the Liddells, the villagers, the Barrows. Now, in the cool shady kitchen, it was just the three of them again, with the woman who had been their governess so long ago, in a time that had meant so much; and with Steven himself, who was now an irrevocable part of it all.

Emily Renner poured fresh tea with a hand that shook. It was Diana who broke the exhausted silence, leaning ashen across the table, her hands outstretched before her.

'Music is the only thing that matters.'

A little movement in his row of chairs. Steven looked up, and saw Priscilla Embleton approaching carefully. He made to rise, but she put a finger to her lips, and sat quietly down: not next to him, but at the discreet distance of another couple of chairs. She gave him a fleeting little smile, then turned to watch the Trio. As he looked for a moment at her profile – that sensitive fine nose, those delicate bones, a face in which he could see both Frank and Diana – he saw how pale she was, too; and, slender as she was, how much weight she too had lost in the wake of Heslop's death.

Today she was wearing a pale blue cardigan and pearls: both looked so lovely against her soft fair hair, but he remembered the jet-black linen she had worn at the funeral, the hat with its little veil, the way she had wept and wept in the closing hymn.

Had she wept more, perhaps, than you might expect from someone outside the family? A good friend, yes. Someone who went back decades, yes. But still.

As the mourners had made that bleak progress through the churchyard, following the coffin out through the gate, down the lane, and round to the field at the back, he had had Margot's arm in his, and been aware only of her desolate vulnerability. But as they stood round the rough field grave he had looked across once to the other side, and seen that weeping go silently on and on, the agonised struggle not to draw attention to it. He had seen Embleton's heavy arm go round her shoulders and her perceptible withdrawal. Then Margot, beside him, was sobbing her heart out, and he turned back to her, holding her tight, and Priscilla Embleton was forgotten.

But now, glancing again at that delicately pretty profile, Steven remembered all of this, and, as he had done so many times since meeting this little group of people, allowed himself to speculate.

'All right, let's take a break.' The Haydn was over. Across the room, George lowered his bow and let the violin rest in his lap. He looked over to Steven, saw Priscilla, and gave her a fleeting smile. 'How did that sound?'

'Good.' Steven cleared his throat. 'Really lovely.' The acoustic must surely be unchanged from previous years – but perhaps, fraught as this rehearsal might become, George had only directed him to sit at the back to keep him at a distance.

'Well done,' said Priscilla. 'Well done, all of you.' She got to her feet. 'I expect you'd like some tea.'

'That would be wonderful. Thank you.'

Instruments were laid down, and they followed her out and into a small sunny sitting room across the hall. Tea things were laid on a tray with a lacy cloth, there were trimmed sandwiches, a cake.

'I'll get the teapot, Mummy.'

'No, darling, you sit down and rest.'

'Is Daddy joining us?'

'I don't think so. He'll be here for the concert, of course.'

Diana sank on to a sofa. 'I used to do my homework in here,' she said, as Priscilla's heels went clicking away across the hall. 'Before we went away to school, I mean.'

'And much good it did you,' said George, crossing to an armchair.

'Thanks.'

'You two,' said Margot, sitting down next to Steven on the other small sofa. He could feel them all doing their best to keep things light, the old teasing and banter.

Then: 'We three,' said Diana quietly. She looked across at Steven. 'And you are our fourth, now Frank's gone.'

He shook his head. 'I could never replace him. And anyway—' he swallowed. 'He'll come back.'

'We can only hope for that,' said George, and closed his eyes, all banter gone as he leaned back in the chair.

Steven looked at him, so pale and drawn, and so much older. He took Margot's hand, and she leaned against him.

And if Frank returns, he thought, feeling the lightness of that dark head on his shoulder, as if even her hair had lost weight; if he returns and finds us together - what might he feel, and do? Had he never considered that this might happen?

Light footsteps came back across the hall. Priscilla appeared with a tray: an elaborate old teapot, a silver jug of water. George was instantly on his feet.

'Let me.'

She flashed him a smile as he took it, such a heavy thing, and set it carefully down.

And they sat taking tea, talking quietly, comfortingly, of nothing very much - 'You must rest, your rooms are all ready, there's lots of hot water for baths,' - looking out now and then at the parkland, the deer, the avenue of beech where in a few hours the first cars would come slowly up to the house.

'Ladies and gentlemen, good evening.' A little pause. 'It is of the greatest consolation to us all to have you here for the annual summer concert at Great Whitton.'

George, in evening dress, stood before the audience. The Lindsays, the Raeburns, the Gills. His parents. Lots of people Steven didn't know. Behind him the sun was sinking, and low shafts of light streamed dustily into the room, already lit everywhere by candles: on the grand piano, at which Margot sat motionless in black; in sconces, on stands on either side of the podium, and on the mantelpiece.

'Our performance this year is dedicated to two people,' George went on, and from his seat in the second row Steven could see that he was trembling from head to foot. 'First, we dedicate it to the absent son of this house, Frank Embleton - gone, as I think most of you know, to fight for the Republican cause in Spain.' His voice shook, as he looked out over their heads. 'The Battle of the Ebro has begun. I need hardly say that we all hope fervently for a Republican victory, and for his safe return.'

A movement in the front row, an angry clearing of a throat. Steven saw Charles Embleton lean forward, as if he wanted to speak, and at once, with a tiny glinting flash of diamond ring, Priscilla's restraining hand was on his arm. George glanced towards them, then out to the whole audience once more.

'Secondly, we dedicate this concert, with the deepest respect and affection, to the memory of Thomas Heslop.'

At the piano, Margot sat so still, and gazed so intently at the score, that you might think she would never move again. At the cello, Diana's lovely face was quite without expression. Like someone in court, Steven thought suddenly, though he had never been in court. Like someone about to be sentenced. To a lifetime of remorse? He glanced towards Priscilla, and saw her gazing up at George unreadably.

There was no more he could say, and he did not say it, only: 'Thank you all again for being here. We begin with Haydn, master of the piano trio.'

A silence, a cough here and there, one or two rustles of programmes. George turned, and went over to his chair. Steven saw his knees tremble as he sat down, saw the struggle for control, the force with which he pressed his feet to the floor. Then he picked up his bow, drew a breath. Diana, her mass of fair hair and black satin dress lit by sun and candlelight, lifted the bow of the cello. Margot rested her hands on the keys. A glance – *we have known one another for ever; we can do this, even now* – ran with quicksilver speed between them. They began to play.

'I will have my say.' In the middle of the crowded hall, Charles Embleton was holding forth to a knot of people. Drinks were going round on trays: Grace and Nellie Barrow, co-opted for the evening, were doing their very best. But where there would usually be a roar of interval talk and laughter, the atmosphere was subdued – how, with such a concert dedication, such knowledge of recent events, could it be anything else? Lovely though the Haydn had been, marvellous though these young musicians were – that was the tenor of things.

But Embleton spoke at top volume, and even on the other side of the hall you could hear him.

'The Republicans are backed by the Soviet Union. The Soviet Union! Is that what my muddle-headed son is after – a European country run by Communists? The sooner Franco beats the hell out of them the better.'

'Charles, please—' Beside him, Priscilla was flushing.

'Please what?' He knocked back his glass, took another as Nellie Barrow came by. 'You think I'm a cold unfeeling bastard—'

'Charles!'

The Raeburns began to look away, but on he went.

'I love my son as much as any father, but if he comes back as a member of the Communist Party I'll cut him off without a penny. "We fervently hope for a Republican victory."' He mimicked George's light voice quite horribly. 'Like hell we do. Bloody pansy.'

Priscilla turned on her heel and walked with trembling speed across the hall.

'He's drunk,' she said to George, who was standing very still with the others. Beside him, his mother was biting her lip. 'He's drunk, take no notice at all.'

'It's all right.' He gave a tight little smile. 'It doesn't matter.'

'It *does* matter!" Diana was on the verge of tears. 'How *can* he? In the middle of the *concert*, when we're all trying so hard—'

'I know, I know, I'm so sorry. Be brave, darling, be brave all of you.' Priscilla flashed a shaky smile around the group. 'Your introduction was so good, George. Really. Thank you. And that

233

was such a wonderful first half – we're all so looking forward to the Beethoven, aren't we Steven?' She was almost babbling.

But before he could murmur agreement, Diana said furiously, 'You're the one who's been brave all these years, Mummy. I can see now exactly why you wanted to—'

'Ssh! Stop it!' And then, with sudden relief at a distraction, Priscilla said quickly, 'Look, here's Miss Renner! She'll help you all stiffen up.' And she gave a tearful little laugh, putting out a hand. 'Hello, Emily, how very good to see you.'

Emily Renner, too, was thin and pale, but she looked handsome as ever in a long summer gown and her features softened as she approached them all.

'That was marvellous. Well done, all of you – I don't think I've ever heard you play so well.'

'Coming from you, Miss Renner—' George gave a little bow, and for a second his old playfulness was there once more, and everyone laughed.

'Where's Nanny?' asked Margot suddenly. 'She said she could come on the bus.'

They looked across the crowd of guests, and through the evening dress, the gowns and pearls and prettiness, saw a stout elderly figure in grey, talking in Nanny fashion to a stiff tall man with a stick.

'Dunn,' said Steven, in astonishment, and Margot said, 'Mr Dunn!' and Priscilla said 'Who?' and everyone laughed again.

'I'd forgotten I'd even asked him.' Steven shook his head. 'How could I?'

'With everything that's happened,' said Emily Renner, 'I should think anyone could forget anything at any time.'

'Miss Renner, I do believe you're mellowing,' said George, and then Steven said he must go and bring him over.

'Bring Nanny, too.'

'Of course.'

And as Margot began to tell the others who Dunn was – 'Another history master at Kirkhoughton, wounded at the Somme, rather difficult, but somehow I like him,' – he made his way through the throng, hearing Embleton roar drunkenly on but thinking, with a rush of affection for all of them – Priscilla, the Trio, Miss Renner, even Nanny, who had been so unswervingly at the Hall since that terrible afternoon: We'll get through this, I know we will.

'David.' He stood before him, held out his hand. 'I'm so glad you came.'

Dunn nodded, shook his hand. 'Good of you to suggest it, Coulter.'

'We've had such a nice talk,' said Nanny, and Steven almost kissed her. 'Glad you came, too,' he said.

'Wouldn't miss it for the world, my duck.'

He did kiss her then. 'Come and join the others.'

And as Dunn came limping alongside, and Margot waved to them all, he saw Emily Renner glance across from the group, and give a little nod of recognition. Of course – she'd seen Dunn once before, after the school Christmas concert. But they hadn't met properly, she hadn't known his background. As Margot fell into Nanny's warm embrace, Steven made the introductions.

'David Dunn. My colleague at Kirkhoughton.'

'How do you do?' Dunn nodded stiffly at each of them in turn.

'And this is Miss Emily Renner.'

She held out her hand, and he took it, with an awkward smile. There was a general pause.

'But surely it must be time for the second half,' said Priscilla suddenly. 'Someone must ring the bell. Oh, dear, perhaps I should. Where is it, does anyone know?'

Dusk was falling.

Now the day is over, night is drawing nigh . . .

As Steven took his seat once more, the little song which Margot's mother had used to sing to her as a child came into his mind, unbidden. There were so many new things he associated with her now.

Shadows of the evening steal across the sky . . .

They were stealing now, beyond the long sash windows. Birds beat by.

The Trio had taken their places. The candles burned brightly in the fading light.

'Ladies and gentlemen.' As George stood once more before the audience, Steven saw how studiously he avoided glancing towards Embelton's glowering presence in the front row. And now there was no beloved face for George to search for in the audience, as he had done so intensely in the past.

'It has been said that Beethoven, more than any other com-poser, deserves to be called the Shakespeare of music,' he went on quietly, 'for he explores human spirit as no other composer has ever done. We conclude this evening's concert with his Piano Trio No. 1 in D major, Opus 70, *Ghost*.' He made a little bow; he walked back to his seat.

There fell the deepest hush. Steven knew that many of the audience would be thinking: How could they choose this? Isn't it asking too much of everyone – and especially of the players – to know that such a title adorns this piece? Isn't it unbearable? He knew that they had made their choice weeks ago, long before Frank's departure and Thomas Heslop's death. But still – they might have reconsidered.

Not one of them had wanted to. Staying at the Hall these last weeks, he had heard the discussions. And with George's quiet invocation now of the composer's grandeur, he knew they had been right.

There were three movements, the programme told him. His real concern now was whether, on first hearing, untutored as he was, it might be possible for him to understand any of them. To like this music, even.

But then the bows were lifted, there came that mercurial glance, and after a fierce little opening flourish a tune began of such mesmerising beauty that all doubt was swept away.

So light, just a handful of notes, it ran from gently calling cello to swiftly responding violin: Diana to George, back again from George to Diana, and at once, on the piano, came Margot, echoing. And now the three players were bound to one another, in an intricate, interweaving conversation – *Hear me . . . I hear you!* – repeating, leaving, embroidering and returning, over and over, to that lovely phrase.

The room was absolutely quiet. Not a cough, not a turning of a programme page. Beyond the windows the sky was darkening; in here the candlelight was more intense, the playing still more vibrant, until came another great flourish, and silence.

There was a pause, filled with anticipation. Then the slow movement, the *largo*, began.

It was dreamy, tentative, mysterious. It was almost other-worldly, the violin soon so soft it was almost whispering. Steven knew that everyone in the room – George, Margot, Diana, every member of the audience – must have their own vision before them now of what this ethereal music meant, of whom they were thinking, and as he began, so astonishingly, to cry, his own past welled up like water.

Who was he thinking of?

Not Frank, risking his life for all he believed in; not a sheet-white boy lying gasping on a row of chairs; not a broken man blowing his brains out.

Remember me . . .

Oh, my love . . .

He saw her bent over her book, he saw her look up as he came into the room, and put out her hand, her eyes alight. He saw her beside him, walking over the moor, singing into the wind, the wind in her hair, and he felt her reach for him as he climbed into bed beside her, naked and warm.

I was real, darling . . .

He saw the bright specks of blood on the little quilt as she sat sewing in the sun while he dug the garden or sawed in the shed, the door wide open to the summer air; he felt her lean on his arm as they went slowly indoors; he heard her coughing, saw her grow pale and thin, the shadows under her eyes growing deeper, until she could only lie in their high iron bed, and all they could do together was hold hands and watch the starry sky.

Don't leave me . . .

He saw himself returning at the end of a winter afternoon, the snow piled high at the door and still falling as he scraped it away and flung himself inside, calling her, shouting for her, stumbling half-frozen up the stairs—

You belong to me . . .

Into the room came the sound of the piano, playing alone. Through a blur of tears, his hand to his mouth, Steven watched Margot's oscillating fingers evoking something unutterably far away, saw George and Diana listening, waiting, until they lifted their bows once more; and as this enthralling music filled the room, evoking human experience at its frailest, most poignant and profound, the Trio played as if they had never heard *Ghost* before, and were discovering it for the first time.

Gradually the movement built to a climax, and gradually faded. There was a final flourish, and then the piano fell silent, George and Diana plucked the strings, quietly, and yet more quietly still, and it was over.

☙

Of the last of *Ghost*'s three movements – hugely energetic and alive – Steven remembered only one thing: the way in which George moved as he played, so intense, so expressive, that the violin was almost a part of his body.

The piece concluded. There was the profoundest silence.

And then the applause filled the room, people getting to their feet until everyone was standing – an ovation for three brave, brilliant young people: that was what Steven heard all around him, as he blew his nose and joined in the endless clapping. Only Charles Embleton had stopped, and turned to his neighbour, talking of who knew what.

'Bravo!' Steven heard himself call out, something he had never done in his life, except on the cricket field. He was calling to all of them, as they bowed, and bowed again, but especially to Margot – yes, especially to her.

'You've been crying,' she said, as she stepped off the podium and into his embrace. 'Oh, Steven . . .'

'You were so good.' He kissed her anxious face.

'But—'

'No buts. Let's go into supper.'

He wasn't going to tell her what had made him weep. Nor that for a moment, flooded with memory, he had thought: I can't do this. Had thought he must write, and tell her.

Forgive me . . . I have nothing to offer . . .

Perhaps she guessed. She slipped her hand in his. And with the simplicity of that gesture, and as he closed his own hand round those slender, miraculously musical fingers, anguish and doubt fell away, became something as evanescent as the music which had so dissolved him. A catharsis – that was how he later understood it. Now, as they walked slowly out through the crowded room, their hands unlocking, intertwining, holding fast, he was filled with the sense of a new life finally beginning.

That night, for the first time, they became lovers.

They arrived at Hepplewick late, the headlamps sweeping down the darkened lanes, and into the drive. The Hall stood before them: huge, unlit, empty.

For weeks Margot had had people staying. Diana, often – 'Of *course* I'll stay,' though Margot had thought wildly that she might want to drive away, race away over the hills, and never return. Nanny, more often than anyone: 'In you get, my duck, and I'll bring you a nice cup of hot milk, that's it.' George once or twice, pacing about in the night and trying, in the morning, to pretend he had slept well, thank you.

Miss Renner had not stayed. 'I can't leave my mother at night – but oh, my dear, my dear.' For the first time ever, she had held Margot to her, stroking her hair.

Barrow had cut the grass for the funeral; Mrs Barrow had come and gone each day, white-faced, saying little, sweeping into every corner, making hot meals, fresh beds.

And Steven had stayed. That first night, there had been no question. While Diana slept with Margot – 'I can't be alone,' – 'Nor me,' – he had taken the spare room, overlooking the back, an unloved part of the place. Bins, a washing line. Who cared? After that, after the first numb breakfast, he'd taken the dog out, and this became the most useful thing he could do, though every time he came back he could see Margot seeing her father, returning from those endless lonely walks.

'Darling, come here.' He held her as she wept.

'Don't go, don't go.'

He stayed, but he was rarely alone with her. There was the funeral. There was the concert approaching. That they might sleep together at any point in all this was unthinkable, wasn't even spoken of. There were others in the house. It was too soon.

But as supper at Great Whitton ended, and people began to leave:

'Come home with me.'

'Who else is staying?'

'No one.'

Now Margot switched off the headlamps. At once, they were swallowed in darkness, and he reached for her hand.

'I'm frightened.'

'Don't be.' Up on the moor he was used to the blackness of the night, sometimes even craved it. He stroked her hand, and now they could make out the moonlit outline of the house.

'Come on.'

They got out, crunched over the gravel to the terrace. The moon, just on the turn, had risen to its full height and hung, steady and calm, over the silvery garden.

'And look at the stars.' He drew her to him, and they stood gazing up.

'Do you know them?' he asked her, and at once knew the answer.

'A little. My father taught me.' She bit her lip. 'And Miss Renner showed us star maps.'

'Show me the Plough. Very good. And Orion?'

They turned, they craned their necks.

'Where's the Great Bear?'

She pointed upwards. 'He was my favourite.'

'And mine.'

A light wind stirred the branches of the cedar; she shivered.

'Let's go inside.'

As soon as they opened the porch door the dog was up and before them, wagging, greeting, eager.

'Hello, hello, we're home now. Poor old boy.'

He took their embraces, then pushed past them and out into the garden.

'He'll be back in a minute.' Margot opened the door to the hall; they stepped inside. Sonorously, in the darkness, the clock began to chime.

Since Heslop's death, Steven had been the one to wind it: another useful task. They stood there listening: the three-quarter hour, waiting for completion.

'Dah-dah-dah-dah,' sang Margot softly, and began to cry. 'Oh, Steven—'

'I know, I know.' He held her close as the last chime faded. The dark house stretched all around them, filled to every corner with enormous absence.

At length she stopped, detached herself with a kiss, and by the moonlight at the open doors made her way across to the table by the fireplace, and switched on the lamp. The hall became human, filled with possibilities again, as the clock ticked steadily on. In came the dog, making for his basket, and Steven went to close the doors behind him, then draw across the immense old curtain.

Margot watched him, and felt misery begin to fade. 'Do you remember?' she asked, as he walked back towards her, 'being here after that autumn concert? Telling the dog how beautiful he was?'

He nodded. 'I think so.'

'It made me notice you,' she said. 'I think that's when I began to fall in love.' She moved into his arms. 'And do you remember our first kiss here?'

'I do.'

'Kiss me again.'

He slipped his hand round her head, and lifted her face to his.

The moon slipped down the sky, and filtered through the dense, stirring branches of the cedar. It pierced a gap in the bedroom curtains, and a thin line of silver fell brokenly on to the bed where they lay, where everything was a muddle and tangle: sheets, quilt, blankets.

'I love you,' said Steven, words he had spoken only to one other woman, and thought never to say again. He said it again.

She lay in his arms with her head on his chest: the timeless pose of lovers.

'I love you,' she said, and kissed his naked shoulder, loving it as much as any part of him.

Outside, the wind was rising, the summer night growing colder. It hadn't rained for weeks, but as they got up, and made the bed straight again, and climbed in again to smooth linen, they heard the first pattering on the glass.

'Come here.'

He drew her back into that eternal pose, and they lay there, listening. The rain began to fall faster, harder, as blowy and ceaseless as it had been on the autumn night they met, when she had had no thought of meeting anyone, and he could only think about the past.

'My love.'

'My darling.'

His eyes closed first. She lay listening to his breathing grow steady and slow, gave his hand a squeeze, felt an answering squeeze. Would there always be that steadiness, that swift response? She felt her own eyes begin to close.

They began to drift towards sleep, little snatches of things – the music, George's voice, Diana's lifting of the bow, the way the dog had run to greet them – blowing about on the cusp of different dreams, as the rain poured on and on.

7

THE SUMMER OF 1938. On flags in every German and Austrian town and city, on town halls and balconies, the swastika hung above the streets, or fluttered in a sudden gust of wind. It blew above the open spaces of Berlin: over the Platz der Republik, from the roof of the Reichstag, and all along the Unter der Linden, where the lime trees stirred. It adorned banners twice the size of a man in medieval Nuremberg, where preparations for the 10th Party Congress had begun: the Rally of the Greater Germany. In every German and Austrian town and city, every Jew now carried a marked identity card.

In Spain, the British battalion of the International Brigade had crossed the River Ebro. *Anti fascista! Proletaria!* The red flags swung as they marched. Now, with their American allies, in the scorching heat, they were fighting a last desperate battle for the town of Gandesa.

In London, the government had ordered a thousand Spitfire fighters.

And in Leeds, Australia had beaten England in the fourth test of the Ashes.

You read about these things, or some of them, in *The Times*, or the *Morning Post*, or the *Northumberland Journal*. You listened to the news, if you had a wireless.

Or you tried not to listen. You imagined, and that was worse.

In the breakfast room of Great Whitton, Charles Embleton

turned irritably to the cricket, and Priscilla looked out of the window and dreamed of seeing a fair-haired, sunburned figure suddenly come walking up the long beech avenue, swinging a kitbag. 'Mother! I told you I'd be back.' She put her hand to her mouth.

'What's the matter?'

'Nothing.' She reached for the butter dish. Cold toast lay on the plate before her.

It wasn't only her son, her darling. Last night she had lain awake for hours, imagining, over and over again, those last moments in the pele tower at Hepplewick: the striding in, banging the door behind him; the taking down of the gun, the hesitation. Then—

It came back to her now, on this beautiful morning, and she gave a little gasp.

The Times was flung down across the table.

'If that boy had thought for a moment of how he would make you suffer—'

She shook her head. 'It doesn't matter.'

'Of course it bloody matters. And where's Diana?'

'Gone over to Hepplewick. You know she has.'

A grunt, a return to the paper.

Enormous, unspoken things lay between them. Priscilla, her cold toast untouched, gazed out of the window once more, thinking now of her daughter, who had finally, in a storm of tears, confided.

'I didn't know – I never knew – he was like a father – a much nicer father than Daddy – I'm sorry, but it's true – and to think of him thinking all those things all these years – I was so *shocked* . . .'

No more shocked than I, thought Priscilla, rocking and stroking her, up in her pretty bedroom, with its view of the reed-fringed lake, the island.

'But I didn't want to hurt him like that - I never thought - I never, *never* thought he would—'

'Shssh, darling, shssh. No one could ever have thought such a thing.'

At last the weeping stopped.

'Oh, Mummy.'

'I know, I know.'

The breakfast-room clock struck nine. A figure was walking up the avenue, small and dumpy: Mrs Chapple, from the village, coming, as every day, to clean. Priscilla pushed back her chair, and made herself - *made* herself - turn her mind to buckets, polish, flowers for the hall.

You thought about the news, of the increasing threat of something terrible about to happen; of things that might, even now, be happening. Or you shut it all away, not wanting to know, and turned, as you had done all your life, to music.

'Can we try those last few bars again?'

Every morning in the shadowy drawing room: it gave shape, purpose and meaning; it gave something alive. Schubert and Schumann; Chopin, Ravel. The divine Mendelssohn, offering the most tender consolation. How they needed that.

No one was giving lessons. No one talked of a concert, just as no one talked of war. But this - this they could do.

'Just once more. Yes! Much better.'

While they played, Barrow worked in the garden, as usual; Mrs Barrow cleaned and made lunch. Everything was being kept going, though no one knew for how long. And Steven - Steven went walking with the dog.

'Come on, old fellow.'

Out past the cedar and down the drive, the strains of music following: Haydn, Mozart, that lovely Mendelssohn. He was beginning to know it all. Once they spent two mornings with Beethoven, the *Archduke*, a miraculous thing. But not the *Ghost*.

'I don't know if we'll ever be able to play that again.'

Out along the lanes. The trees were dark and full: high summer. Since the downpour of rain on the night that he and Margot became lovers, the freshness of verge and ditch was wonderful. The fields stretched away for ever: as he walked, looking out over corn and cattle, he felt his boyhood come up to meet him – all those summer holidays, out with the dog and a sandwich.

But it wasn't only his own past, walking alongside him beneath the trees. Heslop had walked here, over and over, with this dog or that, so often down the years that to retrace his paths felt almost like having his coat around his own shoulders.

How would things have been between himself and Margot, had Heslop lived? They had lived together for so long, father and daughter: would he have found it difficult to lose her? Or had his secret, obsessive inner life been the only thing that really mattered?

'Here, boy!'

The dog came bounding out of a ditch. He had recovered, as dogs did.

'Home.'

He turned back, to walk towards the house. He was living there now, loving and sleeping with Margot each night in that single bed, turning as the other turned, murmuring sweet nothings as they fell asleep. Except for going to fetch clean clothes, he had hardly visited the cottage. Margot had never asked to go there: perhaps she didn't want to. In these long quiet weeks before term began again, they could easily do it, but did he want to take her there? What a huge thing it would be.

The Hall came into view, a place where he was still a visitor.

He walked up the shady drive, hearing the last strains of something float bravely out of the open windows.

You scoured the paper, searching for the only piece of news you cared about. There was no knowing where Frank was fighting, only the guess that it would be by the Ebro, a river crossed by pontoon bridges.

Severe fighting has continued today on the Ebro front . . . Nationalist planes have unceasingly bombed and machine-gunned the Republican positions around Gandesa . . .

You read, at the breakfast table, and pushed away your toast. 'George? Darling?'

The battle rages north and south of Gandesa under a burning sun . . . Blood is mingling with the waters of the Ebro . . . tons of explosives have been dropped on the makeshift bridges . . .

Up from the table, out to the hall. Each day the post brought, once again, nothing that mattered.

George walked along the riverbank on the long hot afternoons. Beside him the Coquet babbled and sang, newly filled from that sudden storm. Little fish darted in and out of the shade of flat stones; moorhen tugged at this and that in the reeds. Everything was restlessly alive. Now and then he met a mother and children on the towpath, skimming stones or running a stick along from tree to tree; sometimes they hung over the bridge, and dropped twigs into the racing water, dashing to the other side to see which bobbed out first.

'That's mine!'

Occasionally it was just one child, doing these things alone, and as he nodded and smiled, and bade them good afternoon, he saw himself as a boy, out with his mother, in years he hadn't realised were lonely until he went to Hepplewick. An only child, and Margot another: she and Diana had become the sisters he hadn't known he needed, and Frank – Frank had become everything. And now Margot had found Steven, another only child. In and out it all wove, like a fugue.

George walked on, running phrases of music through his mind, as he had done all his life. Sometimes he struck the air before him, or sang out a line, and a mother with her children smiled uncertainly. He asked himself what would become of them all if there really was a war. There was a paragraph or two about Spain in *The Times*, there were columns about Czecho-slovakia, and Hitler's rages. He yelled on the wireless, and you shrank. George thought: I want no part of this.

And as the aching weeks went by, he began to ask himself how modern music might respond to modern times, which were beginning to feel so hideous.

At home, after tea – 'Nice walk, darling? More cake?' – he went up to his room and stood looking through scores, and books, and records. Almost everything they played in the Trio was at least a hundred years old. Almost every concert was given to people they knew, or to friends of the people they knew. They were living hundreds of miles from London, and he the only one of them to know what that meant. Chamber music in a drawing room, country house concerts. Nothing wrong with that, music should be made everywhere.

But in London—

He read, he sat listening to Schubert and Beethoven through the scratch and hiss. He wondered if the Trio might ever make a recording of their work. Might that be possible? Other names began to push their way towards him, through reviews and articles: Stravinsky, Prokofiev, William Walton. In London they would surely be listening to their newest works, blowing the past apart.

The weeks went by. The creeper at the window began, here and there, to turn from green to crimson. Soon it would be time to start lessons again: cycling from house to house with a pannier full of music; answering the doorbell here, letting in the pupils, with their violins and anxious faces.

'How have you been getting on? Well done – that's so much better.'

Nothing wrong with teaching: an honourable life. Passing music from generation to generation: what more should a musician want?

But he thought: I came back for a reason. Now that reason is gone.

Steven and Margot walked the long track up the moor, leaving her car at the foot, and the dog went bounding before them. Once more it had rained, a couple of days ago, and the cropped tough grass, even as summer began to end, had a bit of a gleam about it. The sheep were spread out everywhere.

'Here, boy, here!'

'I don't think he'd hurt them,' said Margot.

'But still—' As sheep began to scatter, Steven was conscious of the farmer, and his own trained sheep dog, and the laws of the countryside. 'Here!' He shouted again, and the dog came nosing back.

'Good boy.' Margot took him on the lead, and tugged him to her. She slipped her other hand in Steven's, aware of the momentousness of this occasion: her own nerves, and surely his, too. 'How far?'

'We're close.' And then, as the rise grew steep, and they rounded the bend, 'That's it.'

She looked, saw a square plain cottage with a blue door, the windows shining in the sun. There was a shed. There was a thorn tree. She knew there would be a memory everywhere, and she said nothing, just walked on beside him, the dog straining on the lead.

'Heel!'

As they drew nearer, getting thirsty now, she saw the little fenced-in plot of garden, grass overgrowing unweeded earth.

'I haven't had time—' said Steven, following her gaze.

'Of course you haven't.'

They had reached flat ground, and for a moment they stopped, and he turned her gently round. 'Look at that.'

Far away in the haze of heat she could see the distant town, the church tower. She tried to make out the Square, and the long stone buildings of the school. She turned round again, saw the great slope of the hillside to the farm below, looked up at the limitless sky.

'I'll show you inside,' said Steven, and they walked slowly over the grass towards the door. As he turned the handle she felt suddenly afraid. Should she really be here, in this private place?

'Stay,' she told the dog, unhooking the lead, and he flopped down by the water butt. She followed Steven inside, lowering her head, as he did, then straightening up in the little room.

Two windows, one at the front, one at the side, both hung with print curtains, both thick with dust. A stone sink, like the one in the kitchen at home; plates in a rack. A range, with things on the mantelpiece. A table, two chairs, a dresser, a bookcase. The clock on the wall had stopped. A staircase led to the single room above. She looked away from that. Everything was good and plain and well made.

'Did your father make all this?'

'Some of it.' He stood tall in the middle of the little room, his hair flopping down in the way it did, and he looked so vulnerable that she wanted to go over and kiss him. She held back, waiting. 'Some I made myself,' he said. 'I made the door.'

Margot turned round, saw the winter coat hanging on the

peg beside it, next to his. A pair of small shoes stood beneath, next to his walking boots.

'Oh, Steven.'

He gave a flickering little frown.

'I'm sorry. Is it – is it too much for you, being here?'

She shook her head. 'Is it too much for you?'

'I wanted you to come. I want you to see. I suppose it does feel a bit—'

He had wanted her to come, yet it felt almost as outlandish as the copy of *Homage to Catalonia* had done, with its fist smashing into the foreground, while buildings behind it crumbled to ruins. The book was still on the table: he saw her look away from him and see it there, with her letters, and the pile of textbooks.

Soon the term would begin again.

Outside the door the sheep were calling: not in the urgent way of lambing time, but enquiringly, as if something new were happening. Perhaps it was.

'Listen.'

They listened, they went outside, and the dog got up at once. A little light aircraft was buzzing over the moor. Then came another. Private planes? A few rich chaps enjoying themselves on a summer day? Perhaps. But they were flying low, and it felt like an omen.

'Steven? If there were to be a war, what would you do?'

'I don't know. I think teachers might be exempt. I think that's how it is.'

It was growing cooler, a light wind blowing now over the huge empty space all round them.

He closed the cottage door behind him. 'Let's go and walk a bit. Come on, boy.'

The sheep bolted into the bracken, just as they had when he and Margaret went walking. He took Margot's hand, and pointed things out to her: the river which raced far below on the other side of the hill, the plantation which had been there since the time of William IV. 'And there's a Roman fort,' he said. 'Quite a bit of it left. It's too far to go there now.'

Clouds were beginning to gather. The little light aircraft had flown into the distance.

'Shall we go home?' Steven asked.

Margot turned towards him, reached out to straighten that flop of hair, and kiss him. Nothing here, nothing in the way in which he had lived his life, could be more different than Hepplewick.

'Does it feel like home to you now?'

Behind them, the windows of the cottage, that haunted little place, were darkening in the drift of cloud. He glanced towards it, then back at her. If she had not loved him before, she loved him then, as his eyes filled with tears and he drew her towards him.

September, the first leaves in the Square just beginning to drop in the cooler air. In Nuremberg, the Rally of the Greater Germany had begun. The photographs in *The Times* and *Morning Post* showed crowds of unimaginable size. Armed troops awaited the order to march into Czechoslovakia.

'Sir? Sir, if that happens, will we go to war?'

'It's possible. Let's hope not. Get out your books.'

'Sir? Is Mr Embleton coming back?'

'I hope so. Now, then—'

'Sir, are you Head of Department now?'

'Until Mr Embleton comes back, yes.'

'Have you heard from him, sir?'

'Not yet. Turn to Chapter One.'

Chamberlain flew out to Bad Godesberg, on the Rhine. The younger boys sniggered.

'There's nothing funny about it.' Straughan stood on the stage in his gown like a glowering old eagle. 'Bow your heads. Let us pray.'

Suddenly: sandbags in the Square. Outside the Museum, and heaped up in two corners.

'Any boy found playing about on those bags will be sent to my study and asked to account for himself.' The cane ran through smoke-stained fingers.

Then: 'Sir, we got a leaflet yesterday. Me Dad's digging a shelter in the garden.'

'So's mine.'

Everyone had had a leaflet. Everyone was suddenly after corrugated iron.

And then the gas masks came. In every classroom, throughout the lunch hour, came the struggle to fit the things on, the coughing and heaving at the rubbery smell, the helpless laughter as the trunks were waved about; the trumpeting.

'Look at you, Hindmarsh!'

'Look at yourself, Potts. You look prehistoric.'

'All right, boys, that's enough.'

No one was laughing in the staffroom, as the news got worse. But at the end of September Straughan lifted his hand at Assembly and a hush fell over the hall.

'Boys. You will have heard, I hope, that Mr Chamberlain has returned from Munich with tremendous news. An Agreement has been signed between this country and Germany which guarantees peace for our time.' He paused, to let it sink in. Then he told them all that the great hymn 'Now Thank We

All Our God' had just been sung in Westminster Abbey, that they would all sing it now, that he hoped it would be sung in every school in the country. He looked out over them all, an old eagle surveying his young. Then he glanced towards the piano. 'Miss Aickman?'

She gave her little nod; with the usual clatter and scrape of chairs the boys all got to their feet, as she struck the first chord. And they were off: a mighty tune, and they gave it their all.

'Now thank we all our God
With hearts and hands and voices,
Who wondrous things hath done,
In whom this world rejoices . . .'

October, and Steven left school late: a meeting with Easton, the temporary teacher Straughan had appointed to take Frank's classes. Even now, boys glanced up and down the street when they came out of the gates, as they used to do: waiting for the toot on the horn, the sight of the shining red Imp.

'Hop in!'

Would it ever be standing there again?

Steven turned left into the Square for the bus to Morpeth. And then he saw something which made him stop: a grey-haired couple making their way to the tea shop on the far side. The woman was tall and handsome; the man had a stick, and his gait was stiff, as always, but there was nothing stiff about the way they were talking to one another, walking slowly, arm in arm beneath the yellowing trees.

BOOK TWO

BOOK TWO

I

WINTER WAS CLOSING in. Puffs of wood smoke rose from the houseboat chimneys along the canal, and quite a few curtains were drawn. Sunday: sleeping in. A young man in need of a shave was out on deck in a holey old jumper and scarf, a scruff of a little dog at his side. Geoffrey nodded to him as he walked along the towpath.

'All right?' asked the unshaven one.

All the young greeted you with that, whether they knew you or not; the first time he'd heard it he thought the boy in the hardware shop had actually wanted to know. After a while he realised it was a form of 'Hi,' or 'Can I help you?' or almost anything, really. If he said, 'Yes, fine, thanks,' which wasn't true, they just looked blank.

There were one or two runners up ahead, their breath streaming out on the air; cyclists wove alongside. Mostly, it was just him and the ducks, trailing a V in the icy water.

Cold cloudy weather, but he couldn't stay in the house.

Up ahead, gulls wheeled over the tower blocks, swooped down towards the park off the New North Road. Here, in the gardens running down the sloping embankment, pigeons sat motionless in bare trees. The gardens were beautifully kept: everything pruned and cut back for the winter, leaves swept up; here and there a bonfire smoking in a corner, well away from the house. He liked all that: stuff done properly, things in order. When you felt like death you needed that.

Though a bit of family muddle would be good.

He glanced up through one of the leafless gardens, saw

lights behind French windows, people moving about. Sunday in Islington: coffee grinder whizzing away, organic bread in the toaster, unsalted butter. *The Archers*, or Radio 3. The papers, the dressing gowns. People coming for lunch, but plenty of time. Or the children coming for supper, hours yet, and a casserole ready to go in the oven at six.

There was that kind of Sunday, which had once been his, and there was Sunday Bloody Sunday, which was now, with the memory of Glenda Jackson shoving a cup of Nescaff under the hot tap, knocking it back with a shudder. Why had that moment so stuck in his mind?

The next house had a Christmas tree up, pale lights shining through the grey. Most people round here had the tree in the window at the front, so passersby in the street could see it: bit of a competition for height and general glory. The select few didn't have a tree at all until Christmas week, though on the estates round Packington Street they went up in November, with Santa clambering up the balcony and Babycham reindeer prancing at the windows. The sight of this tree now was difficult: it made him feel better, and it made him feel worse.

'Excuse me.' A cyclist swished past on wheels as slender and light as a dancer, and Geoffrey stepped back, moved closer to the garden wall, with its good wooden gate in the middle. He had an eye for good things: gates, kitchen tables, antiques. You could spend a fortune in Camden Passage once, before most of the dealers gave way to boutiques and restaurants, and on one or two pieces he had done, when he'd started to make proper money: a round Georgian table to go in the drawing room window, a lovely old desk lamp with opaque fluted glass.

But the desk he had now had come from home, like the mahogany dining table, and the fender, one of three: everything divided up between him and Evie on a couple of long wet autumn days. She had the piano; he took the grandfather clock.

She had the sub-Gainsborough painting of the couple in the misty landscape, he had the hunter. It all had to go: the rugs, the teaspoons.

'Oh, Geoffrey.'

'I know.'

That was in 1983, the parents gone, and no way they could do anything but let the Hall go too. The little mine at Morpeth, which had kept the place going for so long, had been part of nationalisation after the war. No income from there for decades, and how his father's salary and his mother's old investments had kept the place going it was hard to understand. They'd all lived frugally, that was all he knew. Now it was over. And now the children were settled at school, and his firm doing well. There was no question of coming back.

Still – it was even more painful than he'd imagined.

'You are quite certain, Evie?'

There were tears in her eyes as she nodded. She and Mike had the farm, and the boys; she had her teaching. She'd stayed up here, while he went down to London – 'Northumberland is in my blood, I could never live anywhere else,' – but a long way from Hepplewick: a hill farm on the far side of the Cheviots, overlooking a tributary of the North Tyne. She wasn't going to give it all up – Mike wouldn't give it all up – to come back to the Hall.

'Oh, Geoffrey,' she said again, standing in the cold, half-empty drawing room, the rugs rolled up, boxes everywhere. The rain poured wildly on to the garden, and the windows shook. The huge great branches of the cedar darkened them, as always, and their childhood swing moved back and forth in the wind.

'*Careful, Geoffrey, careful! Not too high.*'

'*But I want him to push me, Mummy! I like going really high.*'

'What's going to happen to that?' he said, flooded with memories as he had never been while the parents were still

261

alive, the place filled with talk and music, the children racing about. They'd loved coming here.

Evie was walking over to the piano, her shoes echoing on the bare floorboards. 'It'll stay, won't it? I think it helped sell the house – they've got children themselves.'

He didn't like to think of them, the new owners. You could give yourself to a place as much as a person: he saw that, now he was about to lose it.

The sound of the piano began to weave in and out of the pattering rain, something thoughtful and slow which he couldn't think he'd heard before, and he stood listening, looking out over the terrace and the endless stretch of lawn to the ha-ha and the fields beyond. The cattle were sheltering beneath the lane-side trees: another marker of his childhood, and his children's childhood, up here with Becky in the long summer holidays, thinking it was great, all this space. Perhaps, if they came in their teens, the countryside would be just boring.

The gentle piano piece was changing: sprightly now, tuneful and innocent. He turned to watch Evie, who looked so like their mother, and their grandmother, that photograph now packed away with all the others. Three generations had played that piano, and thank God she wasn't selling it.

'Of *course* I wouldn't sell it.'

Bygate Farm was high up a track, sometimes impassable in winter. It led from the village of Craikhaugh, off the A68, up to that great grey stone place which looked, like the sheep on the hillside, as if had been there for ever, and could weather anything. Exposed as it was, the light poured into the big draughty rooms at the front. He tried to imagine the grand in one of them, thought it would look rather fine. Evie could get rid of the old upright, and perhaps having a grand would get Will going properly – he was the musical one.

The piece came slowly to an end. Evie leaned back on the piano stool, and gave a sigh.

'What was that?'

'Elgar.'

'Good God.'

'I found it in a heap of old scores in the library. '

'Lovely thing. What's it called?'

'*Dream Children.*'

He'd never heard of it.

'I think a lot of the stuff in that cupboard must have been Granny's. I don't remember Mummy ever playing it, do you?'

He shook his head, suddenly exhausted. All these boxes, and more to be done, and already it was growing dark. Out in the hall the clock was beginning to strike. Something else he couldn't have borne to sell.

'Let's leave the rest of this to Pickfords. Let's have tea.'

They walked down the long cold passage to the kitchen, passing the row of bells with their worn old lettering. Library. Drawing Room. Master Bedroom. As he'd done when he was little, standing on a chair, he reached up and gave them a ping.

They'd never been back since the sale. Why would they? Too much going on: family life; work. He'd been made a partner in 1973, soon after Nina was born, and in 1973 Islington was full of run-down houses needing people like Becky and him to do them up. They sold the top-floor flat in Barnsbury - a pretty scruffy place in those days - and moved to a street behind the Angel and Camden Passage.

Early nineteenth-century terraced artisan houses, built, they realised after moving in, in the wrong relation to the sun: the street ran north-south, so for much of the day you had to have the lights on, never had a proper sense of the day beginning and ending. But never mind: he could walk to work and they'd been happy there. It was great to have room to swing more than a cat in the kitchen and bathroom, Charlie and baby Nina with their own bedrooms, and a street filling up nicely with young families.

A cheerful primary school a couple of streets away: both the children had gone there. Hadn't learned a huge amount, but came home in a good mood. And then Charlie, who'd always had a sweet voice, got a place as a chorister at St Paul's Cathedral School. Terrific – but he'd have to board. Becky was doubtful.

'*Board?* It's practically down the road.'

'It's only until he's thirteen. And we'd see him at weekends.'

'Only between rehearsals.'

'And after Evensong.'

'I don't know, Geoffrey. He's so young.'

'So are all the other boys. He could have a great time.'

And he had. Anxious at first, and then loving it. And they'd loved going to hear him, Christmas suddenly really special, and Choral Evensong on Sundays – well, you might not believe, and they didn't, but music was at the heart of the family again, as it had been for him and Evie. Everyone missed it, when Charlie left, as everyone had to, and went to City.

But then they could leave the house together in the mornings, swinging bag and briefcase up to the Number 4 bus stop at the Angel, where other City boys were gathering. Quite a few had been at St Paul's.

'Bye, Charlie. Have a good day.'

'Bye, Dad.' The 4 had pulled up, he was moving up the queue: taller than any of his friends, and sometimes so like his grandfather – that flop of hair, that hesitant smile – that it stopped you in your tracks. Geoffrey turned away, off to the office two blocks from here, his name on the brass plaque on the door. Smith, Moore & Coulter: Solicitors.

The plaque was still there, though he wasn't.

'The law, Geoffrey? That's a new one for us.'

His father had thought he might follow him into teaching, his mother had concentrated on Evie and her music, but it was Andrew Ridley who'd fired him up for the law – not even a relative, just someone from the past whom his father had kept in touch with. Old brother-in-law, in fact.

There was a photograph of his father's first wife in the library. She'd been a teacher, too, before their marriage, and died very young. That was all he and Evie had been told, really: that they'd lived halfway across the county in a moorland cottage, and she'd died of TB in a snowstorm.

'You mean, you were married before you married Mummy?' Evie had looked incredulous, and then upset – Geoffrey could remember that, and even at nine or ten he'd felt that they were being told out of some kind of duty, that this was a piece of history they should know: it wasn't something his father really wanted to talk about, nor his mother to hear. And he and Evie hadn't wanted to hear it, either, when they were young: it just felt so strange, and anyway, when you were young the past really was another country.

When you were old it mattered hugely.

They'd sold the Hall. They'd sold it. He'd said goodbye to Evie after breakfast, rain dripping from the trees, the Pickfords men heaving stuff out through the porch. It was half-term: she'd stay to see it all done, take the keys to the agent in Morpeth. But he had a case on: he had to get back.

In the car, driving away down the lane towards the village, passing the cattle moving slowly over the soaking fields, passing the little church where the parents were buried, he felt numb for a bit. Then he'd turned on Radio 3. Brahms. He was suddenly sobbing his heart out.

A fine eighteenth-century house, with gardens designed by Capability Brown. Stables and outbuildings. Tennis court . . .

The sale enabled him to move the family to a better Islington street, a better house, tall and roomy. It faced east-west and now the morning sun poured into the bedrooms overlooking the garden, and the afternoon sun into the drawing room – when there was any sun, of course. It was all much lighter, anyway, did them all good. In 1984 Nina got into Camden Girls, the best school for girls within striking distance, and now it was the three of them setting out in the mornings together, striding up to the Angel. And now Nina had her violin, as well as her school bag, to take on the bus, nipping over four lanes of traffic to catch it.

'Bye, Daddy.'

'Bye, darling. Mind how you cross.'

'Bye, Charlie.'

'Bye.' Tall and lanky, his voice quite broken now, he barely turned from greeting his mates to look at her. Little sisters: who needs them?

He himself had needed Evie, a lot. And Nina had missed Charlie when she was little, suddenly an only child in term-time.

Now she stood at the lights, not caring. Over she shot, and ran for the bus down to Highbury. Then it was the filthy little over-ground, crammed with commuters and other Camden girls.

Life in London – it was where they belonged, and where he'd belonged for a long time now, where his adult independent life had begun.

Walking back along the towpath, thinking about the past because he couldn't bear to think about the present, he saw himself in sixties Bloomsbury, sitting on the pillared portico steps of University College in shades, hair flopping over his collar. Someone was strumming a guitar, everyone was singing.

'The answer is blowin' in the wind . . .'

The end of term. A hot summer breeze was stirring the trees in the quad; girls in long cheesecloth skirts and kaftans were spread out over the grass. One of them was Becky, making a daisy chain on the lawn outside the Slade, fastening the last link and setting it like a halo on her long dark hair. The sweet smell of weed drifted into the air, though if the pigs had shown up there wouldn't have been a joint in sight.

'The times they are a changin' . . .'

They were, they were. Behind his shades, beneath the long floppy hair, Geoffrey still felt a bit of a square, really, though not as much as when he'd first arrived, three years ago. London had been overwhelming then, and his grandfather's name felt like a weight round his neck, though he'd loved his grandfather, loved making things in his workshop.

'Well done, lad.'

But Geoffrey Coulter: it sounded so middle-aged.

'Geoff,' he told girls at the student disco.

'Like Jefferson Airplane.'

'No, Geoff with a G.'

It felt so square.

Now he had a bit more confidence, was hoping for a 2:1 in the History finals, and then a year of Law. The history had pleased his father, and he'd enjoyed it, but the law was for himself. Andrew Ridley had got him going, down from Edinburgh for a visit to his ageing parents in Cawbeck, then driving over to the Hall, the first time for ages.

'It's a good profession, the law,' he said, as they walked round the garden after lunch. It was the Easter holidays, Geoffrey in his last year at school, talking politely to his father's old friend

- old brother-in-law. That still felt so strange. 'You can change people's lives,' said Andrew.

Wind rippled the grass; daffodils blew in the ha-ha. In the bright spring sky the clouds were racing. Geoffrey had never really thought of the future like that, but in that conversation something in him came to life, something he hadn't really known he had.

Andrew Ridley was a bit of a radical - it wasn't really a word they used then, but Geoffrey began to use it in the sixties, and against all the odds it was the sixties that made him a serious person. Looking back on it, he did realise that a lot of it came from his father, and the school in Kirkhoughton: you could change children's lives through teaching.

But he'd joined Smith & Moore, though not to do conveyancing. As well as all that, as well as matrimonial and criminal, they had an immigration department, their clients on legal aid. When he wasn't working there, he was in the Law Centre on Upper Street, dishing out advice for nothing to some pretty desperate people.

All unimaginable now, of course. Legal Aid? You'd be lucky. Law Centres?

God, it was cold. He was back at the foot of the towpath steps, stood aside for a young mother bumping down a buggy. For a moment he had a flash of Becky, pushing Charlie along Barnsbury Street, hauling the pushchair, as they called it then, up the grotty stairs to their grotty little flat.

'All right?' he asked this young woman, and he really did want to know, reaching out to help her down on to the muddy path.

'Yes, thanks.' She gave him a smile, and was off. He could hear her pointing out the ducks. As he climbed the steps himself, and a swirl of sleet came suddenly out of nowhere, he had a flash again of Becky putting daisies in her hair as she sat on the summer grass, looking up as he came down the portico steps, giving him a smile as he took off his Dylan shades and approached, about to ask her out for the first time. At last he'd found the courage.

It all made him want to weep.

2

I F THERE WAS something worse than entering a silent empty house on a Sunday, Geoffrey didn't know of it. And he wouldn't do it. He left the radio on all the time: it murmured goodbye when he left, greeted him as soon as he unlocked the front door and slammed it and the rain behind him. Sunday morning: Radio 3, *Private Passions*; Radio 4, *Just a Minute*. Today he'd left it on Radio 3, and as he hung up his coat Michael Berkeley was talking with his guest about The Sixteen, whom he'd heard with Becky when the new concert halls had opened at King's Place.

That was a good place to spend a Sunday: now and then they'd taken the papers, had soup and a sandwich while everyone milled about, going to a lunchtime recital or wandering through the gallery. On her birthday in the spring he'd treated her to lunch in the restaurant overlooking the canal, children and grandchildren coming to join them.

'Happy birth-day, dear Gran-ny . . .'

'Thank you, my darlings.'

She blew out the candles in two great puffs, and no one would ever have imagined what was lying in wait.

The heavenly voices sounded as he went into the kitchen.

'*Laudem dicite Deo nostro omnes sancti eius, et qui timetis Deum . . .*'

Today he couldn't bear it, retuned to *Just a Minute*. There had to be something wrong with you if you didn't laugh at Julian Clary, and he did laugh, as Becky had done, both of them helpless sometimes. Sleet spattered the windows. He dug about in the fridge.

Last Sunday he'd been to lunch with Nina and David and the boys in Camberwell; the week before to Charlie, Jo and Robyn in Herne Hill. South of the river: a different world, but they were settled there now.

You couldn't land on your children every Sunday.

'We love having you, Dad.'

'I know, but—'

But they had such busy lives, Sundays their only respite, and he had to face it, being alone. Hideous. But had to.

Out in the hall the clock began to strike. *Dah-dah-dah-dah!* Even now he sometimes heard his mother singing that out to him and Evie when they were small. She'd sung it to his own children, too, on those holiday visits, and Charlie's pure high echo had made her stop in her tracks. 'He could do something with that voice.' It was his father who'd suggested a scholarship.

'We had a boy at the school before the war – Alfie Stote. Sang solos. Funny little fellow, but what a voice.'

Here came the pips, the headlines, *The World This Weekend.* The world now was another kind of hideous.

He and Evie had been wartime children, too young and too shielded from everything, deep in Hepplewick, to know what was going on. The air-raids on Newcastle, Churchill's sudden surprise visit in '41, the Fusiliers seeing action at Monte Casino and Dunkirk, the Victory Parade in '45 – all this they were told about afterwards.

He'd been five when it ended, had just a handful of memories. His mother and Mrs Barrow standing on chairs, putting up the blackout at those great high windows: did he really remember that, or had he been told about it?

He did remember finding a bit of spent shell on the village

green, a different kettle of fish altogether from the cartridges you found in the fields now and then from the local shoot.

And he remembered his father coming home from school one day and shutting himself into the library, and his mother going in there and closing the door behind her, but it wasn't until much later that he found out why that had been such a dark day.

As he and Evie grew up, they began to learn properly about the war, from their parents and at school. Sometimes now, listening to the headlines, he thought that little they had ever heard or read about compared with today's barbarities.

He put on a carton of soup, got the bread out, went to the lav in the hall. The clock struck the quarter hour as he returned, and he stood for a moment looking up at its comforting, lovely old face. Charlie and Nina had loved it, too: not just the deep slow chime but the rosy pink smile of the sun, the sleepy, dusky moon – their rise and descent, and then the weekly winding.

Tick-tock, tick-tock. His residue life stretched ahead: somehow he'd have to get through. He gave the case a pat and went back to the kitchen, turned off the soup, retuned from Syria to the lunchtime concert.

The Wigmore Hall, a piano trio. Ah.

And as he sat down with his lunch, and the kitchen filled with Haydn, he was once again back in that great airy drawing room, bunched up on the sofa with Nina, listening to the three of them rehearsing, day after day: their mother at the piano, Diana Embleton bent over her cello, George Liddell lifting the violin aloft. Now and then they'd given a wartime concert at the church, raising funds for the Red Cross, who were camped out in the village hall. And after the war the house had been filled with music once again.

Now the players were long gone, and their music with them: not a single recording ever made. Listening to a trio on the radio, or down at the Wigmore, somewhere else he and Becky had liked to go on a Sunday morning, was the only way he had to reconnect with it all. He drank his soup, nodding in time to the concert; he lifted his hand from the soup bowl, conducting as he'd seen George Liddell do, just walking about the garden. That had been a good thing to see.

Rain and applause melted into one another as the Haydn came to an end.

He took the paper through to the drawing room, put a match to the fire.

Half a degree up, as Becky used to say in her hospital bed. A little bit better today.

Geoffrey fell asleep over the paper, woke as it was growing dark. The empty day was almost over: thank God for that. He made up the fire, drew the curtains, went back to the kitchen for tea things. As he stood waiting for the kettle to boil he asked himself again how Becky would have managed, if he'd been the one to go first. He thought she'd have had friends round all the time, have probably gone to concerts and things with them, not maundered away on her own. But then she was a woman, and women were better at organising. Look at Evie: Mike gone, the farm sold, she moving into the pretty little house in Otterburn. Children and grandchildren nearby, of course, but she didn't spend all her time with them, she was out and about, and still teaching a bit, still playing.

He made tea, toasted a crumpet, took it all back by the fire. Becky might have been lonely as hell, as he was. He hated to think of that. Of course, he could see more people than he did: a man on his own was always wanted, and he wasn't short of invitations. One or two women seemed to be making some kind of move towards him: Rachel someone. Earrings and floaty scarves. Rachel Yates. Background in theatre?

Everyone's background was a bit hazy these days, most people retired for well over a decade. But none of them was sitting about: everyone was in some kind of book group, or Amnesty group, or choir, doing voluntary stuff, keeping up with things. Good company, most of his friends, as he hoped he was, when he made the effort. And everyone being so kind, of course, these days. Come for drinks, come for supper.

Liz Peake. Kind round face, good haircut. She and Rachel had been at one or two dinner parties, both of them interesting and bright. Was one of them widowed? Liz had been at a party a couple of weeks ago, the first of the season. Sweet smile. At first he hadn't noticed her tentative approaches. Then he had.

'I don't know why you're so surprised,' said Nina.

'I'm getting on for eighty.'

'So?'

He shook his head, unable to believe it, really. Anyway, it was much too soon.

And after those dinner parties or little drinks dos you still had to come back to an empty house, pretending that the voice on the radio was waiting just for you. Sometimes that felt so awful – he'd called out 'Becky?' once, without thinking – it hardly felt worth going out to things in the first place.

And now there was Christmas, both children inviting him, and half of him wanted to be with them, and the other dreaded it. Just the thought of it all, without her.

'Oh, bloody hell.'

The phone was ringing. That would be Nina: she never missed. He must sound cheerful. And he got up from the wing chair – another thing from the Hall, an old friend reupholstered – and went across to his desk. The fluted glass lamp still pleased him as he switched it on.

'Hello, darling.'

'Geoff,' said a voice.

'Evie!' Ridiculous, how glad he was to hear her.

'Just thought I'd give you a ring. Sunday, and all that. How are you?'

'I'm fine,' he said, 'Fine. Well, you know. All the better for hearing you, Evie. How's things?'

As he listened to talk of the weather, the grandchildren, her piano lessons, he could feel himself thawing out. She had the radio on, too, he realised, and tuned to Radio 3: he could hear in the background, as well as from his own kitchen, some marvellous choir.

'It's so good of you to ring.'

'I was wondering,' she said, in the clear light voice which still reminded him of their mother's, 'I was wondering about Christmas. Of course it's such a long way up here, and I expect you're seeing Charlie and Nina, but - what are your plans?'

Did he imagine it, or was she making an effort to sound so light and bright?

'My plans,' he said slowly.

'I mean - if you did feel like coming all this way - it'd be just the two of us. We'd see the family, of course, but - well, I just wondered—'

Out in the hall the clock was beginning to chime. Five o'clock on a winter's evening. Snug as anything, or bleak as hell.

'Evie,' he said, feeling his blood begin to move again. 'I'd love to.'

3

H E'D DRIVE: HE loved driving. Heater on, radio on, flask of coffee and a sandwich: your own little world. And somehow not as lonely as the empty house. Views and vistas. It would save Evie from coming all the way over to Newcastle to meet the train. And he liked the idea of ringing her doorbell, seeing her face light up.

'It's an awfully long way,' said Nina.

'You're sure about it, Dad?' asked Charlie.

'We used to do it all the time when you were little.'

'I know, but—'

Neither of them spelled it out: that he was getting on and perhaps not the driver he was; that they didn't like the idea of him trying to do it all in one hop, as the winter nights drew in.

'Thought I'd stay in a B&B,' he said. 'Break it up a bit. Thought I'd take a look at the Hall, after all this time.'

'Is that a good idea?'

Charlie could be a bit of doom-merchant when he felt like it.

'Hope you don't talk to your patients like that. You should be cheering me on.'

'Sorry, Dad. It's just - well, you know.'

He knew. Going back wasn't always a great idea. And he was vulnerable: no question about it. If he saw something he didn't like, if it upset him - not much fun on your own. Even so, he couldn't help a little thrill of excitement at the thought of seeing it all again. He said so.

'I wouldn't mind seeing it again myself,' said Charlie, getting

276

up from Sunday lunch to give Jo a hand with the dishwasher. 'I loved it there.'

Well, that was good to hear.

He might stop in Gateshead and have a look at the Sage, some-where he'd never been. It had made a big splash in the papers when it opened in 2004: swanky Norman Foster, concert halls housed in a great glassy animal, crouching in three dramatic humps beside the Tyne. Seemed silly, to go all that way and not take it in.

There again, he might not. He could press on to a B&B near Hepplewick, if he left early enough. Somewhere in Morpeth, perhaps: lovely place, the county town, with a castle, a court house, good churches, a medieval bridge – and not without family history. The deeds of the Hall had been lodged in a bank there, with the plans by Capability Brown – the solicitor had had to send for it all when they'd sold. And the mine which had kept the Heslops going for generations had been not so far away. He could have a look round, he could please himself.

He sat at his desk doing Christmas cards, the fire at his back. When he got to the Ps he came upon Liz Peake's card, given to him after the drinks party and tucked rather absent-mindedly into his address book. That was quite forward of her, now he thought about it. He reached for a Raphael angel.

Spending Christmas with my sister in the frozen north. Perhaps we might meet up when I get back.

Was that a good idea? Well, he'd done it now, wasn't going to waste a Raphael. And she did have a very sweet smile. He signed it and sealed it, moved past the empty page of Q<u>s</u>. Now then, R. Andrew and Rose Ridley, up in Edinburgh, long ago crossed out. Andrew had gone first, not so long after his father; Rose had hung on, as widows do. As he was doing now. He ran his finger down the page.

Robson, John, old friend from Law School. Hadn't seen him for years, but they always sent Christmas cards. He took a snowy Monet off the pile and wrote the annual message.

Hope all is well with you and Philippa and to see you in the New Year. They'd been saying that since about 1990. But now, as with so many of them, he had to add: *Very sad to say that I lost my darling Becky in the summer . . .*

He stopped, took another sip of his drink. Exhausting, to have to keep saying it, and to people who meant little to him now, except that they had always been there, and at Christmas that somehow did mean something. He looked at the piles of cards, done and yet to be done. The desk was capacious, had room for lots of stuff on the worn old leather top: the computer, the fluted lamp, the telephone. In here he still had the old-fashioned kind with a receiver, probably fetch a bit in a vintage shop. Classic black: he liked that. Then there was the letter rack, the paperknife from Nina, the little Indian box from her boys where he kept his stamps.

'Just what I needed: thank you!'

At one time, of course, the desk had been in the library at the Hall, heaped up with ledgers, employment records, records of coal production, minutes of meetings, everything relating to the mine outside Morpeth over which his grandfather had presided until his death before the war. It had gone on being useful in wartime, was nationalised in '47, had finally bitten the dust – as it were – in 1985. That had been under Thatcher. He still had a mug in the kitchen somewhere, bought in support of the miners' strike.

And all those documents: his mother had boxed them up, put them up in the attic. It was only when he and Evie were packing for the sale that they'd found them, dusted them off and gone through a few, looking at copperplate managers' hands, and the hand of his grandfather, distinctive and firm, initialling accounts, and minutes, signing endless letters.

Thomas Heslop, Director, 1913 . . . Thomas Heslop, Director, 1925 . . . Thomas Heslop, Director, 1936 . . .

The last was dated July 1938: he had died, very suddenly, two weeks later.

'Where's grandpa's grave?'

That was Evie, walking through the churchyard after the Sunday service one summer morning. In boring sermons they'd grown so used to gazing up at all the Heslop plaques.

Evelyn Heslop, 1884-1916

That was their grandmother, whose photograph they knew from the drawing room at home, who'd played the piano to their mother when she was a little girl. She still sang a favourite song to them sometimes, at bedtime.

'The day is coming to a close, the night is drawing nigh . . .'

'She was my namesake,' said Evie, with a touch of pride.

And his own middle name was Thomas, after his grandfather – a name which had far less of a period feel than Geoffrey. At university he'd sometimes thought of calling himself Tom.

But out at last in the fresh air again, looking up at the great old family tombs, one with two stone angels silhouetted against the sky:

'Where's grandpa's grave?'

A silence. Then: 'He was buried outside the churchyard.'

'Why?'

Silence. You remembered silences more than words, when you were little, just because they were unusual. The day his father had come home from school in the war, and shut himself into the library. This summer day, cow parsley lacing the shady borders of the churchyard, butterflies dancing over the lichened gravestones. At last:

'It was what he wanted.'

'Why?'

Birds sang away in the yew, car doors slammed in the lane.

'That's enough now, Evie. I'll tell you when you're grown up.'

'That's ages away.'

When they were finally told, about the accident in the pele tower, a gun going off without warning, he couldn't really understand why that had been held back for so long.

Behind him, the fire was dying down. He got up, put on more smokeless coal,

'What are we going to do with all this?' Evie had asked, blowing the dust off another ledger, with its marbled endpapers and fading ink.

He shook his head. 'Must be a company archive somewhere.'

Still hadn't found the time to find it, and the boxes were still up in his own loft. He'd hardly given them a thought for years: poor show, Coulter.

Time for another drink. Try and finish the cards before supper. On and on they went.

Out and about, doing Christmas shopping, trees for sale on every corner and fairy lights in the windows, he had good days and bad days. The good ones were when he found just the right thing: in a good children's shop on Upper Street a beautiful doll for Robyn, with three sets of clothes: pyjamas, slippers and dressing gown; jeans and T-shirt; a party frock.

'Nothing pink,' Jo had instructed him. 'Nothing plastic. We don't do Barbie crap.' Jo could be formidable, but she was right, of course. He hated five year-olds done up to look like teenage tarts. Robyn, born when Jo was thirty-nine, was seven now, still into dolls. Just. And football, apparently, but he didn't feel like getting her football gear.

The party frock was a very *pale* pink, and so pretty: he bought the doll and the outfits, crossing his fingers, and went to have lunch in the Camden Head. A tree in the corner, piping hot shepherd's pie and a pint, the remains of the Sunday paper.

Becky had been a brilliant shopper: though they both loved choosing books, in truth he'd left a lot of Christmas and birthdays to her. Now, with a hot lunch inside him, walking along Camden Passage afterwards with the nice posh tote bag, he felt quite proud of himself.

Waterstone's on the Green was a different matter. He'd thought books for the boys, but Nina said they just didn't read.

'They must read *something*.'

'Not much. We do try, but once bedtime story went out of the window—'

It was all computer games, video games, Playstation. X-box.

'What's X-box?'

He didn't really understand the answer, didn't really care. He knew he sounded curmudgeonly and old. On days like this, gazing round neon-lit acres of shouty kids books, he felt it.

'To be honest, Dad, you'd be better doing it all on-line.'

He gave in. 'Give me a list.'

At home, he gazed at games on Amazon. What would Becky have thought of all this? She'd probably have been kinder, more lenient. Played with them, even – he could remember her on the sofa last Christmas, Ben and Ollie on either side, showing her stuff on the screen. Their fingers flew. Both now needed glasses.

'Just do it,' he told himself, and did it, ordering two games of Minecraft, which Nina had said they liked best. Then, in need of something he actually knew about, he went to the books pages.

Naomi Klein: that would do Jo. Raymond Tallis for Charlie, who could be a doom-merchant - like Jo, in a different way - but was still a bloody good doctor. He thought about things, and Tallis was a bloody good thinker. He'd do Nina and David tomorrow; tomorrow he'd think about wine. And wrapping. Something else Becky had been so good at.

And Evie, he thought, getting up from the desk and going to the drinks cupboard. Must get her something special.

What he really wanted, of course, was to buy everyone music. Well, there was still time. He turned on the news, poured a whisky.

And now his own Christmas cards were pouring on to the mat: he didn't think he'd ever seen so many. Of course, it was the first on his own – everyone was being extra kind.

Thinking of you so much . . . Extra special wishes, dear Geoffrey . . . We must meet up in the New Year . . . Thinking of you so much . . .

He put them all up round the drawing room, slipping the Happy Christmas side into books, with the pictures of robins, sheep in snowy fields, Nativities and peaceful doves sticking out: another trick of Becky's, so they didn't all blow over every time someone opened a door, and you could get lots more up for your money. As it were. He stood back and looked at them: lovely. All he wanted now was for Becky to come in and say: 'Beautiful, darling. Now when are we getting the tree?'

Standing there in the middle of the room he blew his nose hard. Sobbing in an empty house: he'd done enough of that. No holly, no tree in the hall, no Becky: that's just how it was.

And though there were invitations in several of the cards – *Christmas drinks. Mulled wine & mince pies. Just having a few people round* – it was the thought of going home which was keeping him going now. Yes, he'd go and raise a glass; yes, he'd take all the presents over to Nina and David's, where everyone was gathering for a pre-Christmas lunch on the 20th. The Wine Society case had arrived: that was always cheering. He'd go on to auto-pilot, tuck Becky into the darkest, closest and most secret pocket in his heart, do his best to enjoy it all. And if he was hurting his children and grandchildren by choosing not to be with them – *Gosh, Dad, it's our first Christmas without Mum, too, are you really sure?* then he was sorry. He'd make up for it next year, have everyone here, give them all a good time, like the old days. He blew his nose again.

But what he wanted now was to go back to his roots: to visit his parents' double grave in the little churchyard at Hepplewick, to stand at the gates of the Hall and remember everything he'd loved: racing with Evie down to the ha-ha; walking hand in hand with his mother through the kitchen garden, choosing things for supper. God, that garden had served them well, when the family must have had hardly three farthings to rub together. Swinging high beneath the cedar, smelling that resinous scent in summer; sitting with his father in the library, watching him reading, and marking, looking up with that heart-stopping smile. Hearing music, and music, and music, pouring out of the windows in summer, filling the whole house in winter, sinking into his soul.

He had to go back. And then he'd drive over to Evie, who'd fitted the grand into that little house in Otterburn, overlooking the garden whose birds she fed all through the winter, as he did in London, as Becky had always done. He'd listen to Evie play.

Lunchtime. From the kitchen he could hear the calm tones of Penny Gore, announcing a concert from St John's Smith Square. In one of those moments which really could only come in a novel, where the thoughts of the character are suddenly echoed in life, he heard that a piano trio was about to play. And as the tuning up began, as he walked through, thinking of his mother, so utterly, magically intent at the piano, of Diana Embleton sweeping her bow with such force across the cello, of George Liddell lost in rapture, he realised, hearing the first notes, that what was being performed now was something he had never heard them play, but which his father had once told him and Evie had been the greatest performance they had ever given, after their grandfather's death: Beethoven's *Ghost*.

He knew it, he knew it from listening to recordings many times, he loved it, and Becky had loved it too. How could you not? And standing in the kitchen now, winter sun at the window, blue tits swinging away on the coconut outside, he heard that sublime second movement begin, and then he did weep with longing.

4

H E WAS OFF. He was packed, the car loaded, the
Thermos filled, a box of sandwiches and a heap of CDs
beside him. And the mohair rug: you never knew. At eight in
the morning, he was off and away.

Very cold, air misty, the street just getting its act together, a
tree in every window now. Elegant doors swung open and shut.
In came the milk – fantastic, in this day and age, to have your
own milkman, as he did, tucking a card and a socking great tip
every Christmas between the empties. Out came the suits, with
their briefcases and their smart phones. He patted his pocket,
made sure he'd got his own old thing.

'Please, Dad, just in case.'

The suits were walking briskly up towards the Tube in shiny
black shoes and three-inch heels. 'We're talking two point five,'
they told the air. Banking. The City. That was Islington now,
and who else could afford to live here?

In Camden Passage last Saturday he'd slipped a
twenty-pound note to the other side of Islington, a sad-look-
ing man he thought probably Kurdish, sitting on the freezing
ground with stuff spread out on a square of blanket. A cheap
alarm clock, coloured glasses, trinkets. Nothing he wanted, but
he hated to see such need.

Right: off we go. And he eased the car out of the street, and
up towards the roaring Angel. Right at the traffic lights, and
head down towards the Holloway Road for Highgate and the
AI. As the news ended, and John Humphries told him it was
ten past eight, he settled down into it all: a long drive ahead full

of news and music, the prospect of the B&B he'd booked for tonight in Morpeth, a nice-looking place on the river.

St Albans, Northampton, Leicester. You bypassed them all on the A1, the M1, lorries thundering up the slow lane, the sky clearing to a pale winter blue. Service stations, sheep: with the sight of the first sheep his spirits began to rise. He thought of hills, and hill farms, of Mike and Evie's old farm, which Charlie and Nina had loved, feeding the lambs when they were little, hurling a ball for the sheepdog: nought to sixty in ten seconds.

He passed plough land and bare trees, kestrels hovering above the verges, Radio 3 his companion. *Essential Classics. Composer of the Week.* Haydn at Esterhazy – he practically knew it by heart, but it didn't matter, you could never have enough Haydn. And he raised his hand now and then, conducting.

It was all as he'd imagined it, except for the overtaking. He'd always been a fast, confident driver, but it was a long time since he'd gone the distance and now – you couldn't stay stuck behind lorries for ever, but he found he was nervous as he pulled out and overtook one, then, two, then three, each longer than the last. After the third, he pulled back again, got flashed for doing it too quickly, and found he was shaking. Couldn't have that. He raised a hand in apology, slowed down, took a few deep breaths.

What to do? You couldn't hog the middle lane, and he didn't feel up to the fast, though in the old days he'd never have left it. Well, he was in a different kind of old days now: his own. Time for a coffee. And he pulled off at a slip road, and drove until he found a lay-by overlooking farmland. More sheep, grazing timelessly.

'Hello.' He unscrewed the flask and sat watching them, wondering when they'd been taken into lambing sheds, which was what happened now, though in the old days – here they were again – they'd often be lambing out on frozen hillsides all through the winter.

The coffee restored him: should have stopped miles back. Only now he needed a pee, of course. He eased open a field-gate, stood behind a hedge just as another couple of cars pulled up.

Right, off we go again.

When he saw the Angel of the North silhouetted against the cloudy sky he made a decision. He'd stop off at Gateshead, and visit the Sage. The newest and most exciting concert hall in the north of England: he couldn't come all this way and not have a look at it. The older you got, the more you should try to keep up: do stuff, do new stuff, have things to talk about. This feeling, which Becky had shared – always something new on the go in the book group; always a new exhibition; all that volunteering – had been so utterly eclipsed by her death that he was astonished now to find himself thinking like this. A good sign.

And he turned off at the roundabout and followed the signs. It was early afternoon: he could look round, have tea, press on to Morpeth in time for supper.

Above him, the Angel spread its mighty wings. That felt like a good sign, too.

'Oh, Becky.'

He still said her name aloud, still wanted her there to share it all. She'd have loved this trip.

'I'll tell you all about it,' he said, before he could stop himself, and then he made himself concentrate on the route. Heavy traffic now, accompanied by Bach Partitas, just what he needed. And if he didn't want to overtake, he wouldn't. Plenty of time.

He parked in the Sage car park and walked slowly up to the entrance. It was indeed an extraordinary place, those glassy panels reflecting the slowly-moving clouds, everything about its drama and size and modernity proclaiming: Music matters! Look what we've done! And its position, beside the great Tyne Bridge, riverboats passing, gulls wheeling, lights coming on in the buildings across the river – fabulous.

'I'm a Northumbrian,' he thought, as Evie had always said she was, and felt London, which had come to mean so much to him, just slip away. And yes, it was doing him good, to do something new at last, for the first time since Becky had gone.

A vast Christmas tree stood in the foyer. Inside, it was like being on board a liner: great white curving balconies, views of the river everywhere you looked. He strolled about, one of dozens of visitors, found the two concert halls, heard someone blasting away on a trumpet. There were lots of children skidding about on the polished boards – it was the holidays, of course, and reading the notice boards he saw there was a lot going on for them, the place an education trust as well.

He should bring the grandchildren here. He stood looking at flyers for workshops and jam sessions, reading the concert programme. The Newcastle-upon-Tyne Bach Choir. Blues, brass, Indian classical. Young Musicians Live, lunchtime recitals; the Endellion Quartet; piano in the afternoon – it was endless, it was terrific. But no trio, he noticed, not in this season, and he thought how wonderful it would have been, for the Hepplewick Trio to have played somewhere like this, somewhere really on the map, and packed to the gills. It was only George who had ever played at somewhere significant, and that was before the war.

Had he done enough, he wondered now, had Charlie and

Nina done enough, to tell Robyn and the boys about the trio their great-grandmother had played in for so long? About how good it had been to grow up with the sound of his mother practising, the Trio rehearsing, students coming for lessons. The music talk at mealtimes, all those concerts. Of course, it had been Evie who had really followed in their mother's footsteps. He'd loved it all, but been no good, not really, not put in the hours. But he'd listened, he'd listened all his life – like his father, who'd had not a shred of musical education until he and his mother met, and fell in love.

'Then music began to mean everything.'

He heard himself sigh. Time for tea. He made his way to a café, settled down with a pastry and a pot for one. Fortified, he got out his phone and texted Nina.

Having tea at the Sage, terrific place. We must bring the boys.

Would they want to come? Would they want to hear, if he went on about the Hepplewick Trio, and how good they'd been? Their uncle had had a voice to die for, sung the solo of 'Once in Royal' at St Paul's one Christmas, still sang in a choir, his one relaxation from hospital and family life. Ben and Ollie had both started off on piano and violin, but – like him, let's face it – they didn't practise as they should.

Well. He'd give it a go. Bring them up in the Easter holidays, perhaps, take them to a concert, take them to the Hall. And he saw them, London children used to tower blocks and street after street of terraced houses, looking through the open gates of the Hall, as he would do tomorrow: at the drive, the tree, the terrace; at the lovely old house with the pele tower, overlooking lawn, tennis court, stable yard—

'You mean you used to live here?'

What about Robyn? Could he bring her? His little girl, his darling.

'Grandpa!' Her arms round his neck.

'Granny!' Snuggled up on her lap.

Did he dream it, or was she, even at seven, beginning to withdraw? Was Jo's crispness, and briskness, and general – oh, what would you call it? – he was feeling tired now – making her less demonstrative? Less loving?

God knows what they'd make of that doll.

Enough. Better get going. He made his way out through the throng.

5

B Y THE TIME he got to Morpeth it was dark; by the time he'd found the B&B he was shattered. No two ways about it. He parked the car behind the house, feeling the chill of winter air from the river, and carried his overnight bag up the path. A cheering light shone on to it; a Christmas tree smothered in stuff stood twinkling away in the hall.

'I've driven up from London,' he told the landlady. 'You couldn't by any chance do supper.' He gave her his most winning smile.

She couldn't, she was ever so sorry. But a couple of roads away was a nice little place. She gave him the card, and carried his bag up the stairs. A marmalade cat was sitting on the landing.

'That's Orlando.'

'I thought it would be. Hello, puss.'

His room was warm, that was the main thing. Too many beaded cushions on the bed – what was he supposed to do with that lot? Otherwise: fine. He threw the cushions on top of the wardrobe, had a pee and a wash and brush-up. Not quite so bad once he was done. He splashed on a bit of cologne and felt better.

Okay, supper. Supper, shower and bed. He could sleep for England. And he went downstairs, took directions again, and walked out into the street.

Everything felt quiet and solid, Christmas trees in every window. Perishingly cold. He could hear the river lapping beneath the old stone bridge. But it did him good to stretch his legs, and the restaurant was festive and welcoming.

'A *table for two, sir?*'

That was how it had been for ever.

'Can you squeeze me in?'

He was squeezed into a table for two in a corner. Everything was candlelit and jolly, other tables laughing away. A few paper hats.

Oh, darling—

He stopped himself. None of that. He scanned the wine list, ordered a half-bottle of Chateauneuf and fell upon the bread basket. Famished, he was famished. He'd driven three hundred miles on a couple of ham sandwiches and a Danish; time to tuck in. And he ordered warm goat's cheese, and a rack of lamb, raised his glass and let this very good wine hit the spot.

God, that was better. He felt for his book, just as a text went ting in his pocket.

Hi Dad, thinking of you. Glad the Sage was good. Where are you now? xx

Having supper in Morpeth, he texted back. *Everything going fine. xx*

He got out Orwell's essays, and settled down. If you had to be on your own there were worse things than reading a good book over a good meal, and Orwell had sustained him since his teens. He turned the pages, found 'Death of an Elephant'. You could never read that too many times. And he began to read, deciding on sticky toffee pudding to polish off the meal. If you couldn't have sticky toffee pudding in Northumberland, where could you?

He woke next morning to the bluest of blue skies. Everything looked fresh and good, and now, as he dressed, he could see the river from his window, rushing along and glinting. The Wansbeck. He remembered leaning over the bridge in childhood visits, racing sticks with Evie. He'd love to see it again.

No time to drive out and visit the site of the long-gone mine, and what would be the point? But he'd have a bit of a walk in the sun after breakfast.

Breakfast was the usual B&B extravaganza, and if he hadn't eaten so well last night he'd have had the works. As it was, he had coffee and scrambled eggs and a small mountain of whole-meal toast, nodding to the other guests, then reading the paper.

'Terrific. Thank you so much.'

He left a large tip, and went up to pack. Left a fiver on the chest of drawers, too, imagining some poor little Polish thing, her eyes lighting up; feeling expansive and – yes – happy. Just the thought of the drive, the sight of the hills, and then, at last, the village, and the Hall.

He looked at his watch. Half an hour's look-about, and he'd be on his way. And after the Hall, on the way to Evie's, he'd drive over to Kirkhoughton, see the school. That would be a fine thing. Have a pub lunch, then off to Otterburn. No need to rush, and he'd be there by teatime.

'You made it! Come in, come in.'

Tea by the fire, and then all the talk could begin.

Downstairs, he paid the bill, stroked the cat, swung out with his bag to the car. It might be sunny, but God, it was cold. He wound his scarf twice round his neck, pulled on his gloves. Okay: just a quick look.

He walked along good clean streets. As he came into Castle Street, and looked around, he saw the court house, something else he remembered from childhood: a mock medieval castle, complete with battlements, a mighty thing. He turned towards it, and walked up the broad tarmac path, remembering Evie skipping along, holding their father's hand, and he wanting to wear chainmail, and march about.

'It's not as old as it looks,' he heard their father tell them. 'It was built in the early nineteenth century – an architect called

John Dobson, quite famous. This was a court house and also a jail.' Everywhere they went, he told them stuff.

'Has it got dungeons?'

'No. But there were plenty of prisoners, plenty of cells. Pretty imposing, isn't it?'

It was. He'd thought about clambering about on that roof, whizzing arrows into the air.

A lot of cars were parked outside it now. Well: it was a popular tourist destination – there would be. But as he drew nearer, he realised: No, not visitors. Residents. The whole thing had been made into flats. He stopped on the path, rather taken aback, and then, as a young man came hurrying out of the building, late for work by the look of things, he recalled something he hadn't thought about for years.

This was where George Liddell had had to face a tribunal, in the early months of the war. This, as the Magistrates Court, was where they had heard the appeals from conscientious objectors.

How could he not have thought of that, when he was planning this trip? Well – losing Becky had wiped a lot of things from his mind, that was all there was to it. He thought about the past all the time, but this – he just hadn't made the connection.

He was making it now. And pacing up and down in the cold, in front of the great arched entrance, he tried to imagine the scene.

'Mr Liddell? Come and sit down.'

George walked across the bare floorboards towards the desk. Three men were sitting there, their backs to the light. On this spring morning the huge panelled room was sunlit, and beyond the leaded windows trees were in full fresh leaf. A beautiful day, but the men at the desk looked sombre. He pulled out a chair, and sat before them.

The man in the middle cleared his throat.

'Mr Liddell, we must introduce ourselves. My name is Michael Ingham, and as a barrister I am chairing this Tribunal. To my left, Dr Hetherington, who practises in this town. To my right, Mr Ferries, town councillor.'

There was a general inclination of heads. Ferries, thought George, looking at a mean narrow face: he's the one to watch.

'Now, then,' said Ingham. 'Your full name?'

'George Edward Liddell, sir.'

'And your date of birth?'

He gave it, with his address. Tile House, Coquet Bridge. His mother, as he left this morning, had looked ashen. His father, too old for call-up, had stopped speaking to him.

'And your occupation.'

'Musician, sir.'

Ingham was writing, though he had all this information before him already.

'Instrument?' He pronounced the word as if it were something deeply distasteful. George had a sudden flash of how he would be in court, cross-examining.

'The violin.'

'And who do you play with? Where do you play?'

He began to explain, knowing at once how it sounded. He and two young women, far from the swim of manly life. Country house concerts, churches, church halls. Perhaps church halls were good. Church halls and schools.

'And I teach quite a lot,' he said. 'I'd like to teach more.'

'And you wish—' Ingham gazed at him. 'You wish to be exempted from military service.'

'Yes, sir.'

'On what grounds?'

George took a deep breath. 'I'm a pacifist.' It was true, though until war was declared he had not known how deeply pacifism ran in every cell of his body. He had never fought anything, never wanted to. If he had anything to give the world at all, it was not through combat. He cleared his own throat, and it sounded horribly loud.

'I love my country,' he said, and that was true, too. 'But I've joined the Peace Pledge Union. And I believe I can best serve England by doing what I do best - uplifting people's lives through the transforming power of music.' Did that sound grandiose? It was how he felt. 'Especially,' - he hesitated. 'Especially in these dark times. People will need music more than ever now.'

'I see.' Once more, Ingham made it sound as if he'd heard something unpleasant, outlandish, even. 'You're not married,' he said suddenly. Did George imagine it, or was this said with particular, meaningful emphasis? 'You don't have a young wife you're anxious not to leave.'

'No, sir.' He struggled, and failed, to quell a rising blush.

Ingham gazed at him, and the blush deepened. 'I thought that was probably the case,' he murmured, and George thought: it's not Ferries, it's this man. This man is someone to fear. And he was afraid now, and his knees began to tremble.

'If I may—' Hetherington was looking through papers.

'Of course.' Ingham gestured towards him.

'You have people who have testified on your behalf?'

Another deep breath. He clenched his knees together. 'Yes, sir.'

'And they are?'

'My tutor at the Royal College of Music. In London. I studied there between 1926 and '29. I believe my violin tutor has been kind enough to speak well of me.'

'Anyone else?' Hetherington had his hands clasped before him, as if in prayer, and again it sounded as though some music tutor could barely be given the time of day, even if he did teach at the Royal College.

'Mr Harold Straughan,' said George. 'The head of the boys' school at Kirkhoughton. Kirkhoughton Boys,' he added, and began to feel steadier. Just a bit.

Since the outbreak of war, Straughan had presided over assemblies as if he were Winston Churchill: that was what Steven had told him, delivering each fresh piece of news in a way which made every boy in the hall thrill with patriotism. And yet—

'Go on,' Steven had urged him. 'You know what effect that concert had. Ask him - he can only say no.'

He'd said yes, and his letter was there on the desk, George could see that great black flourishing signature, beneath Miss Aickman's typing. And with Straughan's name, and the passing of the letter from man to man, came a microscopic change in the atmosphere, he was sure of it.

'Mr Liddell.' Ingham leaned forward, and clasped his hands. 'You are aware of the decisions we can make at this Tribunal?' And at George's uncertain nod, he went through them, slowly and deliberately.

'Unconditional Exemption from military service - as I am sure you know, this is extremely unusual. Exemption on condition that you undertake civilian work, under civilian control. Or you could be registered for call-up for non-combatant duties - fire-watching, for example. You will be aware that there have already been air-raid warnings in Newcastle. Finally, if the Tribunal is not convinced that your application is genuine—' he paused. 'Then you would simply be liable for military service. A refusal would mean imprisonment.'

There was a silence. Russet leaves blew past the window: he would always remember that: such beauty, and such fear.

'You may leave,' said Ingham. 'We will write to you with our decision.'

'Thank you, sir.' He did not think to nod to the other men,

just got to his feet, his legs like water. He could feel their eyes upon him, as he walked slowly across to the heavy, brass-handled door.

'*Not anxious about leaving a young wife . . . No, I thought not.*'

Outside, he leaned against the arched stone walls of the entrance, lined with sandbags, and shut his eyes, winging a message to his beloved, wherever he might be in earth or heaven.

Was that how it had been? Returning to the car, Geoffrey thought back to the time when he and Evie, beginning at school to learn about the war, asking about it at home, had been told about George, and his refusal. Conchies had had a hard time of it: the Fusiliers had seen action at Dunkirk, at Monte Cassino. Northumberland had lost some 17,000 men by the end of the war, and grieving families didn't want to see a man out and about when they'd lost husbands, brothers, sons. On the streets of Newcastle such a man could have a white feather thrust into his hand, could be hissed at, spat at, even.

'But George is so *nice*,' said Evie, clasping her knees by the fire. 'I love him! They shouldn't have spat at him.' She put her hands to his mouth. 'He didn't go to prison, did he?'

'He didn't.' Their mother got up, and went over to the piano, as almost every evening. 'And no one spat at him, as far as I know. He didn't think he had a hope, after that awful tribunal, but they gave him exemption, as a music teacher.'

'Old Straughan's name must have carried some weight,' said their father, throwing another log on the fire.

'George was a wonderful teacher, actually.' At the piano, their mother began to play. 'And he joined a sort of wartime council for promoting music and the arts. He organised lots of concerts, all through the war, not just for the Trio, but with other musicians, and children – in a way, his life went on as before, but busier. He did fire-watching, too.'

'So did I,' said their father. 'Don't forget that. Up on the roof of Kirkhoughton Town Hall, night after night. Grand stars.'

'The Peace Pledge Union?' Geoffrey remembered asking, as he reached the riverside now. A boy and his father were setting a little sailboat on the water, nudging it with a stick. 'What was that, exactly?'

And his father had begun to talk about the artists and academics who'd been a part of it - Bertrand Russell, Eric Gill, Sybil Thorndike. Benjamin Britten.

The piano music suddenly changed: no longer a sonata but loud rhythmic chords which made them all sit up.

'The Young Person's Guide to the Orchestra,' said Evie, leaping to her feet and conducting madly. She stopped. 'George didn't know Benjamin Britten, did he?'

'No,' said their father. 'But he knew all about him. He took a whole lot of Kirkhoughton Boys to see *Peter Grimes* once, in London - that was right at the end of the war, the first production.'

'Did you go?'

'No.' A wry smile. 'It was bang in the middle of exams, as it happened.'

'Dad,' Geoffrey had said, as their mother stopped playing, and Evie flopped back in her chair. 'You were exempt from call-up, weren't you? Like the miners.'

'Miners, teachers, farmers - reserved occupations.' His father was watching a log break up in the fire. He leaned forward, gave it a poke. 'Like the dockers, and the railway workers - had to keep the country going.'

'But did you—' he felt himself tread carefully, not wanting to hurt or upset. 'Did you mind not fighting?'

There was a silence. Their mother was turning on the piano stool, looking across the room.

'Dad?'

299

His father leaned back in the high wing chair. 'Of course I wanted to stay alive,' he said slowly. 'For your mother, for all of you. For myself. But – well, there's a lot to be said for fighting for what you believe in. You must read George Orwell, Geoff. Part of me felt I should be there with the rest.'

6

MORPETH WAS BEHIND him, and now, as he drove along the old roads he'd once known so well, he felt a rising happiness. The morning was still fine, the sun striking bare tree trunks in a way which even in childhood had lifted his heart: that greeny-grey, that winter stillness – the fields stretched away in the sun. But the hills to his left were speckled with white on the tops. In the north, you could have two kinds of weather within a few miles.

Composer of the Week: still Haydn. A quartet danced with him as he drove. He slowed to drive over a bridge across the river, passed a farm. A dog on a chain began to leap and bark wildly at the sound of the car. 'Quiet!' The farmer crossing the yard gave a shout, then raised his hand, and Geoffrey raised his own in greeting, glimpsing a young woman washing dishes at the kitchen window. And from thinking so much about George, who had been Evie's godfather, and written to her until his death, he found his mind turning now to Diana Embleton, who had spent the war as a Land Girl.

'Imagine it! Me! Driving a tractor, digging up swedes. Milking! Gosh, I did love milking. Some of those cows were so sweet.'

If Evie had loved George, he had adored Diana. How could you not? So gorgeous to look at – in his teens he'd woken from dreams about her which had made him flush with mingled happiness and embarrassment. She was forty-five! How could he think of her in that way?

He could. Lots of men could. She was beautiful, funny and

kind. As she grew older, the pale mass of her hair began to grey, yet it was still something you wanted to touch, to stroke, to unpin. Her skin had never lost its English rose pink and cream; her clothes were always the kind of clothes which made you think about the underwear beneath, imagining satin, silk and lace. She had such spirit, she was such fun. But there was more than that, a dreaminess, a thoughtfulness. Now and then you'd look up from a game of croquet in the garden, or draughts by the fire, and see she was miles away. And when she played—

'Of course,' she told him once, when they were out for a walk, 'I've always been the weakest of the three. George lets me know that, though he never actually says. But if anyone has to do everything three times, or keeps missing an entry, or just fluffs things - you can count on me.'

'I think you play fantastically.'

'Darling.' She put her hand on his arm and he felt a tingle run through him from head to foot. She had called him darling. Could he - might he - might it ever be possible . . . 'You're so sweet,' she said, as they came to a stile. 'Help me up, would you? I'm getting so creaky now.'

He knew that without him she would almost have vaulted it, she was so graceful and strong. And all those years in the war as a Land Girl: that must have made her really fit. But he put a hand under her arm, in its soft tweed jacket, and helped her up, and over. She dropped down onto the grass.

'Diana?' He followed her over the weathered planking.

'Yes, darling.'

The wind was blowing strands of hair across her face; he reached out and brushed one away. Her dreamy grey eyes regarded him.

'You're so like your father.' And then, as he opened his mouth to speak, to make, at last, his declaration: 'Don't,' she said quickly. 'I'm old enough to be your mother.' She laughed.

'I almost *am* your mother, if that's what godmothers are. Come on.'

And she was striding away, over the grass still glossy from yesterday's rain. He followed helplessly.

She was beautiful, she was unattainable – by him, or by anyone else, it seemed. It was Evie, always the one to ask questions, and go on asking them, who had said to their mother one evening at supper;

'Mummy? Why isn't Diana married?'

'I don't know. Who wants a second helping?'

'Me,' said their father, at the other end of the table, and then it was all pass your plate, and is that enough, and who wants another potato.

'She's so lovely,' said Evie, and he looked at his plate, feeling no one but he had the right to say that. 'I'd have thought lots of men would want to marry her.' She turned to look at him. 'Don't you think so, Geoff?'

'S'pose so.'

Evie groaned. '*Honestly*. Boys.' She turned back to their mother. '*Lots* of men,' she said again.

'Oh, Evie. Perhaps lots of men did want to marry her. Perhaps she just didn't want to marry them.'

'But why? I mean, there must have been *someone*.'

He saw a glance run between his parents down the table.

To this day he didn't know its meaning, and to this day he had not thought of it for years. Decades. When you were as old as he was, everything was decades ago.

'I just don't know,' said their mother at last. 'But I do know you haven't done your practice yet. Straight after supper, yes?'

'Oh, *Mummy*.'

The evening sunlight slanted through the window. Here in the kitchen, here at the back of the house, it was always full of shadows.

'Diana,' Geoffrey said now, slowing as Hepplewick village came into view. Apart from Becky's, it was the first time he'd said a woman's name aloud for years. And he thought of another conversation with her, much later, when he was married, and everything was easier between them. There'd been a rehearsal, soon there would be supper. Becky and his mother were clattering about.

'Music is everything to me.' She was sitting in the drawing room, a glass in her hand. Outside, a blackbird was singing away on the rooftop – there was always a blackbird at the Hall. 'I might not have been as good as I wanted, or everyone else wanted, but – it saved me. Without it, I'd have been just a silly girl.' She looked out at the garden, and again he saw that faraway look fill her eyes. It was a look which could drive a man mad.

'We all need something to give our lives meaning, don't we?' she said slowly. 'I mean, I know that's a cliché, but – music is mine. Just as it is for your mother. And the wretched George.'

'Did someone mention my name?' He was crossing the hall, as the clock began to chime. In he came, lifting his hand in a sweep. 'I see everyone has a drink except me.'

There was the village green, with its handful of houses. A few new ones, stretching out quite a way behind them. A Christmas tree stood in every window, some flashing lights, though it was barely mid-morning. There was the church. Geoffrey pulled up, got out on to the verge. It was cold, he was stiff. He shook himself, pulled on his gloves.

Then he walked up and opened the lych gate, remembering that lovely click, though surely there must be a new latch now. He closed it behind him, looked round, trying to remember. It was over thirty years.

One or two of the graves had fresh flowers out of season;

some of the headstones were that black shiny granite he didn't like, though you saw it everywhere.

And there were the two Heslop tombs, there were the angels. Evie had loved them, Nina and Charlie had loved them: that billowing hair, those gowns, those upraised hands. One was stern, one had a gentle smile. All nonsense, of course. And yet – he had loved them too.

He walked along the path towards the west end of the church, feeling more confident now. Yes. There it was. His feet sounded loud on the flag-stoned path.

In loving memory . . .

His father had gone first, so suddenly, so shockingly – but then, how hard he'd worked.

Steven Geoffrey Coulter, 1910-1979

His mother, weeping unstoppably, had clung to the Hall.

'Don't make me leave it, I couldn't bear to leave it.'

A cleaner came, one of the Barrow girls: Grace, the first to marry. A gardener, Nellie's husband. There weren't many families who'd stayed together as these two had: Heslop – Coulter, as his mother became – and Barrow; he and Evie knew they were lucky, not to have to worry too much. But then, as with Becky; as with their long-ago, long-dead grandmother; cancer came to call.

And of his beloved wife, Margot, née Heslop

1912-1982

Weeds were growing round the base of the headstone, and he bent to tug them out, straightening up with difficulty. Then he just stood there, thinking.

'I'm here,' he said to his parents, and felt he need say no more.

Up on the church tower a jackdaw was making its sharp metallic sound – you couldn't really call it a cry. *Chip. Chip-chip,* into the raw morning air. The country in winter: filled with emotion as he was, he was very glad he'd come. And he walked back through the churchyard, dropping the weeds in a metal basket, and wondering whether to look in the church. Yes, just for a minute or two. The Trio had often played here.

He walked up to the south door, turned the handle, pushed at the old oak door. But it didn't give. It was locked - you couldn't even get into the porch.

Had it ever been locked in his childhood? He couldn't remember. But just as well, perhaps: he still had a lot to do. He walked back to the car, got in, and drove away. No music now: he didn't want it, didn't want anything except this rising tide of anticipation, rounding the bend in the lane, slowing down to prolong the moment.

He was almost there. And now he was driving really slowly, his heart beginning to thump in his chest as the lane straightened out and he saw the line of trees.

They'd been thinned, they'd been thinned quite a lot. He looked through them and frowned. He'd misjudged the distance - he wasn't as close as he'd thought. And he drove on, passing a lot of new build, a housing estate, and rounded the next bend. This was it.

No it wasn't.

For a moment he felt himself quite lose his moorings. He was older than he thought, he was more forgetful. Somehow he'd made a mistake. And he pulled into the verge, and switched off the engine.

'Get a grip, Coulter,' he said aloud, and got out of the car once again. Perhaps he should walk, perhaps that was better. The fields to the left stretched away, just as he remembered. But there was nothing to see on the right except more fields, ones he remembered walking through on Sundays with the family, remembered that quite clearly. So where was the Hall?

He turned back, walked past the car to the bend, and on to

the next. Here were those new-build houses again: where had they come from?

Then he knew.

He stood in the lane and beheld not the tall iron gates, not the drive or the terrace, not the towering cedar, nor the grey stone house overlooking that limitless lawn, with its rose beds and summerhouse. Not the ha-ha, nor the tennis court, nor the stable yard. It was gone, all of it. He was looking at houses you could see anywhere in the country: bright red brick, the dark brown window frames and little porches which every builder in the land used now; tarmac paths and cars where there should have been front gardens. Instead, just a strip of grass, running from house to house. And a Christmas tree in every window. From somewhere he could hear cartoon voices, laughing away in the quiet.

He could not move. He could not move a muscle. How could he have been so foolish, so unthinking, all this time? Developers were everywhere, the price of land was soaring, people needed somewhere to live. In a great spacious county like Northumberland there was every opportunity to give it to them, and make a fantastic profit.

When had it happened? How soon after they'd sold it had it happened?

'Oh, Jesus.' He covered his eyes.

Back in the car, finally back there, though it felt like an hour before he made it, he reached for the Thermos. Something else he hadn't thought of – to ask the landlady at the B&B to refill it. He slowly unscrewed the cup, then the lid, drank a cold mouthful and almost spat. But he had to have something, or die. That was what it felt like.

Caffeine stirred in his veins. It was better than nothing. At last he stopped trembling. Then he started the car. He'd drive to Kirkhoughton, which surely could not have been razed to the ground. He'd look at the school, have a good hot lunch. And then he'd be over to Evie's, fall into her arms.

Cars were parked all round the Square, and all of them on meters. Of course they were. He drove round, finding almost the last space, not far from the Museum, and felt in the little compartment for coins. Another thing he hadn't considered, but he wouldn't be staying long, and he found a couple of pounds and some fifty pences. He got out, fed the meter, and looked about him.

His millionth Christmas tree stood outside the Museum. Posters of Roman antiquities were pinned in a glass box at the entrance. At the top of the Square stood another, a mighty thing, a terrific tree, as tall as the one at the Sage, if not taller. He knew where it had come from, as it had come every year since for ever: from Harwood Forest, up in the hills, brought down by lorry. Even as he thought this, he wondered if it were true. The world he once knew had moved beneath his feet – that was how it still felt, and even the lights on the tree were not as they used to be, but that planet-saving cold bluish-white, as they had been at the Sage. Never mind, never mind. There were some things you had to get used to.

All along the street, beneath the bare trees, people were doing their Christmas shopping, children racing about on scooters, every second person on a phone. He passed a gift shop, full of stencilled cushions, distressed chairs, blankets tied up with ribbon. Enamel jugs of holly stood on distressed chests, before rag-rolled walls hung with prints. In truth, the whole thing could have come straight out of Camden Passage. He supposed that retro was where it was at now, wherever you were. A computer shop stood next door, stuffed with smart phones and iPads: straight out of Tottenham Court Road. It was packed. He walked on, past a butcher hung with game – well, that was something he did remember.

What had he expected? That the town would be frozen in time, as he had imagined the Hall? He stopped on the pavement, gazed out at the great ring of hills beyond the town. Snow on the tops, and it was colder here, much colder then Morpeth. He stamped his feet, wondered if Evie could lend him extra socks.

Now then: the school. Might that have gone, too, that shabby old Victorian thing? He looked across the Square, searching for the line of railings, along which many a boy had run many a stick. They were there, but smartened up no end. And beyond them, across the playground, he saw that the old façade had been re-faced: shiny grey oblongs hung over the brick, and a great glass extension jutted out into the playground. A science lab? Probably. He went slowly over the road.

The gates in the railings were padlocked for the holidays. He looked up at the sign which stood next to them.

Kirkhoughton School
Head Teacher Barbara Mason, BA (Hons), Cert. Ed.

Of course: it was a comprehensive now. It was mixed. Even as he realised this, a couple of girls came down the street towards him, scrolling away on their screens. They were out of uniform, but he knew straight away that this was their school.

Well: that was all right, wasn't it? It looked like a damn good modern school, as good as anything you might find in London and possibly better. Why should he feel such a stab of sadness, that what he had remembered was, like the Hall, now utterly erased? Again he asked himself: what did you expect?

'Excuse me—'

The girls stopped, looked up from their screens. They were

309

young, they were cool, they were of their time. It just wasn't his time, that was all.

'All right?' asked one of them.

He wasn't all right, he was still shocked to the core.

'Are you at school here?' he asked them, and they nodded. 'My father,' he said slowly, 'My father was Headmaster here. Head Teacher.'

'Oh, yeah?' He could see the girl trying to be polite, to take an interest. 'That must have been a long time ago,' she said, and then, 'Sorry, that sounds a bit rude.'

'Not at all. You're quite right,' he said, and then, 'Everything was a long time ago.'

He sounded an idiot, even to himself. A very foolish, fond old man. 'Sorry. I'm a bit shaken up.' He got some kind of a grip, and smiled. 'Take no notice,' he told them. 'I'm fine, really.'

'No probs,' said the friend.

'Happy Christmas,' he said, turning back to look through the railings.

'Merry Christmas.'

They were back on their screens, arm in arm.

For a little while he stood looking across at this shiny new building. If he shut his eyes he could half-see the old one, with boys pouring into it, boys pouring out of it, off down the hill to football and cricket, his father as a young teacher bringing up the rear.

'Sir? Sir, when are we playing Hexham?'

He'd struggled to concentrate, his mind on other things. Was that how it had been?

'I never thought I'd be Head,' he said once. 'There were people much better than me, all lining up for when Straughan retired.'

'You made a brilliant Head,' said their mother.

Had Geoffrey disappointed him, choosing the Law? Would

he not have wanted him to follow in his footsteps, not those of another man?

He was getting cold again. Just one more thing to revisit, before he had lunch. And he walked up the hill, passing the bus stop at which, he knew, his father must have stood a thousand times, waiting to go back to that moorland cottage.

He walked on, came to the war memorial, right at the top of the Square. Even now, though it was almost Christmas, a couple of scarlet wreaths stood on the plinth. Someone had tucked a sprig of holly beneath the one on the left. He walked slowly round the grey stone obelisk, with the words engraved as they were on almost every such memorial.

To the memory of the men of Kirkhoughton
who gave their lives for their country.

He searched for the names he knew. On one of the three sides dedicated to the First World War he found the one he was looking for.

Capt. Edward Gibson. Fusiliers. The Somme. 1916

There was a window dedicated to this young man in St Mary's at Hepplewick, rather a lovely thing: had the church not been locked this morning he would have looked at it again for the first time in thirty years. Now, he stood gazing at the lettered name, remembering Mrs Dunn, Miss Renner as she had been once, visiting the Hall with her husband, who had survived this very battle.

'*Miss Renner meant everything to us when we were little. I'm so glad she's happy now.*'

He remembered being a little afraid of her husband, who walked so stiffly, and had that rather strange laugh.

'You should have seen him before he was married,' his father had said drily. 'He's a new man now.'

And now he, like Emily Renner – Emily Dunn – was gone,

as everyone was gone. Geoffrey walked round to the fourth side, looked for the two names he had first seen when he was a boy, and learning about the war in which he, and then Evie, had been born.

Capt. F. C. Embleton. Int. Brigade. Ebro, Spain, 1938

Frank Embleton: at last he thought of him.

'He made us a quartet. When he was killed—'

His mother had been unable to finish the sentence.

'My brother. My darling brother. Oh, how I wish you had known him!'

'The best teacher the school ever had. He was the one who should have been Head.'

'Everyone loved Frank.' George spoke so lightly, when he said this, but you knew, though nobody ever said so, that he was the one who had loved him most. Adored him.

Had he really been as wonderful as everyone said he was?

'Every generation has people like that, and he was ours. In our group of people, he was ours.'

He looked on down the list of names.

Pt. D. Hindmarsh. Fusiliers, 2nd Batt. Dunkirk, 1944

His father's favourite pupil. You shouldn't have favourites, but he had.

He'd lost a boy once to TB, it was everywhere, then. It had upset him terribly, his mother had told them once. But when the news came of Donald Hindmarsh - that was the day he could just remember: the library door shut tight, and he and Evie told to shush, and not to dare to knock.

'He wasn't very clever, he wasn't great at sport. He couldn't do anything, really, but he made us all laugh, and that counted. But that's not why I liked him so much. He was just a good lad, that was all.'

In front of the memorial, Geoffrey bowed his head. After this horrible morning, it gave him such relief.

He had lunch in a pub in the Shambles, the oldest part of town, and less crowded with shoppers, though there was a little bookshop he liked the look of. In the snug they were playing darts, as his father had said they did in his day, when he and Frank Embleton had a drink here now and then. At least that had survived.

Amazing, what good a piping hot meal could do you. He sat by a proper fire with a pint and vast plate of steak-and-kidney pie. A tree flashed away by the bar, and carols were playing on a loop.

Oh, come, all ye faithful . . . .

He would not get any more sentimental. He would not. He blew his nose and made further inroads on the pie. Then he sat back for a bit, resting before he resumed the journey, listening to the carols and the thud of the darts.

'Wha-hay!'

Apart from the flashing lights and the recorded singing – not quite King's College, Cambridge, but never mind – he thought that perhaps little had changed here in all these years. A pub was a pub, after all. In the old days the bar would have been thick with smoke, of course, as his father had said the staffroom always was. 'You could hardly see across the room, sometimes.' Well – that was one thing that had changed for the better. He shut his eyes, let the carols drift over him, felt himself falling asleep.

'All right?'

He woke with a start, as the barmaid cleared the table.

'Fine, thanks. Very good pie.'

'That's good.'

He looked at his watch: he must get going. He dug out his phone, texted Evie.

Should be there for tea. And then: *Oh Evie. Lots to tell, alas.*
G.

He texted Nina. *In a pub in Kirkhoughton. More tonight.*
Dad. xx

To his surprise, he sent a text to Jo. *Wanted to visit Emily*
Davison's grave in Morpeth. No time. Hope all well. G.

Emily Davison, one of Jo's heroines. If you could still call
them that. She was a woman after all. Was she a hero now? A
brave mad woman, anyway. 'Deeds, not words' was inscribed
on her gravestone. He thought about that, as he got up to pay,
and then he went out into the Shambles and took a quick look
at the paperbacks in boxes outside the second-hand shop. One
of the boxes was full of old orange Penguins: he riffled through
them. Good Lord. Orwell. *Down and Out in Paris and London.*
Keep the Aspidistra Flying. 1984. He pulled out a dog-eared copy
of *Homage to Catalonia,* 75 pence pencilled on to the flyleaf.
Well, well, well.

And as he went inside to pay, remembering everything
his father had told him about this book, he remembered
his first reading of it, when he was fifteen, and falling in
love with Diana. He still had that edition at home – the
first one, the one Frank Embleton had sent to his father,
urging him to read it. Already, he had been on his way to
Spain.

He still remembered that cover, that fist smashing into the
foreground. Now, the edition he paid for seemed anodyne: a
watercolour of soldiers at the window of a train. They were
holding up their fists, but they were smiling, might almost have
been going on holiday. But he had to have it: it was too much
of a coincidence, to find it here, on this momentous day. He
leafed through the pages.

I have no particular love for the idealised 'worker' as he
appears in the bourgeois Communist's mind, but when I see an

actual flesh-and-blood worker in conflict with his natural enemy,
the policeman, I do not have to ask myself which side I am on.

'Deeds, not words.'

Orwell was one of those rare people for whom both were important. Like Frank Embleton, perhaps.

Geoffrey walked back through the Shambles, and into the Square. A bus rumbled out of it, down the hill, and once more he thought of his father, and those endless journeys, to and from school. He crossed over, just in time to see a traffic warden stick a ticket on his windscreen. God, how had he managed to obliterate all thought of the bloody meter? Very easily, came the answer, and then he made two decisions.

The first was that he wasn't going to argue, and make a scene. He was too tired: to hell with it. The second, reached as the warden walked away, was that on the way to Evie's he would try to find Hencote Moor. Was the cottage was still there? The Hall might have been bulldozed and utterly destroyed; up on the moor there might still be something that once had mattered.

He tore off the ticket, got in, got out the map.

Even a few miles out of town he saw that the weather was changing, the sky beginning to darken. Was he mad, to do this? He drove slowly, for a good half hour, *Afternoon on Three* interrupted now and then by a blast of local traffic news. He banged on the knob, got Penny Gore back again, listened to some Hungarian thing she liked.

The road climbed, climbed further; he scanned it for signs. The Cheviots went on for ever, and how did he really think he was going to find one little bit of them, just because he wanted to? One thing made it easier: the fact that it was winter. Passing the leafless trees, and verges stripped of summer grass and weeds, he could make out a sign or two: Public Footpath. To Hadrian's Wall. Wark Fell. Probably none of these had been there in his father's day. Now, Tourist Information wanted to tell you everything, and he was glad of it.

Public Footpath. Hencote Moor. He almost missed it, couldn't believe it, braked suddenly and was hooted at by a car behind he hadn't even noticed. He flashed his lights in apology, let it speed past. Then he pulled over, and parked by a ditch.

Three o'clock. It couldn't take more than half an hour to walk up there, half that time to walk down again. He texted Evie: *Stopping at Hencote. Shan't be long.* He got out, locked the car, had a pee behind a bush. Then he wound his scarf round his neck once more, did up every button on his winter coat, and pulled on his gloves. He walked to the foot of the track, he began the climb.

It was incredibly cold. He was stiff and slow, and halfway up, as a wind began to rise, he almost turned back. But the moor stretched away so magnificently, and every now and then a fitful sun made an appearance. He climbed on, breathing hard, stopping when he had to, feeling the misery of the morning slip away. He was up high. Up high was good. And there were the sheep, moving slowly in and out of the browning bracken, stopping to stare at him, as they always did. He greeted them, climbed on, determined to find the place now.

Ten minutes later, there it was, in profile. That must be it. A little grey house miles from anywhere. He stopped to get his breath, take it all in: even from here, he could see there were holes in the roof; a bit further on, he saw the broken windows. Across the grass, a thorn tree was bent almost double: relentless moorland wind would have done that. A tumbledown shed stood beneath it. Slowly he walked on, walked round it all. A sheep bounced away at the back.

He returned to the front, and looked down the hillside. Far below, smoke rose from the chimney of a farm – a good-looking place, with a barn and good outbuildings. It made him think of Mike and Evie's place. And it made him think that his father would have looked down on this farm every day, would probably have known the farmer, whoever had been there then.

He let quietude sink in. Lapwing were beating their way across the valley; as soon as he heard it, he knew their high sad piping. Other than that, there was nothing: only the wind, the sheep cropping the tough moorland grass, rustling through the bracken. Only the soaring sky.

The sun had gone. He clapped his hands on his arms, feeling the cold bite deeper. He must go. But just for a few minutes longer he'd stay here, in this forgotten place which must once have meant everything: to his father, to his first young wife.

In loving memory of Margaret Coulter, née Ridley . . .

Just once he'd seen her grave, out at Cawbeck.

He turned, now, the cottage behind him, and stood looking out over the leafless trees far below on the road, trying to see the distant town, the school. He could just make it out, standing there where his father must often have stood, looking down on the track where he'd walked day after day in all weathers.

The wind was rising. It felt all at once as if it were blowing right through his life, summoning everything, and he began to think of all the people he'd loved, knowing he was nearing his own end now, bringing them all to mind. His parents. Diana, and George, in quite different ways. Becky. Becky above all. And she was gone: the wind had taken her, as it had taken everyone he'd cared about, except for his children, and grandchildren, and blown them to the farthest reaches of creation. Where were they?

The cold was numbing him. He looked back at the cottage for the last time. He had spent the whole day looking back, yearning for what could never be recaptured. But still. The historian within him began to stir: he was his father's son, after all, and how he had admired him. And he knew that in the great hush of the past probably nothing was as you'd imagined it to be; as you had heard, or not heard: there would always be something forgotten, or misremembered, or untold.

The wind moved like music over the moor. It began to snow.